Praise for
LITTLE TINY TEETH

"Elkins makes the reader feel the heat." —*The Boston Globe*

"A series that never disappoints."
—*The Philadelphia Inquirer*

"An ingenious story well-told . . . that leaves the reader not only well-entertained but somewhat better educated also."
—*The San Diego Union-Tribune*

"Grips the audience . . . filled with foreboding and thick suspense." —*Midwest Book Review*

UNNATURAL SELECTION

"Engaging . . . Elkins excels in making his hero's skills plausible and accessible." —*Publishers Weekly*

"The forensic accuracy is admirable, and the plotting compelling." —*Booklist*

"Elkins's plotting is devious, and the forensics information is thoroughly terrific." —*The Olympia (WA) Olympian*

continued . . .

Other Titles by Aaron Elkins

Gideon Oliver Novels

UNEASY RELATIONS*
LITTLE TINY TEETH*
UNNATURAL SELECTION*
WHERE THERE'S A WILL*
GOOD BLOOD*
SKELETON DANCE
TWENTY BLUE DEVILS
DEAD MEN'S HEARTS
MAKE NO BONES
ICY CLUTCHES
CURSES!
OLD BONES*
MURDER IN THE QUEEN'S ARMES*
THE DARK PLACE*
FELLOWSHIP OF FEAR*

Chris Norgren Novels

OLD SCORES
A GLANCING LIGHT
DECEPTIVE CLARITY

Lee Ofsted Novels (with Charlotte Elkins)

ON THE FRINGE
WHERE HAVE ALL THE BIRDIES GONE?
NASTY BREAKS
ROTTEN LIES
A WICKED SLICE

Thrillers

TURNCOAT
LOOT

*Available from Berkley Prime Crime Books

LITTLE
TINY
TEETH

AARON ELKINS

BERKLEY PRIME CRIME, NEW YORK

THE BERKLEY PUBLISHING GROUP
Published by the Penguin Group
Penguin Group (USA) Inc.
375 Hudson Street, New York, New York 10014, USA
Penguin Group (Canada), 90 Eglinton Avenue East, Suite 700, Toronto, Ontario M4P 2Y3, Canada
(a division of Pearson Penguin Canada Inc.)
Penguin Books Ltd., 80 Strand, London WC2R 0RL, England
Penguin Group Ireland, 25 St. Stephen's Green, Dublin 2, Ireland (a division of Penguin Books Ltd.)
Penguin Group (Australia), 250 Camberwell Road, Camberwell, Victoria 3124, Australia
(a division of Pearson Australia Group Pty. Ltd.)
Penguin Books India Pvt. Ltd., 11 Community Centre, Panchsheel Park, New Delhi—110 017, India
Penguin Group (NZ), 67 Apollo Drive, Rosedale, North Shore 0632, New Zealand
(a division of Pearson New Zealand Ltd.)
Penguin Books (South Africa) (Pty.) Ltd., 24 Sturdee Avenue Rosebank, Johannesburg 2196,
South Africa

Penguin Books Ltd., Registered Offices: 80 Strand, London WC2R 0RL, England

LITTLE TINY TEETH

A Berkley Prime Crime Book / published by arrangement with the author

PRINTING HISTORY
Berkley Prime Crime hardcover edition / June 2007
Berkley Prime Crime mass-market edition / July 2008

ISBN: 978-0-425-22250-8

BERKLEY® PRIME CRIME
Berkley Prime Crime Books are published by The Berkley Publishing Group,
a division of Penguin Group (USA) Inc.,
375 Hudson Street, New York, New York 10014.
The name BERKLEY PRIME CRIME and the BERKLEY PRIME CRIME design
are trademarks belonging to Penguin Group (USA) Inc.

PRINTED IN THE UNITED STATES OF AMERICA

10 9 8 7 6 5 4 3 2 1

Acknowledgments

I owe particular thanks to two scientific papers: a case report by Abdulrezzak Shakir, Steven A. Koehler, and Cyril H. Wecht that appeared in the *Journal of Forensic Sciences*, vol. 48, no. 2, March 2003; and a monograph by M. S. Olin, H. A. Young, D. Seligson, and H. H. Schmidek that appeared in *Spine*, vol. 7, no. 5, 1982.

Without these two excellent monographs (I can't put in the titles without giving away too much), Gideon Oliver wouldn't have been half so smart down there in the Amazon.

My friend, retired FBI Special Agent David Hill, kindly dug up some hard-to-get data on the South American cocaine industry.

Another knowledgeable friend, Carlos Cordero, helpfully straightened me out on my shaky Spanish.

The title, *Little Tiny Teeth*, came from the imagination of Mary O'Rourke.

I should probably mention that the Chayacuro and Arimagua tribes are fictional. All other Amazonian groups that are mentioned do exist.

And there really is such a thing as a Goliath spider.

PROLOGUE

Peru: The Upper Amazon Basin,
August 4, 1976

THEY knew, being Chayacuros, that the waking world, the world we think we see, is nothing but illusion. The real world, the true bonds between causes and their effects, is revealed only through the ritual drinking of ayahuasca. This they both had done under the ceremonial ministrations of old Chaya. The bitter brew had first purged and purified them, and then the Other World beings had come to guide them.

"They have killed all the plants in their own land, these white people," the bird-headed spirit-helper had told them through the shaman's mouth. "Now they come to destroy ours. And then the government will come and burn our village. It is up to you to see that this does not happen."

They had agreed to undertake the task. For the last three hours, silent and unseen, they had been observing the three white men who had made camp not far from the village the night before and were now stirring. But in the true world, as in the false, there were separate realities; there was room for differences of opinion.

"I say kill them now." Matsiguenga, the younger of the two, spoke in sibilant whispers, but he smote his naked, hairless chest with his fist for emphasis. "We have wasted enough time."

The older man, Jabuti-toro, took his time replying, as befitted someone wiser. "No. They may not be from the government. They may be blameless."

"So what? They are strangers; they have no relatives. Who would avenge them? Who would even know?"

They did not look at each other as they talked, for among the Chayacuro, for one man to look openly into another's eyes is a deadly insult. They lay, propped on their elbows, peering narrow-eyed through giant, insect-eaten banana leaves and gnarled liana vines at the three men, who sat on the ground in a tiny clearing, their backs against a fallen tree trunk, breakfasting on manioc pancakes and cold coffee. Fifty feet farther out, in a rough semicircle, lay another six Indians—younger men and boys, less skilled at hiding, and trailing, and killing, proud to be in the company of the two leaders and eager to learn from them. The youngest, and perhaps the most eager of all, Matsiguenga's nephew Shako, was not yet twelve.

In La Cosa Nostra, the two leaders, Matsiguenga and Jabuti-toro, would have been known as "made men," men who had murdered—"made their bones"—to prove their worth as members of the Family. In the equally elliptical language of the Chayacuro, they were *kakaram*, "powerful ones." Their power derived from their success at assassination. Both had killed enemies. Both had taken heads.

They were dressed almost identically. Of anything that we would describe as clothing, they had only woven kilts of dyed cotton. But they did not think of themselves as naked. Heavy necklaces of jaguar teeth, boar tusks, nuts, and shells hung in layered profusion around their necks. Their faces were dyed orange-red with achiote, their chests painted in ancient designs with white clay. Sharpened quills of blue and green macaw feathers pierced their nasal septums, and thin bamboo tubes and more feathers ran through their earlobes. Their glossy, black hair had been carefully trimmed into neat bangs and tightly bound with headbands.

Beside them lay nine-foot-long hardwood blowguns, meticulously carved and hollowed out and lovingly polished. Around each man's neck was slung a palm-frond quiver of darts from which dangled a small woven bag of cottonlike kapok. They were totally unafraid. The ayahuasca had made their bodies hard; they could not be harmed by others.

"I say again," Jabuti-toro whispered forcefully. "We wait. We do not kill those who are not our enemies."

Matsiguenga grunted his acceptance, but he had already made up his mind. The intruders would die. Jabuti-toro was getting old; he was more concerned about his wife and his four daughters than he was about protecting the village. His *arutam*—the soul that sustained and protected him and gave him the courage to fight—was leaving him; everyone could see that. He no longer had the stomach for killing. But Matsiguenga did. It would be up to Matsiguenga to teach the young ones how a man should act.

With the ayahuasca still coursing through his body, he could distinguish the future as if it were the present. Behind the lids of his closed eyes he saw how it would be. He would take the heads from the fallen whites, each with a single, slashing stroke of his machete. If Jabuti-toro wanted none, Matsiguenga would take all three, why not? He would run pieces of *cincipi* vine through their mouths and out their throats, and sling two of them over his back. The third he would allow young Shako to carry. Shako was impatient to take a head of his own, but he was still too young, too reckless, too out of control for that. Perhaps the honor of carrying a head would slake his thirst for blood for a while.

At the crossing of the River Yapo, where they had cached pottery jars, the shrinking process would begin. He would have Shako assist him. Shako was his sister's son; Matsiguenga was responsible for his learning. Among the Chayacuro, it was the maternal uncle, not the father, who was responsible for the education of a boy. They would slit the skin on the backs of the heads, then slip out the skulls and put them in the river as gifts for *pani*, the anaconda. They would boil the skins in river water, dry them, and then turn them inside out to scrape away the—

"They are moving," Jabuti-toro said. "They are leaving. We will follow them." His voice hardened. "If they do not approach the *hayo*, we will let them go, do you understand?"

"And if they do?"

"Then they must be killed. But wait. Watch. They may not be what they seem."

INDEED, they were not what they seemed. They were two brothers named Frank and Theo Molina and their friend Arden Scofield. A trio of adventurous, young Americans, they had no interest in *hayos*, the coca-leaf gardens that the people of the Amazon had grown for a thousand years but were now deemed unlawful by the Peruvian government. All three were promising Harvard graduate students in ethnobotany, the study of how the world's peoples make use of local plants for food, drugs, medicine, clothing, and anything else. Since getting their bachelor's degrees, Arden and Theo had continued at Harvard, working toward their master's degrees, with specializations in South American flora. They had arrived in the Amazon only ten days earlier. Frank Molina—six years older than his brother and five years older than Arden and the most serious scholar of the three—had been living in Iquitos for the past ten months, completing the fieldwork for his Ph.D. dissertation on the Amazonian Indians' use of *Brunfelsia grandiflora*, a member of the potato family, for curing gum disease.

But it was not this plant that these ambitious young men were after, nor any other medicinal botanical. It was *Hevea brasiliensis*—the rubber tree, and through it they meant to make a great deal of money.

In all its existence, the Amazon had known something resembling prosperity but once: during the rubber boom of the late 1800s, when the strange, new, bouncy substance was king. The finest rubber in the world came from Amazonian trees, and huge fortunes were made in the rowdy, knockabout jungle towns at either end of the great Amazon river, Manaus, Brazil and Iquitos, Peru. But the seeds of ruin—the literal seeds—had already been sown. An English botanist named Henry Wickham had smuggled seventy thousand seeds out of South America in 1870 and gotten them to Malaysia. Five years later, the new plants were being tapped, and in thirty years they had become great trees superior even to those of the Amazon. By 1913, Malaysia and Singapore were the new capitals of the rubber market. The Amazonian boom had gone bust.

But in the early 1970s the Malaysian plantations of the giant Gunung Jerai rubber conglomerate were having troubles of their own; their trees were being decimated by a vicious disease that was known as South American leaf blight but was capable of attacking *Hevea* anywhere in the world. As it happened, Arden and Theo, who followed such things, had heard from one of their professors about an isolated region near the junction of the Huitoto River and the Amazon, only about thirty miles upriver from Iquitos, where rubber trees grew that were remarkably resistant to the blight. Arden, the quickest-minded and most decisive of the three, had contacted Gunung Jerai to determine if they were interested in seeing some of the seeds from these trees, the location of which he sensibly kept to himself.

They were interested all right, enough to cover the costs of a three-week expedition to the Amazon for Arden and Theo, who would pick up Theo's brother Frank in Iquitos. Gunung Jerai would pay two thousand dollars for a viable sample of one thousand seeds. If they proved on testing to be truly blight resistant, there would be another ten thousand dollars. And in five years, when the young trees were tapped for the first time, they would pay an additional one hundred dollars for every surviving, productive tree. The money was to be paid to Arden, who volunteered to split it evenly with his two partners.

The likely total was upward of a hundred thousand dollars, and it was as good as in their bank accounts right now. In Arden's backpack was a net bag layered with gauze, in which nestled twelve hundred blight-resistant *Hevea brasiliensis* seeds. Collecting them had not been easy. In the Amazon, as almost nowhere else, trees did not grow in stands, but rather in widely scattered ones and twos, often miles apart. It had taken the three Tikuna Indians they had hired five days to harvest them. The Indians had been paid the equivalent of two American dollars a day per man, and had chuckled among themselves at the foolhardiness of the white men, who paid good money for things that anybody could go out and find just by walking around the jungle and keeping his eyes open.

"Let's get going," Arden said, standing up and hefting the precious backpack onto his shoulders. "If we get moving, we should be back in Iquitos by tonight."

"Iquitos," Frank said with a sigh. "Hot food, cold beer, showers . . ."

"Clean shirts, shaves . . ."

"Girls who wear clothes," Theo put in with an eyebrow-waggling leer, and they all laughed.

It took only a few minutes to roll up and pack their hammocks and mosquito nets, and they were soon once again on the rough path—an old deer or capybara track, probably—that led back to the shore and the broken-down old Bayliner they had rented in Iquitos. Its outboard engine had coughed and stuttered worrisomely all the way up, and even died on them a half dozen times, but the way back would be easier. Iquitos was downriver. They could float back if they had to.

After just a few minutes, the path took them to a large, cleared, relatively orderly patch of head-high shrubs with bright, yellow-green leaves, tiny yellow flowers, and red, coffee-bean-like fruits.

At the entrance to it, Frank put up his hand. "Whoa, hold it. You know what this is, don't you? It's *hayo*. Coca. I think maybe we want to go around it."

"Around it," Arden said with an edge to his voice, "means around the swamps on either side of it. That's a lot of extra ground to cover. I don't know about you, but I'm bushed. And I want to have my dinner tonight in Iquitos. I never want to look at another piece of manioc."

"Sure, me too, but we're on the border of Chayacuro country here," Frank said. "This could easily be theirs, and they're not exactly as, shall we say, "hospitable" as our Tikuna friends. I've worked with them once or twice, and trust me, you don't want to make them mad."

"Our good Tikuna friend Tapi," Arden said, referring to the Indian guide who had brought them this far and then returned home the previous night, "told us to just stay with the path, and we'd be back at the boat in a couple of hours. With the compass not working right, don't you think we ought to just follow his instructions? You really want to chance getting lost again?"

"Well, no, of course not, but I think I could find the path again—"

"You *think*. Oh, that's just great."

"Look, Arden," Theo said. "Frank's got a point. We don't want to mess with the Chayacuro. I like my head the size it is."

"For Christ's sake, what is it with you two?" Arden erupted. "It's five o'clock in the goddamn morning. You think these guys have guards out this time of day, monitoring the hordes of people that come through here? They're still asleep, which is what I intend to be at this time tomorrow."

"Yeah, sure, but—"

"Look, we'll be in and out of it in less than a minute.

We've spent more time arguing about it than it'll take to get through the damn thing."

"I don't know . . ." Frank muttered, chewing on his lip. Although the oldest of the three, he was by nature the least assertive. "Theo?"

Theo's shoulders rose in resigned submission. "What the hell, let's do it. Arden's the boss."

"I am?" Arden said. "Hey, thanks for telling me. How about letting your brother in on it?"

Frank gave in too. His open face relaxed into a smile and he waved Arden on with a flourish. "Lead on, Macduff. Just walk fast, will you?"

THE Chayacuro had followed at a hundred feet, slipping silently through the undergrowth and hanging vines like the jaguars they revered. They watched as the strangers entered the coca garden. With only a look between them and a barely perceptible dip of the chin from Jabuti-toro, each man pulled from his quiver a dart dipped in poison before they had left the village. A pinch of kapok was taken from each woven bag, moistened with saliva, and wadded onto the back end of the dart. This was partly to make it fly true, but mostly to stop up the hollow interior of the blowgun so that the coming puff of air would not pass uselessly around the dart but would instead propel it forward. The long tubes were lifted to their lips and aimed. Both men gathered in quick, shallow mouthfuls of air, and . . .

Ffft.
Ffft.

A Chayacuro blowgun dart is made by cutting away the leafy part of an ivory nut palm leaf, leaving only the straight, slender central rib, which is then whittled to a point with a few expert strokes. It is about ten inches long and not much thicker than a toothpick. If it were to appear beside a barbecue grill among the wooden canapé skewers, no one would look at it twice. The poison into which it is dipped is a curarelike extract pressed from the skin of the poison-dart frog, *Phyllobates terribilis*, and is among the most potent poisons known to man. A bird struck with such a dart will fall paralyzed from a tree in ten seconds and be dead in thirty. A squirrel or small monkey will take three or four minutes to die, a sloth or tapir fifteen, a human being anywhere between thirty minutes and three hours, most of which is spent in total paralysis. Death results from asphyxia. Curare and its relatives are neuromuscular blockers that first turn the muscles limp and unresponsive, then paralyze them altogether. When the muscles that control the lungs are no longer capable of inflating them, the victim suffocates. It is a particular horror of curare poisoning that consciousness is not affected until very near the end. A human victim can think clearly and feel himself becoming progressively incapacitated, but is very soon unable to speak, to call for help, or even to gesture.

In the hands of a Chayacuro marksman, the dart can be accurate at over a hundred feet, a distance that it travels in a shade under one second. Once it leaves the blowgun, there's no sound. An entire troop of monkeys can be brought down before they grasp the danger. Browsing animals who are narrowly missed continue their peaceful grazing, unafraid. But Chayacuro marksmen don't often miss.

"OUCH," Theo said. "Damn."

Arden glanced at him and saw, to his horror, the slender dart protruding from the back of Theo's neck. Theo, possibly thinking he was brushing off a stinging insect, reached for it and plucked it out. He and Arden and Frank stood staring at it for a second, then looked up at each other, their eyes frightened. All knew what it was. All knew what it meant. Theo uttered a half sob and flung it to the ground.

When a second dart struck Arden—but miraculously

lodged in his backpack—they broke for the cover of the jungle.

"I don't . . . think they're . . . following us anymore," Theo gasped.

They're following us, all right, Arden thought, but said nothing. His heart was pumping crazily and he needed all his breath to keep going. The three Americans had been running for almost ten minutes, pushing clumsily through the jungle and hacking inexpertly away with their machetes when they had to. Moving along what they thought was a diagonal track, they should have reached the path by now, but if they had they must have gone right through it without realizing it. But there was no doubling back to look for it. All they could do was keep going in what Arden thought— prayed—was generally the right direction. The only one to carry a sidearm—a little Beretta semiautomatic—he had pulled it from his holster and now clutched it in his right hand.

There was no doubt in his mind about the Chayacuro being on their trail. In the early morning hours, once the god-awful dawn racket from the birds and howler monkeys had died down, a tropical rainforest was very quiet. Sounds traveled a long way, and several times he had picked up the Indians' voices, frighteningly calm and monosyllabic. Unlike the Americans, they were in no hurry. Unlike the Americans, they knew what they were doing. Besides, Theo's increasingly dragging feet were making enough noise to be heard down in Iquitos.

"Maybe . . . maybe they just . . . wanted to . . . scare us off," Theo managed, following it with an "Uff!" as he tumbled headlong over a fallen trunk.

Sure, Arden thought grimly, *and maybe they forgot to dip their darts in poison. And maybe your poor gray face and your uncoordinated movements*—this was the third time Theo'd fallen—*are just in my imagination.*

"Jesus, Theo," Frank said. "You have to watch . . . where

you're going." He said it with a kind of teeth-clenched jauntiness, trying to convince himself—to convince all of them—that there was nothing the matter with his brother aside from simple, frightened clumsiness.

Theo knew better; Arden could see it in his eyes as he and Frank pulled him to his feet.

"Well, let's go," Theo said, but he just stood there. His speech had slowed perceptibly now and was more mumble than words. He could no longer put his lips together. His system was shutting down. "Oh, hell, I need to . . . I need . . . lie down." He sagged against Frank.

"Theo," Frank said urgently. "You can't lie down. Come on, we have to keep going."

"B . . . bud . . . I can't . . . I can . . ." His eyelids were drooping; saliva ran down his chin.

Frank wiped it away with his fingers, his eyes filming over with sudden tears. "Theo, you can make it, we'll get you there, bro."

"Don't worry, Theo, we can do it," Arden said. "Come on, buddy."

Quickly, they each hooked one of Theo's flaccid arms over their shoulders and got going at as close to a trot as they could manage. Theo was as inert, and as frightfully heavy, as a corpse.

"Artificial respiration," Arden panted, as they struggled on. "Get him . . . to boat . . . artificial respiration."

This was mainly for Theo's benefit, if he could still hear them. As they all knew, if artificial respiration could be applied until the effects of the toxin receded, the victim could recover, and Arden wanted him to know they hadn't forgotten.

"Right," Frank said brightly. "We'll take . . . turns. All . . . have dinner in Iquitos . . . tonight." But his eyes were rolling back in his head and he had begun to stagger with Theo's weight. He was more delicately built than Arden, and he was clearly in agony, at the very end of his rope.

As was the stronger Arden. His lower back shrieked with pain, and every breath drove shards of glass into his lungs. His legs were beyond pain; he was no longer running, only driving each leg one excruciating, slogging step at a time. How many more could he force them to take? And were they really getting any closer to the boat, or were they going deeper into Chayacuro country?

Again, seemingly from a few hundred feet behind them, came a casual, softly spoken syllable or two of the Chayacuro language.

Frank slowed, struggling for air. "Can't . . . carry . . . anymore!" he groaned. "Got to . . . put him down."

Arden wouldn't have been able to haul Theo much farther either, and it was with mixed guilt and relief that he slipped out from under Theo's arm and helped Frank lay him gently on the mossy ground.

Frank crouched beside the supine, inert body and looked up at Arden. "We have to hide him. We can't let them . . ." He couldn't bring himself to say it. "You take his legs. I'll take—"

"Are you out of your mind?" Arden cried in a hoarse whisper. "They're right behind us. Do you want us *all* to die?" He was tugging at Frank as he spoke. "Come *on*!"

Frank resisted, slapping angrily at Arden's hand. "He's still alive. He can hear us."

Theo's eyes were open, though unmoving. He could see them too. But there was nothing they could do. Hauling him farther was out of the question. "The hell with you then," Arden said, straightening and turning away. "I'm going."

"Wait! I'm coming, I'm coming!" Frank bent quickly to kiss Theo's forehead. "Don't worry, little brother, we'll be back for you," he said, choking on the words. Tears dripped from the end of his nose, but he let Arden drag him to his feet.

They had hurried on for only another minute or so before they stopped dead at the sound of Chayacuro voices carried on the still, heavy air; not the laconic syllables they'd been hearing till now, but an excited jabbering.

Frank squeezed his eyes shut. "Oh, God, they found him. Oh, please, no."

"Not necessarily. They—" Arden's voice died in his throat at the unmistakable *chunk* of a machete chopping into something that didn't quite sound like wood. "I'm sorry, Frank."

Frank turned stricken eyes toward the sound and actually began to stumble blindly in that direction.

Arden grabbed him by the collar. "What the hell are you doing? There's nothing we can do for him now. Come on, snap out of it. We have to keep going."

Frank let himself be turned around by Arden and goaded into moving forward again, but he was like a man in a trance now, going wherever Arden pushed or pulled him. They had thrown off their heavy backpacks—the precious bag of seeds now hung from Arden's belt—and they were crossing a less thickly overgrown area where the going was easier and quieter, and they were less likely to be overheard.

But the same was true for the Chayacuro.

"Oh!" Frank exclaimed as a dart struck him in the soft, V-shaped space just below the left ear and behind the jawline. "Oh, no."

Like his brother before him, he plucked it out and threw it away. As with his brother, it made little difference. Half paralyzed already, perhaps with grief or despair, he stumbled after Arden into a heavier, more concealing thicket, but made it only fifty yards before collapsing in a heap across Arden's legs, sending them both sprawling. Arden got quickly to his feet, but Frank lay where he was. One trembling hand reached up to Arden.

Arden recoiled from it as if it were a snake. The skin on the back of his neck tightened instinctively against the prick that must surely come at any moment. "Frank—"

Instead of a dart, a slender, naked Indian burst out of the brush only five yards from them and froze, staring shocked and openmouthed at them. He carried an immensely long blowgun, longer than he was, but he was only a youth, thin and unmuscled, Arden saw, no more than twelve or thirteen.

"Hahhhh!" He shook the blowgun at them.

Arden, in a sort of dull shock of his own, raised the Beretta and shot him in the chest, then shot him again as he crumpled with a sigh.

Whether Frank was even aware of what had happened was unclear. His gaze was loose and unfocused. "Arden, don't leave me here," he said thickly. "I can make it. Just help . . . just . . . uhh . . ."

Arden turned and fled, but quickly came to a stop. Hesitating for only a moment, he ran back to where Frank and the boy lay. The boy's eyes were open, staring at the sky. A pool of blood was spreading out from under his shoulders, but the two black holes in his chest were almost bloodless.

"Arden . . . ," Frank said, his eyes shining. "Thank . . . thank you. God bless you . . . I knew . . . I knew you wouldn't . . ."

Arden tried not to look at him. He snatched up the bag of seeds that had come untied from his belt when the two of them had fallen and dashed back into the jungle, toward the river.

August 12, 1976

Mr. A. K. Chua
Executive Vice President, Research and Development
Gunung Jerai Industries Sdn. Bhd.
Level 3, Amoda Building, No. 22 Jalan Imbi
Kuala Lumpur

Dear Mr. Chua:

It was a pleasure meeting with you in Miami earlier this week. I hope that you (and the Hevea *seeds) had a safe flight back to Kuala Lumpur.*

As you requested, I am putting into writing the tragic events that attended the securing of these seeds.

On August 4 of this year, having acquired the thousand blight-resistant Hevea brasiliensis *seeds which we* had contracted for (plus another two hundred as backup in case of spoilage), my companions, Theodore and Franklin Molina, and I were attacked without provocation by Chayacuro Indians as we returned to the boat that we had left on the Amazon for the return journey to Iquitos. The first sign of them was when Theo was struck in the neck by a poisoned blowgun dart. A second dart hit my backpack.

We immediately fled toward the boat, which we believed to be some two miles farther on. For several hundred yards we hacked our way through the jungle with the Indians in pursuit some distance behind. When Theo was no longer able to run, or even walk, Frank and I carried him between us for a few hundred feet more, until it became inescapably apparent that he was dead. With our own strength failing and the Indians closing in, we had no choice but to leave him and continue our own escape.

A few minutes later, Frank was also hit by a dart, and at once showed signs of hysteria. I was unable to stop him from running wildly off through the jungle in what I was sure was the wrong direction. Nevertheless, I ran after him, catching up to him only when he stumbled and fell. At this point, one of the Indians suddenly appeared, brandishing his blowgun. I managed to shoot him just as he was about to release another dart.

By this time, Frank was completely paralyzed, able only to move his eyes. Apparently his frantic activity had hastened the circulation of the poison. He died in my arms.

Using the failing strength I had left, I again made for the boat, where I started up the engine and arrived in Iquitos that evening.

Once there, I made a full report to the police and waited for five days at our base hotel in the faint hope that I might have been wrong about my companions having perished, that I might have mistaken paralysis for death, and that either or both of them had somehow *survived and would show up. Needless to say, neither of them did.*

If you require further information, I would be glad to provide it.

In closing, I would like to thank you for your prompt initial payment. I wish you the best of luck with the seeds, and I look forward to accepting your kind invitation to visit the Gunung Jerai plantations to see the new plantings for myself.

Sincerely yours,
Arden Scofield

ONE

WHAT with pitchers of beer at not much more than half price and hot buffalo wings at ten for a buck, Brothers on a Wednesday night was not the best place in the world, or even in Iowa City, for quiet, sober reflection. The place was jammed with students—the university campus was a scant block away—and the noise level was enough to rattle the windows up and down Dubuque Street.

Nevertheless, quiet, sober reflection was exactly what Tim Loeffler, a graduate student in the University of Iowa's prestigious Ethnobotanical Institute, was shooting for. Unfortunately, the "quiet" part had been out of the question from the start, and the "sober" part was beginning to get away from him, inasmuch as he and his four buddies were working on their third pitcher of Bud. But with his friends now taking their turns at the nearby foosball table, he was able to more or less collect his thoughts and sort through what was bothering him.

He'd gotten cold feet; that was it in a nutshell. When he'd first heard about the upcoming Amazon cruise and learned that none of his fellow grad students had signed up, he'd jumped at the chance. Almost a full week in the wilds under the direction of his major professor, Arden Scofield, with no other students competing for Scofield's attention; it would be a heaven-sent chance to get on his good side, and—at long last—to get his Ph.D. dissertation topic approved, maybe right then and there. The other two members of his committee—Maggie Gray and Dr. Gus Slivovitz—had signed off on it six months ago. Only Scofield had held back his approval, merrily sending him back to the drawing board each time Tim had submitted it to him, always with one niggling, incredibly time-consuming "suggestion" or other. And the ironic thing was, Tim had taken on the miserable topic specifically to please Scofield, who went in for such subjects: "Agrobiodiversity conservation relating to consumer-driven strategies as they pertain to chick pea cultivation in the central Midwestern United States." Just looking at the title practically put him to sleep, and here he'd been laboring on the wretched thing for almost three years, with no end in sight as long as Scofield kept waffling.

But this was it; he'd had it. Three years of classes and three more years slaving over the damn dissertation were enough. It was now or never. He'd been offered a fantastic postdoctoral fellowship at the Harvard Botanical Museum— Harvard, for God's sake, the granddaddy of ethnobotany!— scheduled to begin the next academic year, the catch being, of course, that he had to be a bona fide postdoc himself to accept it. His coursework, comprehensive exams, and language requirements had been gotten out of the way long ago. All that remained now was Scofield's squiggle of a signature on the title page, and he was determined to get it from him before the trip was over. There would never be a better opportunity.

So why the cold feet? Because it had finally dawned on

him that a big part of his problem with Scofield—or more accurately, Scofield's problem with him—was that the man simply didn't like him, had never liked him. Who knew why? Maybe Scofield, who loved center stage and thought he was the greatest lecturer on God's green earth, didn't like him because Tim had once or twice inadvertently stepped on his punch lines. (It was hard not to when you were hearing them for the tenth time.) Or maybe Scofield, underneath the hail-fellow-jolly-well-met act, disapproved of Tim's interest in ethnopharmacology. Tim's original choice for a dissertation topic had been an examination of the preparation and use of hallucinogenic plant extracts among the Indians of Southern Ecuador—now *that* was something he really could have gotten his head into. But at the idea, Scofield's caterpillar eyebrows had come together, he had stuck his pipe in his mouth, and he'd made one of his friendly, phony, well-now-let's-you-and-I-think-this-through-together faces that meant anything but. Cravenly, Tim had caved in and accepted the agrobiodiversity topic the moment Scofield suggested it. He had even more cravenly thanked him for it, though his heart had been plummeting.

For the ten-thousandth time he mentally kicked himself for not choosing Maggie Gray as his major prof. Maggie, despite that hard-shelled, sarcastic bitchiness of hers, was not only a hell of a lot easier to get along with ("Call me Maggie," she'd told him the first time he'd met her. "Call me Arden" was something he was still waiting to hear and probably never would), but Maggie, unlike Scofield, had a strong interest in ethnopharmacology herself and would have welcomed his Ecuadorian project as a thesis subject. But no, he'd leaped at the chance to get the famous Scofield as his major professor, imagining all the good it would do him in his career.

What a laugh. And the really irritating part of it was, everybody knew that the supposedly straight-arrow Scofield himself was a damned druggie, or near enough to it to make no difference. His everyday tea of choice after dinner was known to be something called Mate Celillo, which he claimed was an ordinary Bolivian *mate*—a popular tea, often recommended for altitude sickness and stomach problems, and made from coca leaves from which the addictive alkaloids had been removed. He drank it, so he claimed, because of its digestive properties and because it was a soothing way to end the day and thus helped him sleep. But Tim, who had his suspicions, had once swiped a couple of his tea bags and tried it, and he'd been a lot more than soothed. For an hour or so there had been a wonderfully relaxing, extremely pleasant sense of floating and well-being, and then, without seeing it coming, he'd suddenly plummeted into a deep, nine-hour sleep—in his chair, while watching television. Despite a little morning-after letdown—nothing new there—it had been a great trip, and Tim had made several efforts to locate some of the stuff on his own, but so far, no luck.

Getting back to Scofield, maybe the problem was that the guy just didn't like his face, or his nose, or the shape of his ears—just a matter of chemistry, at bottom unexplainable and irreversible. Well, if so, it went both ways by now; he could hardly look at Scofield without feeling his stomach turn over. But whatever it was, it was there, all right, and earlier tonight, when he and his pals had been talking about it, one of them had raised a pertinent point: "If he just plain doesn't like you after three years of knowing you, what makes you think that being around him twenty-four hours a day is going to make him like you any more?"

It was a reasonable question, and Tim was worried. He couldn't imagine coming out of this detesting Scofield any less than before, so why should it work the other way around? The thing was, he was never at his best around the guy—clumsy and stupid, saying the wrong thing, usually overly obsequious, but sometimes (the wrong times, inevitably) overly assertive, even blundering. His meetings with Scofield invariably left him feeling hollow and sick to his stomach. What if he picked the wrong time to present him with the latest incarnation of the dissertation? What if Scofield turned it down yet again?

Well, if that happened, that was the end of it. Enough of his life had been wasted. He would throw in the towel. With his master's degree he could certainly teach botany at a junior college, or maybe get some kind of job with a company that made herbal products or natural nutrients or something. But good-bye, "Dr." Loeffler; farewell, Harvard; so long, big-time research.

He gave his head a shake and poured another glass from the pitcher. What the hell, the die was cast, he couldn't get out of it now, and maybe that was a good thing, all things considered. One way or another, he was headed for a life-altering experience on the Amazon. By the time it was over he would know exactly where he stood, and that was a feeling he hadn't had for a long time.

A little over three blocks away, in her office on the third floor of the darkened biology building on the University of Iowa campus, Assistant Professor Margaret—Maggie—Gray was also pondering the life-altering possibilities of the upcoming Amazon cruise with Arden Scofield.

One thing was crystal clear. She had no future in the Ethnobotanical Institute or its parent, the Department of Biological Sciences. Once again her promotion to associate professor had not come through. That amounted to a not-so-subtle way of telling her to find another job someplace, because she certainly had no future at UI, especially considering the new, cost-driven plan to cut back Institute faculty next year and fold it into Biological Sciences, with no formal status of its own. There would be funds for only one faculty member in ethnobotany, instead of the current three, and she had no illusions about who that was going to be. She and Gus Slivovitz were history, or soon would be. Gus, seeing the handwriting on the wall, had already applied to and been accepted at some wretched agricultural school in Mississippi, or maybe one of those other equally dreadful states down there . . . Louisiana, Arkansas, Oklahoma . . . which, if we were going to be painfully honest about it, was about where Gus had belonged all along.

Looking out over the lamplit, shadowed campus walkways from her desk, sipping tawny port from a tumbler, she was in a downcast frame of mind and deep in self-recrimination. She was thinking bitterly of how much good her Ph.D. had done her. All that work, and where had it gotten her? At thirty-nine she was still an assistant professor with a reputation (well-earned) as an acid-tongued, going-nowhere, old spinster with no life outside the lab. And the sacrifices she'd made, the wrong turns in the road! If she'd gone to Los Angeles with Curt all those years ago instead of insisting on hurrying back to finish her oh-so-important coursework at Cornell, maybe now she'd *have* a life.

She swallowed the rest of the port and, grim-faced (she'd feel like hell in the morning), poured two inches more. Make that three. What the hell. Her past was all water under the bridge; nothing to be done about it now. It was her future she had to think about.

And Arden Scofield, unlikely as it seemed, held the key to it. In addition to Arden's professorship—his *full professorship*—at UI, he was a more-or-less permanent part-time prof at the Universidad Nacional Agraria de la Selva in Peru, where he supervised an extension program for local farmers. That university was creating a new position of full professor of medical ethnobotany the following year, and according to Arden, he had already recommended Maggie; the job was as good as hers if she wanted it. She didn't doubt that this was true. A recommendation from the great, the celebrated Arden Scofield would be sure to carry a lot of weight. Besides, the job was made for her. Medical ethnobotany—the study of how indigenous peoples use local plants for curative purposes—was her area of expertise, and the closest thing she had to a consuming interest . . . her one interest, really; she had published several well-received papers on it (and *still* no associate professorship!). So all that remained was for her to go down with Arden to Tingo Maria, where the school was located, and have Arden introduce her to some of the administrators.

And that was the plan. She would come along on the Amazon cruise, paying her own way, but assisting Arden as needed. That part of it was quite appealing, really. She had done her graduate fieldwork on the Rio Orinoco in Venezuela fifteen years ago and had made several subsequent trips there, but this one would be to the great Amazon Basin itself. She would do some collecting—a lot of collecting—and she was eager for the chance to sit down with local shamans and *curanderos*. These "uneducated," unworldly Indian healers, carrying in their heads the results of thousands of years of experimentation with barks, roots, leaves, and flowers, were the world's first and best medical ethnobotanists.

So many medically useful herbs and drugs had already come out of Amazon Indian healing practices: analgesics, astringents, expectorants, hypnotics, steroids, antiseptics, antipyretics, anaesthetics. Even their poisons—their neurotoxins and paralytics—had turned out to have enormous potential benefit. D-tubocurarine, an extract of curare, was a blessed muscle relaxant that had transformed surgery. Rotenone, the safest biodegradable insecticide in the world, had first been extracted from plant materials used by Amazonian Indians as fish poisons. What untold treasures were still locked up in the minds of those mysterious jungle scientists awaiting discovery? Cures for AIDS? Alzheimer's? Cancer? Delve into their ancient lore, and you unlock the gate to the greatest storehouse of natural medicine in the world. But time was running short. They were a vanishing breed, these old shamans, and no one was taking their place. It was an opportunity she wouldn't have missed under any circumstances.

After the cruise was over (and this was the part that had her grumbling to herself between sips), she would fly on with Arden to Tingo Maria to discuss the details of the appointment: responsibilities, lab facilities, accommodations, and so on. Then, assuming she was interested, in a little less than a year she would fly to Tingo Maria again, but this time on a one-way ticket.

The question was: did she want to? Her Spanish was rusty, but with a year to work on it, that was no problem; it had been one of her two qualifying languages for the Ph.D. And the salary was attractive, more than she was getting at UI, plus all kinds of great perks. Beyond that, it would be a distinct and not inconsiderable pleasure to outrank Arden, technically a mere adjunct professor, in the faculty hierarchy. But, Jesus Christ, the Universidad Nacional Agraria de la Selva? The National Agrarian University of the Jungle? How appealing was that?

And what about the town, Tingo Maria? Arden, who lived down there for a good part of every year, had talked it up, but Arden was the kind of person who didn't much care or even notice where he lived. Maggie did. When she had Googled the city to get some other points of view, the descriptions hadn't done much for her spirits. "Tropical, hot, and wet," "a tatty, ugly town," "the drug-trafficking capital of Peru," "the saddest kind of 'modern,' ramshackle South American town, cobbled together out of nothing in 1938, and already rusting to pieces." Not a lot to draw her there.

On the other hand, what did she have in Iowa City?

"OUCH."

Mel Pulaski gingerly peeled the Band-Aid—well it wasn't a Band-Aid, it was a lump of cotton held on by a scrap of masking tape; the Providence County Health Department was making a point about its dissatisfaction with its current budget—from his beefy upper arm.

Standing at the bathroom counter in his undershirt, he checked the swollen, reddened site of his tetanus booster shot in the mirror and gingerly touched it with a finger. "Ooh."

At the twin sink beside him, his wife Dolly, in the flannel nightgown she'd taken to wearing lately, was applying a squib of toothpaste to her brush. "That last shot's bothering you, isn't it?"

"Oh, a little bit. It's the only one that has."

"No, it isn't. Your arm hurt for a couple of days after the one for yellow fever."

"True."

"And you didn't feel that great while you were taking the typhoid pills. I had to nurse you for two days."

"Yeah, that's right, I forgot. That was not fun. Ah well, such is the life of the freelance writer. Danger, sacrifice, and adventure abound at every turn."

"I still don't understand why you're so keen to go on this trip," Dolly mumbled around her toothbrush. "I don't see the point."

"Well, for one thing, EcoAdventure Travel is paying me three thousand bucks for an article on it, and another five hundred for photos, which will cover the cost and then some."

"Not-much-some, when you figure in the cost of all those immunizations."

"Okay, then," Mel said reasonably. "There's the fact that Arden Scofield will be on it, and I've got some ideas for another book we can do together. I think he's going to be interested."

A few months earlier he had concluded a yearlong ghostwriting association with Scofield on an autobiographical narrative, *Potions, Poisons, and Piranhas: A Planthunter's Odyssey*. It hadn't been that hard either. Scofield had a pretty good way with words himself, and he'd led an exciting, interesting life; he just hadn't wanted to take the time to organize the material and do the grunt work that went with rewriting and editing.

Dolly snorted. " 'Do together.' You practically wrote that whole damned book for him, and he's going to get all the credit."

Big, strong, slow, and mellow, a onetime linebacker with the Minnesota Vikings, Mel Pulaski was a hard man to get into an argument, even when Dolly seemed to be spoiling for one, which had been happening a lot lately. Well, he understood why. She was forty-seven. It was the dreaded Change of Life, and she was having a hard time with it, psychologically as well as physically. It didn't help that she was five years older than he was, something that was clearly starting to bother her a lot more than it did him. Mel had stopped telling her that the age difference didn't matter, because when he did it only ticked her off even more.

"Well, he's the expert, honey," he said. "He's the only reason anybody would buy the book. Me, I'm just a hired hack. Anyway, who cares about the credit? We got fifteen thousand bucks for what probably amounted to maybe two months' work altogether. That's a pretty good paycheck in my line of work."

"I thought you couldn't stand him."

"I never said I couldn't stand him. I said he was a phony, posturing pissant of a prima donna." He grinned. "But for another fifteen grand I guess I can stand him a little longer. Pass me the floss, will you, babe?"

Unsmiling, Dolly passed it, rinsed her toothbrush, and put it back in the rack. "Fifteen thousand. And how much is *he* going to get?"

"He's a name, sweetie; I'm not. It's his life the book's about, not mine. And don't forget, my name *is* going to be on the cover right up there with his. That's not going to hurt my career."

"I'll believe it when I see it," Dolly said. And then, a moment later, as a muttered afterthought: "What career?"

Mel sighed. The moods were worst at night. In the morning she'd shyly and sincerely apologize and say she didn't know what had gotten into her, and surely he knew she hadn't meant it (which he did). And things would go smoothly until the next night, or maybe the one after that.

Mel had been doing a lot of Web research on menopause. Among the things he'd learned was that it typically lasted anywhere from six to thirteen years. He just prayed Dolly's was the six-year variety.

* * *

A seasoned underground commuter, Duayne V. Osterhout knew precisely where to stand on the platform of the cavern-like Smithsonian Metro station in order to be first through the rear doors of the second car, from which he would have a clear shot at his preferred corner seat, wedged in by the window. As usual he had arrived in time for the 5:23 P.M. Or-ange Line train to West Falls Church, in order, not to take it, but to be there when the passengers boarded, so that he could assume his place on the platform the moment the doors slid closed and thus be in position for the 5:37. He did not consider a fourteen-minute wait a high price to pay for a comfortable seat, with no sweating straphangers leaning over him, during the twenty-five-minute ride to Virginia. At this time in the evening on a weekday, planning was essen-tial if he didn't want to stand most of the way home.

When the platform lights began blinking to signal the imminent arrival of the train, a man with a backpack—a little old to be traveling with a backpack in Duayne's opinion—more or less unthinkingly bulled his way to the front of the crowd that had now collected behind Duayne. (Duayne was not the only one who knew precisely where to stand so that the doors opened directly in front of him, but he was one of the few who was willing to wait from the departure of one train to the arrival of the next.)

"Excuse me, sir," Duayne said. "I believe I was here first. So were these other people." His heart was thumping, but there were times when you had to stand up for what was right. Otherwise you invited anarchy, the kind of thing to be found on the New York City subway system.

The man stared malignly at him. "Well, excuse *me*, buddy. I didn't see no sign that said you could reserve a place to stand." But when Duayne unflinchingly returned the stare, the man said, "Ah, the hell with it," and moved off.

"Thank you, sir!" the woman behind Duayne said to him as the doors opened, and Duayne strode to his accus-tomed seat feeling bold and beneficent.

He took from under his arm his copy of the day's *Post*, but instead of slipping on his glasses to read it, he stared out the window at the lights whizzing by as the train left the station, and then at the pulsing black of the tunnel walls. Even after the adrenaline rush from his encounter had receded, he continued to stare unseeing at the darkness. He was thinking about the Amazon River.

He was also thinking, as he often did, about bugs.

Unlike the other members of Arden Scofield's Amazon expedition, Duayne Osterhout was not an ethnobotanist or even a botanist. He was that even rarer bird, an ethnoentomologist. As the senior research scientist in the Housing and Structural Section of the Urban Entomology Bureau of the United States Department of Agriculture, he was an authority on the extraordinary creatures referred to as "pests" by the uneducated general population: silverfish, beetles, ants, and the like. In particular, he was a much-published expert on that miracle of propagation, survival, and resourcefulness, *Periplaneta americana*, the common American cockroach, and its many cousins.

It was Duayne's not-so-secret shame that in all his forty-eight years he had never set foot in the tropics, from whence almost all insects had originally come. Never had he gloried in the sight of a *Blaberus giganteus*, its carapace gleaming brown and gold in the equatorial sunshine; never had he stood among giant jungle plants, eye to eye to eye, or rather eye to metallic, antlerlike mandibles, with a *Cyclommatus pulchellus*. It was not a conscious decision that had kept him from seeing firsthand the insect marvels of the southern hemisphere, it was simply that he hadn't gotten around to it. He'd gotten married before he was out of graduate school, and then his work had consumed him, along with the raising of a family of three. Life had gotten in the way, that's all. Besides that, his wife Lea wasn't much of a traveler aside from luxury cruising, and she wasn't very keen on his going anywhere without her. And—let's be honest about it—he hadn't ever gotten up his resolve enough to press the matter.

However, that had all changed now. Three days after their youngest daughter had left for college in Ohio last year, Lea had up and left him to move into some kind of socialist commune in upstate New York. Although it had been a shock at first, he had been astonished at how little difference it had made in the basics of his day-to-day life, and at how quickly he had been able to settle into a satisfying, fulfilling routine. It was as if he'd been living someone else's life for the last twenty-five years.

It was his eldest daughter, Beth, who was responsible for his upcoming Amazon adventure. Beth had taken after her father from the start, with a gratifying interest in natural history, but somewhere along the way she'd moved from fauna to flora. Now she was a fledgling plant biologist with the National Science Foundation, but last year she'd still been finishing up her graduate work at Georgetown. Someone had told her about Arden Scofield's botanical field expeditions to the Huallaga Valley near Tingo Maria, Peru, and she'd signed up. The trip she'd described had sounded so fascinating to Duayne—there had been so many amazing bugs!—that he had telephoned Scofield to apply for a place in the next expedition if there were any to spare. When Scofield told him that he was welcome, and that they would be exploring the mighty Amazon River itself this time, Duayne couldn't have been more thrilled.

There was, however, an unexpected fly in the ointment. Only a few days ago, he had learned from his ex-wife that Scofield had made some persistent and highly improper advances to Beth during the expedition. She had held him off, of course, but the thought of it made Duayne's blood boil. It wasn't only because his own daughter had been the recipient of Scofield's unsavory attentions, it was the very idea of a celebrated, mature scientist . . . a *teacher* . . . a figure of trust and authority, taking advantage of an innocent, starry-eyed student barely into her twenties—*any* innocent, young, starry-eyed student—who had been entrusted into his care. Duayne knew such men and despised them. Before the expedition was over, he planned to

have a few sharp words with Scofield and give him what-
for. You couldn't let men like that simply think they had
gotten away with it free and clear.

But for the moment, all that was secondary to the inex-
tinguishable glow in his heart as he considered the great
adventure to come.

The Amazon River! He whispered it to himself, just for
the pleasure of forming the words as the train burrowed,
deep and echoing, under the Potomac. *The Amazon River!*

TWO

Set in the sun-drenched coastal splendor of Cabo San Lucas on the Mexican Riviera is the elegantly rustic, eco-friendly Mandalay-Pacific Spa, where you will find the balance between body, mind, and soul that is the key to a wholesome, healthy, and energetic lifestyle. Mandalay-Pacific Spa helps you achieve this goal through the integration of the four vital elements of traditional holistic healing: Water, Fire, Earth, and Air. Our treatments, known since antiquity, will help you to achieve the perfect state of balance and harmony that our harried modern lifestyles cry out for.

During your relaxing, luxurious, seven-day winter holiday, you and your companion will experience the life-renewing pleasures of:

- Traditional Persian clay treatments that cleanse your body of physical, emotional, and spiritual toxicities.
- Herbal body scrub/wraps that break up crystallized nodes and dissolve blocked energy. (Your choices include

coffee bean scrub with crushed turnip wrap and grated coconut scrub with fresh papaya wrap.)

• Antistress, aromatherapeutic foot massages using grape seed oil and lavender, clove, and lemon extracts.
• Naturopathic facials that rejuvenate and revive through the application of yogurt-and-fresh-cucumber masks and deep-penetration limewater-and-sea-salt scrub.
• Ayurvedic total-body massages employing charcoal and frankincense to . . .

"Umm . . ." Julie Oliver stopped reading and slid the peach-colored, almond-scented flyer back across the table. "Are you sure you want *me* to go with you?" she asked doubtfully. "I don't know, Marti, that doesn't really sound like something I'd enjoy all that much."

Marti Lau shook her head. "What, a week in Cabo with enough pampering to last a lifetime? Free transportation, free food, free everything? What's not to like? And *sunshine*! Wouldn't you like to see what color the sky is again?"

To clinch her point, she gestured out the window beside their table, which overlooked Puget Sound, or as much of it as could be seen on this typical early-November day in Seattle. A dismal, freezing mist hung low over the dull gray water, totally closing out everything more than a few hundred yards offshore. As they watched, a big, green-and-white state ferry slid slowly away from Colman Dock and disappeared almost immediately into the murk, looking forlorn and bedraggled and without a single passenger out on the open, wet deck.

"Well, why doesn't John go with you?" Julie said, then turned to address Marti's husband directly. "You're the one who's always grumping about the Seattle weather, John. I would have thought you'd love a chance to be in sunny Mexico for a week."

"Yeah, but not enough to sit still for getting scrubbed with a turnip," John Lau said. "No, thanks, not my kind of thing."

"Julie, I just don't see what your problem is," Marti said. "You already said you could get away."

Julie nodded. She was a supervising park ranger at Olympic National Park headquarters in Port Angeles, she was overdue for some vacation time, and November was a good month to take it. "I could, yes . . ."

"Think of those warm, oily massages—"

"That's just it. Actually, I'm not that crazy about massages."

Marti stared at her. "How could anyone not be crazy about massages?"

"Julie doesn't really enjoy being touched by other people," said Gideon Oliver, her husband and the fourth and final member of the party. "Neither do I, for that matter."

Marti guffawed. "That sure sounds like the recipe for a happy marriage."

Julie smiled back at her. "Well, I make certain exceptions."

"I'm relieved to hear it. Come on, though, will you at least think about it? It'd really be fun."

"I am thinking about it," Julie said, getting back to her wild-salmon-and-tarragon-mayonnaise sandwich. "Quite seriously."

Old friends all, they were lunching at Maximilien in Seattle's Pike Place Market, where Marti had just sprung the surprise she'd so ponderously hinted at on the telephone the night before. She had bought a twenty-five-dollar raffle ticket at a charity event a month earlier, and had wound up winning the grand prize: a one-week, all-inclusive stay at Cabo San Lucas's posh Mandalay-Pacific Spa, to be used anytime before the end of the year. For two. And she wanted company.

She poked impatiently at her cheeseless vegetarian tarte flambé. (Marti was a nutritionist at the Virginia Mason Medical Center in the city and imposed on herself— and claimed to like—the same meatless, fatless, saltless, sugarless regimen she inflicted on her captive clientele.)

"So," she pressed after all of thirty seconds, "have you thought about it?"

"Yes, and it does sound tempting. But, well . . ."

"I know what's worrying you," Marti said. "What would we do with the boys?"

"The *boys*?" John demanded.

"The *boys*?" Gideon said. "Are you by any chance referring to—"

"Well, I wouldn't quite put it that way," Julie said, ignoring them, "but I can't help wondering how they'd get along for a week without us."

In this they were engaging in the affectionate self-delusion of wives everywhere that, in the absence of their domesticating influence for even a week, their husbands would regress to the natural male status of unshaven, uncivilized, antisocial troglodytes, and they, the wives, would come home to find the beds unmade, the ashtrays littered with cigars, the floors with socks and underwear, and the kitchen sink overflowing with beer cans and old, crusted pizza boxes.

In point of fact, however, "the boys" in question were two accomplished men in their early forties, both well able to take care of themselves, and both with highly developed senses of personal hygiene. Gideon Oliver was a professor of physical anthropology at the University of Washington's Port Angeles campus and a highly regarded forensic anthropologist known to the world's press (to his mild dismay and the continuing amusement of his colleagues) as the Skeleton Detective. John Lau, whose relationship with Gideon went back even further than Julie's did, was an FBI special agent with specialties in firearms, ballistics, and international racketeering. John was a powerful, muscular six-two, Gideon a somewhat more slender six-one.

"I think maybe we could manage," Gideon said mildly. "Don't you, John?"

"Well, as long as it's not for more than a week," John agreed. "I'd need a change of socks by then."

The women paid no attention to them. "As it happens," Marti announced, "I have a plan."

"Why am I not surprised?" John murmured. He went back to work on the cheeseburger he had so predictably ordered. "Okay, may as well hear it," he said resignedly.

"It's simple," she said. "Give Phil a call and see what he's got going in the next few weeks. Take a trip. You both have a standing invitation, don't you?"

"I could do that," John said amiably. "I've got vacation time coming."

"It wouldn't work for me," Gideon said. "It's right in the middle of the quarter. I have classes."

"Ask Lyle Spatz to take them for you," Julie suggested. "He owes you, doesn't he?"

Gideon nodded slowly. "Well, that might work, especially if it's over Thanksgiving so we're already skipping a few classes anyway. I'd have to figure some things out."

"Could be fun," John said, "depending on what Phil's got going." He glanced out at the bleak day. "But if it's not somewhere south of here, forget about it."

"At least you wouldn't be moping around by yourselves, and you wouldn't have to scrounge up your own meals," Marti said.

"And it probably *would* be interesting," Julie said. "Don't you think?" And Gideon could tell that she was warming to the idea of her own week in Cabo San Lucas.

All right, then he would help make it happen. "With Phil, it's always interesting," he said. "Okay, let me see what he's got on the calendar."

He borrowed Julie's cell phone, took it to a quiet corner near the entrance, and hit the button to speed-dial Phil Boyajian's number in Anacortes.

Another old friend, Phil's relationship with Gideon dated back two decades, to Gideon's days at the University of Wisconsin, where they'd both been graduate students in the anthropology department. Since earning his Ph.D., Gideon had pursued a reasonably straightforward path up the academic ladder. Phil's progression had not only been anything but straightforward, it had been distinctly peculiar. As he himself had described it, he'd had a career in reverse. He'd started at the top, with a tenure-track position at a major state university lined up even before he'd completed his doctorate in cultural anthropology. He'd lasted just one year. ("Can't stand the politicking!") From there he'd gone on to a community college in Seattle, managing to stick it out two years this time before quitting. ("How can anyone stand all those damn committees?") Then came a stint in a high school, also not to his liking. ("I'm not a jail guard.") This was followed—inevitably—by grade-school teaching. ("Have you ever tried spending all day with eight-year-olds?")

With just about nothing else to descend to, he had hooked up as a tour guide with On the Cheap, a new company that promoted and arranged economy travel. With his scruffy appearance and no-frills approach to life, his natural optimism, his readiness to see the good in everyone, and his love of travel, it was the job he'd been born for. Now a partner in the firm, he still led about twenty foreign tours a year, and there was always space for the Laus or the Olivers. And if they were willing to lend a hand when and if needed, they were welcome to come along at no charge, or rather at cost.

It was a very good deal, and Gideon and Julie had taken him up on it twice now, once on a trip to Costa Rica, and once on a tour of Italy's Lake Maggiore region.

Phil answered on the third ring and immediately came up with a proposition.

"How does Peru sound? Six days, starting in three weeks, November twenty-sixth."

"Peru!" Gideon exclaimed, thrilled. "Fantastic! I've wanted to go for years; I've just never gotten it together to go. That'd be great, Phil, wonderful! Machu Picchu, Sipán—"

"Well, don't get too—"

"—the Moche tombs, Cuzco, Huaca Rajada—"

"Hey, hold your horses, will you? Forget archaeology. That's not exactly what we'll be doing."

"—the ruins at—it's not?"

"Not exactly, no." He cleared his throat.

"IT better be someplace warm," John said as Gideon returned to the table. "That's my one and only condition." John, who'd grown up in Hawaii, loved hot weather. He considered it a cruel trick of fate that he'd been assigned to cold, gloomy Seattle. He claimed to have a standing request into the bureau for a transfer to Mexicali if they ever opened a regional office there.

"Well, then," Gideon said, "you'll be happy. How does eight days on the Amazon sound?"

John's eyes popped wide open. "Seriously?"

"*On* the Amazon?" Julie asked. "You mean on a boat?"

"Yup, an Amazon cruise."

"That sounds fabulous," Marti said. "Hey, maybe *we* should go. I love cruises. Talk about pampering."

"Yes, but this is Phil we're talking about," Julie said. "On the Cheap. Somehow, I don't think pampering will be on the agenda."

"Don't they have anacondas on the Amazon?" John asked. "Headhunters? Poisonous frogs? Giant spiders?"

"I'm pretty sure headhunting died out thirty years ago or so," Gideon said. "About the others, I don't know."

"And what about mosquitoes?"

"I believe there are a few down there."

"And malaria? How many damn shots would we have to get?"

"There aren't any shots for malaria, there are pills you take. Other than that, there may be a couple of other shots, just to be on the safe side."

"Great, I love shots," John said under his breath, but Gideon could see he was just going through the motions. He was intrigued with the idea, and who wouldn't be? "So where would we pick up the ship?"

"In Peru. A town called Iquitos," Gideon said, "way upstream, near the headwaters of the Amazon." He returned to his salad of smoked salmon, Dungeness crab, and avocado, picking it over to see if he'd missed any slivers of crab. "It's not Phil's usual thing, though. That is, it's not an official On the Cheap tour, it's a kind of . . . I guess you'd say, an evaluation visit, and he wouldn't mind having us along to help him evaluate."

There was a cargo boat operator in Iquitos, he explained, who had been trying for some time to convert his rebuilt ship, the *Adelita*, to the tourist trade. The operator/captain, Alfredo Vargas, had earlier contacted Phil about Phil's writing up his would-be cruise enterprise in the next edition of *South America On the Cheap*. Phil had agreed to come down and check out the *Adelita* if and when Vargas got an actual boatload of paying passengers together for a bona fide cruise. That had been two years ago, and not long ago an exuberant Vargas had come through: a professor named Arden Scofield had chartered the ship for a week in late November for a scientific research cruise from Iquitos to Leticia, Colombia, a trip of 350 miles. Including Scofield, there would be a total of five paying passengers. Meals would be provided, and each passenger would have his or her own air-conditioned cabin with private bath. There were at present ten such cabins on the ship, but more would be added in the future as the cruise business prospered.

"In other words, other than telling Phil how we like it, we wouldn't have any responsibilities at all. Nothing to do. Just relax and enjoy it."

"A research cruise," Julie said. "What kind of research?"

"Well, apparently they're all ethnobotanists—"

"Ethnowhatanists?" Marti said.

"Ethnobotanists. Sort of a combination of cultural anthropologists and botanists. They study the way various peoples live with and use their local plants. You know, how they use them for medicine, for food, for clothing, and so on. Phil says they're going to be doing some scientific collecting— there's a tremendous number of unknown, uncataloged flora in the Amazon basin—and talking to shamans along the way to see what they can learn from them."

"Learn from shamans?" Marti snorted. "And these guys are supposed to be scientists?"

"Well, I know what you mean," said Gideon. "A lot of the shamanistic stuff is mumbo jumbo, but they do know an awful lot about the properties of their plants, especially the curative aspects, and some of it's very much worth knowing. It's been put to a lot of use in medicine, and there's still a lot to be learned."

They paused while the waiter cleared their plates and poured coffee for all.

Phil had offered a few other details, which Gideon now shared. Scofield held a dual professorship, spending most of the year at the University of Iowa, but also teaching at the Universidad Nacional Agraria de la Selva in Tingo Maria, Peru, where he ran an extension program that trained Amazonian coffee and cacao farmers in ecologically sound farming techniques.

Twice a year he took some of his American students and other interested people down to Peru on a botanical field expedition. Until now, they had always been treks in the Huallaga Valley near Tingo Maria, three hundred miles south of Iquitos and the Amazon, but this year he'd wanted to do something different: an Amazon River expedition. Hence, his hiring of the *Adelita*.

"So what would this cost us?" John asked.

"Well, Phil says he can get there and back for a six-hundred-dollar fare: Seattle to Iquitos, and then Leticia back to Seattle."

"That's a terrific deal," Marti said to John. "Harvey and Cece Sherman went to Peru in June and just their round trip to Lima was something like eleven hundred dollars."

"And once we're there," Gideon said, "we'll pay the same thing on the boat that Phil will—twenty dollars a day to cover food—a hundred and forty bucks for the week."

"So . . . seven hundred forty bucks for the whole deal?" John said.

"Right. The regular passengers are paying over thirteen hundred just for the cruise part."

John set his cup on its saucer with a decisive clink. "What the hell, let's do it. What's the name of the town again? Iquistos?"

"Iquitos," Gideon said, then added with a smile: "It rhymes with *mosquitoes*."

THREE

CAPTAIN Alfredo Vargas, founder and president of Amazonia Cruise Lines, headquartered in Iquitos, Peru, conducted most of his business meetings with government officials, potential investors, and prospective clients in the bright, pleasant bar of the Hotel Dorado Plaza, self-described, with some justification, as "the only five-star hotel in the Peruvian Amazon." While this practice might seem extravagant to some, it was in reality a measure of thrift on the captain's part, being far more cost-effective than renting a bona fide office full-time, especially inasmuch as his business meetings were few and far between. Of course, once Amazonia was on its feet, once there was a steady stream of passengers for the *Adelita*, once another ship or two had been added to what he fondly thought of as his "fleet," *then* there would be a fine office with an anteroom and a receptionist, and right on the Malecón Iarapacá too, the grandest boulevard in all Iquitos.

But for the time being, the elegant hotel bar served his purposes. It was where he had first met with the famous professor, Scofield, to negotiate the terms for the *Adelita*'s maiden voyage as a passenger ship. It was where he was sitting with him today to iron out the final details. But the meeting was not going well. Scofield had taken exception to Vargas's intention of having three additional passengers aboard: the man from On the Cheap and his two associates.

"I don't know about that now, Captain," he said pleasantly enough, digging at his cheek with the bit of his pipe. "That wasn't the arrangement, as I recall. Didn't we agree that my party would have the ship to themselves?"

"True, professor, very true, you're right about that. But these men, you see, are not passengers at all, not in the usual sense of the word. They will be there only to look at life aboard the *Adelita*. It's going to be in a travel book, you see—that is, if they are favorably impressed—and as you can imagine, this can be a great asset to my business."

They spoke Spanish. Although Vargas could converse quite well in English, he was more comfortable in his native language. Scofield was equally at ease in both.

"We can't have them interfering with our activities, you know," Scofield said. "That wouldn't do at all." He was a stocky, apple-cheeked man, handsomely boyish and twinkle-eyed, and he was speaking, as usual, with a playful, jokey air, but Vargas knew from their earlier meetings that he was not to be taken lightly. Underneath the pleasantries there was a man who was used to getting what he wanted.

"No, no, I can assure you that they won't. They are observers only. You'll hardly be aware they're there."

"All right, but I must require that the ship pursue *our* itinerary. Your eventual aim may be tourism, but on this trip it's strictly botany. Is that understood?"

"Perfectly, perfectly, professor. On that you have my word."

Despite the hotel's air-conditioning, Vargas was sweating. Scofield was a difficult customer, had been from the start. But he was also Vargas's only customer, with no others presently in sight. If he insisted that he didn't want Phil

Boyajian aboard, Vargas would have to accede. But it would be a blow to his hopes and plans. "Flowers and shamans, that's what it will be about," he said jovially. "Don't give it another thought."

Scofield pointed the pipe bit at him. "*Plants*, captain," he said merrily. "Botanicals. Not 'flowers.' "

"Yes, yes of course. Did I say flowers? Plants, I meant to say plants, nothing but plants and shamans." He hesitated. "Well, that is . . ."

One of Scofield's eyebrows lifted. "Yes?"

"Well, I'm sure this is already understood, but perhaps it's best to be perfectly clear. I am at present still in the cargo business. In addition to your group, we will be carrying a consignment of coffee, along with a few miscellaneous items—a little lumber, a little mail, a generator, a few pairs of rubber boots, a dining room table and chairs, a wooden door, and so on. The coffee is bound for a warehouse in Colombia; the other items will be dropped off on the return—"

"You use one of the warehouses on the Javaro tributary, do you not? The one not far from, what is it, San José de Chiquitos?"

Vargas was astonished. "Yes. How is it that you know that?"

Scofield laughed again. "A little preliminary research. Naturally, I wanted to know your regular routes and your stops."

"Oh, *very* few stops, and I can promise you there will be no inconvenience to you, no interference with—"

Scofield brushed his concerns aside. "That's fine, Captain. An excursion along the Javaro will be just the ticket."

Bernardo, the shirt-sleeved, bow-tied barman—very likely the only person in Iquitos who wore a bow tie, let alone owned one—brought their second round of drinks: a bourbon and soda for Scofield, and an Inca Kola for Vargas, who was too nervous to trust himself with anything alcoholic.

"All right then, I think we're all set as far as that goes," Scofield said after swallowing some of his whiskey. "Now

that I think about it, I can see some real advantages to having these guide book people along taking notes on everything. At any rate, I imagine we can look forward to some
excellent meals." He chuckled, shoulders shaking and face
pinkening a bit more.

Vargas played it safe and responded with a neutral
smile.

"So then, on to other matters," Scofield said. "Have you
found us a decent guide?"

"Indeed, I have, *señor*." Vargas was relieved to change
the subject. "There is a local man, a fine guide, much in demand up and down the river. He knows the jungle trails like
the back of his hand. He is—"

Scofield was shaking his head. "Knowing the jungle
trails is all well and good, my friend, but we require something more. We need someone who is something of a
botanist himself, who knows what he is looking at; we
don't want simply to wander blindly in the jungle. And we
need someone who can give us access to the curing
shamans in the area—" He waggled a finger. "I mean the
real shamans, not the ones that stick a feather in their nose
and put on a dance performance for the tourists."

"Yes, yes, I'm trying to tell you. This is a person who
has actually studied with the *curanderos* and who has
learned many of their secrets. The White Shaman, we call
him, the perfect man for you. As luck would have it, he
finds himself available, and I have secured his services for
your cruise. You are very fortunate."

Scofield cocked his head, weighed this information.
"He speaks English? Because some of my people don't
speak Spanish."

"English, Spanish, Yagua, Chayacuro—"

"Chayacuro!" Scofield exclaimed. "I don't want anything to do with the Chayacuro! I don't want to go anywhere *near* the Chayacuro."

"No, no, certainly not, why should we have anything to
do with the Chayacuro? No, I was only describing this
highly accomplished gentleman to you."

"Mmm." Scofield's tone indicated that he was well aware of Vargas's tendency toward hyperbole. "And how much will this paragon of virtue cost us?"

"His fee is one thousand *nuevos soles*."

"A thousand?" Scofield's bristly eyebrows shot up. "For taking us on a few walks and introducing us to one or two—"

"Well, but you see, professor, it's a whole week of his time, after all. He can't very well get off the boat in the middle of the trip, can he? Ha-ha-ha. He has to stay aboard. Really, it's a bargain."

"All right, all right. A thousand *soles*. So in dollars, that's another—"

Vargas was ready with the answer. It was his ace in the hole. "It comes to about three hundred American dollars, professor, but it will cost you nothing. His fee has already been arranged, as part of the service provided by Amazonia Cruise Lines."

Considering that his take from Scofield's people would come to over seventeen thousand *nuevos soles*—more than five thousand dollars—and that there was the sweet, added promise of a possible *On the Cheap* recommendation, it was an investment he was happy to make. Besides, he was, naturally, not paying the guide a thousand *soles*. Three hundred was the agreed-upon fee, and the man was glad to get it.

Scofield had spent a lot of time in Peru. He knew the way things worked here, so he almost certainly knew that Vargas was conning him. Still, he looked pleased, and why not? A thousand, five hundred, four hundred, whatever it was, it wasn't coming from his pocket. "Very good, Captain. I appreciate that."

"It's my pleasure, Professor."

Well, not quite. The man known as *el Curandero Blanco* was in fact a disreputable and notoriously unreliable misfit called Cisco—a fitting name, with its faintly disparaging connotations. What his last name was, if he had one, nobody seemed to know, not that that was any great rarity in Iquitos. He had been hanging around the city, on and off, for as long as Vargas could remember, having come from who-knew-where. His Spanish wasn't Peruvian, but what he was was in dispute. Some claimed he was a *colocho*, a transplanted low-level Colombian drug-dealer who had hurriedly left Colombia in advance of a gangland reprisal for offenses unspecified. Others were sure that his accent was Catalonian; a Spaniard. Still others believed he was Argentinian, which went along with the rumor that he was the grandson of Nazis who had escaped to Argentina in 1945. Cisco himself was known to have told each of these stories at different times. Vargas suspected he was simply one of the many lost souls of the Amazon, a rootless drifter from Ecuador or Colombia who had settled in Iquitos the way a stone settles wherever it falls in a stream. More than likely, Cisco himself might be a little confused as to who he was and where he'd come from, and where he was when he wasn't in Iquitos.

What Vargas had told Scofield about him was mostly true, but there was plenty that he hadn't told him. Foremost among these things was that Cisco's knowledge of the *curandero*'s arts was deep, all right, but pretty much limited to those relating to hallucinogenic plants. He had sat many long hours at the feet of various tribal healers and shamans and learned of the psychedelic virtues of *ayahuasca*, *epena*, *ajuca*, and a hundred others. In return, he had introduced several of his gratified tutors to the similar if less spectacular pleasures of cannabis and LSD. In short, what he was, when you got down to it, was a dopehead, vague and fog-brained, who was thought to live with an Indian woman in a shack down in the mudflats near Belén (where he went in flood season was anybody's guess), and who eked out a living, such as it was, by occasionally hiring himself out as a guide to unsuspecting tourists.

It was true enough that many people—well, a few people—referred to him as the White Shaman, a title he promoted for himself, but others who knew him referred to him sarcastically as the White Milkman. Somehow or other, he had made a friend of a small, local dairy farmer who had taken pity on him and offered him on-again, off-again work with his paltry herd of a dozen or so skinny cows. He was not really a milkman in the sense of delivering milk, since no one in Iquitos drank fresh milk (babies drank thick, yellow stuff that came in cans from the U.S. and Austria), but he did milk and tend the cows, which were used to produce cheese, and so the Spanish term *el lechero blanco*, with its droll, mocking associations of gallantry and adventure, had stuck to him. It wasn't much of a secret that he also made a little pocket money by running menial errands for the petty jungle drug traffickers or carrying messages for them. In Iquitos, this kind of behavior elicited no more than a noncommittal shrug from others. It was hard to make a living in Iquitos.

There had actually been some positive reports on his guide work. Once he'd taken a party of Swedish amateur botanists into the Yuturi wilderness, and they'd come back raving about his knowledge of the ecosystem. But another time he'd up and left a group of English horticulturists stranded in the jungle south of Pucallpa because he'd had a vision telling him to go home at once. So the man was a loose cannon, all right, but what choice was there? Who else could knowledgeably guide Scofield and his people and also introduce them to genuine jungle shamans? No one, only Cisco. Vargas had advanced him a hundred *nuevos soles* to get his hair and that wild beard of his trimmed and to buy a pair of new shoes to replace his disgusting, falling-apart, ankle-high sneakers. Whether he'd actually do any of that, or would even remember that he'd been asked, was strictly a toss-up.

Scofield, ready to leave now, drained his whiskey, smacked his lips, and set down the glass. "All right then, Captain, we have ourselves a deal." His left hand went into the pocket of his neat plaid shirt, from which he withdrew a blue leather checkbook. His right hand clicked the top of a ballpoint pen and held it, poised, above the top check.

"Five thousand four hundred dollars, correct?"

"Perfectly correct," said Vargas, his heart in his mouth.

Five thousand four hundred dollars would almost cover what was still owed for the *Adelita*'s refitting. The pen remained poised.

Write, write, damn it!

Scofield began to scratch away at last. "Let's round it off and say fifty-five hundred, shall we?"

"Thank you, professor." Vargas started breathing again. They were actually closing the deal. "I do have many expenses that—"

Scofield completed the check, tore it off with just about the sweetest sound that Vargas had ever heard, but then practically stopped the captain's heart by drawing it back across the table before Vargas could snatch it.

Now what? "Is something wrong?" he said, managing what he hoped was a smile.

"I wonder, Captain," Scofield said slowly, gently waving the check, "if you would be interested in earning an additional five thousand dollars?"

Vargas's heart started up again. At about a hundred beats a minute. "You're thinking about another cruise?"

"No, not *another* cruise. Something more in the nature of a simple favor on this one. No additional trouble on your part at all." He leaned closer, smiling. "I have a proposition in which I think you might be interested, Captain Vargas."

TWENTY minutes later, the two men stood up and shook hands, Vargas having first used a cocktail napkin to surreptitiously wipe the sweat from his palm.

"We'll look forward to our departure on the twenty-sixth, then," Scofield said. "Thank you for the drinks."

"Thank *you*, professor."

Once Scofield had left, Vargas flopped back into his soft leather chair. With the thousand *soles* he was being paid for the mail and cargo deliveries, he would gross almost $11,000, an incredible sum, enough to outfit his beloved *Adelita* in the manner it deserved, enough for a down payment on a second ship! Yet all the same, an edgy panic, as thick and turgid as cold mud, pressed painfully on his heart. What had he gotten himself into?

He shoved his Inca Kola aside, and limply signaled the barman.

"Bernardo, a double *aguardiente*."

FOUR

IN the elevator on the way to his fourth-floor room in the Dorado Plaza, Arden Scofield was experiencing a mixture of excitement, relief, and self-congratulation. The arrangement he'd just concluded with Vargas was the final element in an elegantly contrived plan. Had Vargas not agreed, it would all have come to nothing. But really, there hadn't been much chance of that. His choice of Vargas was hardly random. He had chosen him with care, had meticulously researched him and liked what he had discovered: a cash-pressed boat owner with big dreams for the future; an ambitious, cunning, but basically simple man; not a hardened criminal by any means—certainly not "connected"—but definitely money-hungry and not above the occasional skirting of the law when expedience demanded it. Perfect for what Scofield had in mind.

And what Arden Scofield had in mind had little to do with ethnobotanical expeditions. What he *was* interested in was the more than $120,000 he would net from the 150 kilos of coca paste "rocks"—the gritty, sand-colored balls of coca-leaf derivative—that the ship would now be carrying. The individually wrapped rocks, grouped into eight-quart, white plastic kitchen garbage bags, would be stowed among the contents of the four dozen sixty-kilo bags of coffee beans that the *Adelita* was transporting to a riverfront warehouse in Colombia. From there, they would be picked up by runners and taken to Cali, where they would be refined into fifty kilos of "white gold"—pure, top-quality cocaine hydrochloride for the high-end North American trade.

In other words, the esteemed professor was a *"narco"* on the side—a drug trafficker, one of the many thousands in Peru that make the international cocaine trade possible. While it is true that the majority of finished cocaine seen on the streets of Europe and the United States is made in Colombia, most of the coca paste from which it is processed comes from Peru, which produces three-quarters of the world's supply of coca. And well over half of that is grown along the infamous "coca belt"—mainly the Huallaga Valley, the main commercial hub of which is Tingo Maria. Which happened to be where the resourceful professor resided three or four months a year.

On Scofield's behalf it had to be said that he'd come with no intention of getting involved in the local drug commerce. But when certain opportunities more or less fell into his lap, his perceptions changed. And opportunities weren't long in coming.

As head of an extension program that trained rain-forest farmers in the techniques of sustainable, ecologically sound farming, he was expected to make periodic trips into the jungle to talk with and evaluate growers of tea, tobacco, and other legal crops. These visits, which generally lasted a week or ten days, were usually made alone, in the university's four-wheel-drive Land Rover. Interesting anybody else in ten days of backcountry, showerless travel, bouncing over remote, rocky roads in the dry season, or wallowing through them, hubcap-deep, in the rainy season, was an unlikely proposition.

A few days after he had returned from his second such

solitary tour, he was invited for coffee to the estate of one Hector Arriaga a few miles north of the city. Scofield had already learned—it was one of the first things that a newcomer had better learn—that one did not idly flaunt the wishes of Hector Arriaga, who was the region's *patrón*, the local boss representing the Medellin cocaine cartel in the Tingo Maria area. As such, he was both feared as the brutal, dangerous man he was, yet respected as one who was generous with his money, who helped the poor and contributed richly to the church, and who "removed" bothersome petty criminals and crazy or violent outsiders far more efficiently than the police. Known by all, he could eat, drink, buy clothes, and entertain his friends with nothing in his pocket. His name and his reputation were more than enough to guarantee payment.

And when he invited someone for coffee, someone came.

All that aside, Scofield's curiosity was piqued. And so three days later, having been picked up outside his apartment by two stony, wordless men in a richly polished maroon Bentley limousine—a refurbished London taxi, Scofield thought—he sat opposite Arriaga at a glass table on the latter's awninged stone terrace overlooking six acres of unbroken, close-cropped lawn. (When you live in the jungle, open space is the most desirable of all vistas.)

Arriaga himself was a disappointment, a long way from the Hollywood version of a drug baron. No gold chains around his neck, no massive gold rings on his fingers. A toad-faced, acne-scarred, lisping man wearing boxy green Bermudas drawn almost up to his armpits by wide, striped suspenders, he got down to business at once, not bothering at all with pleasantries. Over Jamaican Blue Mountain coffee served in Spode bone china cups that had been delivered by another hard, silent man—this one with the checkered grip of a semiautomatic pistol prominently protruding from a shoulder holster—Arriaga bluntly got started. Did Scofield know what the average annual earnings were for a small coffee or tea farmer in the Huallaga Valley?

Scofield did. In American money, approximately four hundred dollars.

True, said Arriaga. In other words, they were working themselves to death for barely enough to survive on. And did Scofield happen to know what that same farmer could earn growing coca leaves and converting them into coca paste?

Probably more, Scofield said prudently.

Much more, Arriaga told him. Something on the order of twelve hundred dollars, a living wage here. And he could do it virtually risk-free, since the local police had been effectively "dissuaded" from pursuing their enforcement responsibilities overvehemently, at least in regard to farmers associated with Arriaga's cartel.

What was more, coca was the region's most sensible crop in terms of conservation and ecology, two subjects to which the professor was so commendably devoted, and to which Arriaga himself was deeply committed. Tea, coffee, palm oil trees—these took years to begin producing, and rivers of sweat. Coca shrubs would be ready for harvesting in one season. And they would thrive in poor soil, where coffee and tea crops would not without constant attention. Moreover, they would not deplete the nutrient-deprived jungle soil, as so many other crops would.

Nod, nod, nod, went Scofield, who in truth was in substantial agreement with Arriaga's arguments but was increasingly anxious for him to get to the point.

And, with the moral and ecological justifications out of the way, here it came. For every quarter hectare of land— roughly half an acre—that Scofield could convince one of his local farmer acquaintances to convert to coca growing, he would receive a onetime honorarium of one thousand dollars. Afterward, there would be an annual payment of five hundred dollars per quarter hectare as long as reasonable production was maintained. If the farmer himself successfully undertook the conversion of the leaves to coca paste (not a simple operation) for further pay, there would be another two hundred dollars per quarter hectare per year for Scofield. Was Scofield interested?

Scofield was fascinated.

That had been nine years ago, and now, with almost no expenditure of effort, he was pulling in an extracurricular income of $55,000 a year, paid in good, green, American dollars, and tax-free at that. By the sixth year, however, he had exhausted his contacts in the Huallaga Valley. His earnings were no longer increasing. Knowledgeable now about the ins and outs of the underground coca economy, he itched to branch out on his own. Naturally, he didn't dare to do anything that Arriaga might perceive as treading on his turf, but that didn't stop him from thinking about other options.

His opportunity had come ten months ago, when the Peruvian government had announced the coming reinstitution of its "air-bridge denial" policy, a drug interdiction program in which military jets hunted and shot down the planes of traffickers hauling coca paste to Colombia for processing into cocaine. The program had been introduced by President Fujimori in 1992 with great success, but it had been halted a few years later because of international outrage over the botched shooting down of a missionary's plane that resulted in the killing of an innocent American woman and her daughter. But now the outrage was forgotten, and the sleek, Russian-made Sukhoi Su-25s of the Peruvian Air Force were again aggressively scouring the skies, hunting down unauthorized airplanes. Air transport was now out of the question. The only alternatives were transport by water and by foot.

This was a staggering blow to Hector Arriaga and his kind. Tingo Maria was five hundred miles from the Colombian border, a four-hour trip in a small plane—but two difficult, risk-filled weeks on rough jungle paths for even the fastest "two-legged mule." And at best, these runners were capable of carrying no more than fifty kilos of cocaine paste on their backs. A disaster.

On the other hand, for the Amazon River Basin itself it was a windfall. Amazon coca was inferior to that grown on the higher, drier slopes of the Huallaga Valley, and therefore brought less money and was in less demand. There were no

Arriagas there, only a gaggle of small-time traffickers who paid low-end prices to their farmers. But with the skies effectively shut down, the Amazon River and its tributaries reemerged as effective means of transport to Colombia, and the coca grown within a day or two's walk of it was about to become a far more cost-efficient commodity.

Arden Scofield realized this before the small-time traffickers did. As soon as the government announced its plans to retake the skies, he contacted a Cali cocaine manufacturer he'd met a couple of times to discuss certain mutually advantageous possibilities he had in mind relating to the transport of Peruvian coca paste to Colombia. Señor Veloso expressed his interest, and they talked figures for a while.

A highly motivated Scofield then set up a university-sponsored trip to North Loreto Province, ostensibly to talk ecology with Amazonian farmers. But it was coca growing he wanted to talk about. This time, however, he wasn't primarily interested in converting coffee or tobacco farms to coca growing. Instead, he sought out the known coca farmers and paste producers, of whom there were many, and offered them all more or less the same proposition: if they would skim off a small amount of their paste production, say ten percent (virtually unnoticeable by their bosses, given the vagaries of jungle agriculture), he would buy it from them at exactly double the prices they were getting from the local traffickers. It was a deal few could resist, especially when it was sweetened with a promised five hundred American dollars up front, no strings attached.

He then got in touch again with Veloso, his new Cali connection, to discuss the specifics of delivery. Veloso would have nothing to do with getting the paste across the border and into Colombia. That was Scofield's job; how did he propose to do it? Scofield, uncertain on this point, asked for the Colombian's advice.

Veloso told him that there were two or three small coffee and tobacco warehouses on the Javaro River, a northern tributary of the Amazon, just over the Colombian border from Peru. They had been used as drug pickup points before, when river traffic had briefly become more practical during the previous air interdiction, and could well serve that purpose again. The one he had in mind—not far from the village of San José de Chiquitos—was somewhat run-down at the moment, but if Scofield could guarantee a steady supply, Veloso would have it rebuilt and made stronger by native laborers. Veloso would also arrange for them to stay on as watchmen. Now, could Scofield make such a guarantee?

His heart in his mouth, Scofield said he could.

Fine, said Veloso; they would begin work at once. But there was one more problem to be considered. Vessels approaching these warehouses were routinely stopped and inspected at the military police checkpoint at the border and would be under even more careful scrutiny now. Scofield's best bet, Veloso suggested, was to somehow get the paste aboard an ordinary Peruvian cargo ship that had been making the run to these warehouses in the past, a ship that was already a familiar sight at the border checkpoint and that was well-equipped with the necessary permits. And most important, a ship with a captain who was known to have standing "arrangements" with customs authorities that would preclude any overzealous searches for items on which the duties had perhaps been inadvertently overlooked, and similar contraband that might be aboard.

Which was where Vargas and the *Adelita* came in.

FIVE

IT is an axiom among airport personnel in Iquitos that *Yanquis* are a cranky and irksome lot. There may or may not be something to this, but in fairness it should be pointed out that nobody arriving in Iquitos from the United States is likely to be at the top of his form when he gets there. There are no direct flights to Iquitos from anywhere in the United States. To reach it, one must fly first to Lima and then change planes for the flight to Iquitos. The problem is that while almost every incoming flight from the States to Lima arrives between eleven P.M. and midnight, nothing leaves for Iquitos or anywhere else until six-thirty in the morning. This means that already flight-weary through-passengers generally spend the night in the airport, inasmuch as the two-hour customs and immigration hassle they went through upon arriving, and the hour or so that would be consumed in getting to and from a hotel, would leave something like an hour and a half for sleeping (or trying to sleep) before being roused by a four A.M. wake-up call, amounting to something closer to torture than rest.

And when you've arrived in Lima by way of a round-trip, bargain-basement $599 itinerary all the way from Seattle, Washington, there are a few additional catches. John, Phil, and Gideon had boarded an American Airlines flight to Dallas at six A.M. the previous morning, from where they'd flown to Miami, and then finally on to Lima's Aeropuerto Jorge Chávez. By the time they cleared customs in Lima they'd been in transit for twenty hours and they looked and felt it: grungy, stubble-faced, and weary. To make things worse, the chairs at Jorge Chávez are famous for being few in number and extraordinarily uncomfortable for sleeping.

Still, four hours later, awaiting departure for Iquitos, they were again in reasonable spirits. Phil was a world-class sleeper. Within fifteen minutes of arriving at the airport proper, he had been snoozing away in a corner of the polished floor on a $1.59 plastic air mattress purchased from a Seattle-area G.I. Joe's for this express purpose. A fair number of other experienced old hands were already doing the same, paying no attention at all to the nighttime floor-polishers moving slowly among them.

As for John and Gideon, they were both enthusiastic trenchermen, and there was an all-night food court at the airport at which they had spent their last couple of hours. John had been joyfully surprised to find that it included a McDonald's, a Papa John's, and a Dunkin' Donuts, and he had happily indulged himself in the kind of fats-and-sugars orgy that was strictly *verboten* on the Lau home table. He had proclaimed the McDonald's *cuarto del libro* every bit as good as what you got at home, and the donuts an acceptable facsimile. Gideon went to the nearby Manos Morenas counter to try his first Peruvian meal and also pronounced it well: marinated chicken brochettes and salsa on a bed of chewy hominy, accompanied by thick slices of boiled potato that had been fried to crisp the surfaces. *Milk shakes de chocolate* from McDonald's and *picarones* from Manos Morenos— wonderful-smelling, deep-fried fritters that looked like onion rings but tasted like pumpkin—satisfactorily finished off the meal for both of them.

At six o'clock the three of them proceeded to the departure lounge for their hour-and-a-half LAN Peru flight to Iquitos, refreshed and upbeat, only to find that they weren't yet out of the woods. They were met with a burst of noise: a long, excited announcement in Spanish. Too rapid-fire for Gideon to understand, but the distressed faces and thrown-up hands of the other passengers told him that the news wasn't good.

"What's up?" he asked Phil. "Please, don't tell me there's a delay. I need a shower *fast*."

"Unfortunately, yeah, that's exactly what's up," Phil told them. *"Un problema grande."*

Phil was something of a language prodigy. He was impressively fluent in Spanish, as indeed he was in several other languages. Gideon could generally get along in Spanish and a few other languages if the other person spoke slowly enough, but John was hopeless. His existing repertory consisted of *sí*, *no*, *por favor*, *gracias*, *buenos días*, and *bueno*, mostly gleaned from old Westerns. Currently, he was working on *"Me llamo Juan."*

"What's the problem?" John asked.

"Well . . ." Phil shook his head, perplexed. "I didn't exactly understand all of it."

"You didn't understand it?" Gideon echoed.

"Well, I thought I understood it, but I must have gotten something wrong. Some kind of local slang or something. I thought he said . . . wait, let me go talk to the guy."

Two minutes later he was back. "No, I understood it, all right. *Cóndors.* Vultures. There's a mob of them circling over the Iquitos airport. It's too dangerous to try to land."

"Vultures!" John exclaimed. "Jesus, Phil, where are you taking us?"

"The thing is," Phil explained, "there's a garbage dump near the airport, and when the wind is right, the smell wafts over that way and brings the vultures. There are also some chicken and pig farms around the airport, and that draws them too. Not to worry, though," he added cheerily. "They're going to try to scare them off with cannon fire. Shouldn't be too long."

"Vultures. Cannon fire." John rolled his eyes, appealing first to the ceiling and then to Gideon. "Can I please go home now, Doc?" Since the first day they had known each other, Gideon had been "Doc" to John, and they'd never gotten around to amending it.

"No, you can*not* go home," Gideon said severely. "You wouldn't want Marti to find out you can perfectly well take care of yourself on your own, would you?"

With an indefinite length of time to wait, they split up. Gideon tried unsuccessfully to call Julie in Cabo San Lucas and then went looking for an Internet café, John went back to the food court to do some more grazing, and Phil went back to sleep.

There was no Internet café, but the bar, which had opened at five, had a few computers set up along one wall. No charge, but order something to eat or drink, and you could use one of them for as long as you could make your order last. Gideon got a good, fresh orange juice and a cup of weak but bitter coffee, and tapped out an e-mail to Julie.

Hi Sweetheart,

We're all safe and sound in Lima—not too bad a trip, although we're a little grubby by now. We're waiting out a slight (I hope) delay on the Iquitos leg. You wouldn't believe it if I told you the reason. It's six A.M. here—nine in Cabo, I guess—and I just tried calling you, but you weren't in the room. Probably at the spa getting your nodes uncrystallized. Don't overdo it now. I really admire your nodes the way they are.

Nothing else to say, really—I just wanted an excuse to "talk" to you. I love you and I'm already missing you, and I'll see you next week. Have a great time, honey.

XXX
Gideon

With a sigh he turned to his e-mail inbox.

* * *

IT took a couple of hours, but the artillery blasts did the job. The vultures flew away, the flight loaded up and left, and by ten A.M.—about the time the attendants were handing out welcome trays of warm, tasty ham-and-cheese sandwiches, orange juice, more bad coffee, and rum cake—the plane had left the coastal plain behind, had cleared the craggy, snowy peaks of the Andes, and was beginning its long descent to the Amazon Basin and Iquitos. Gideon pressed his face to the window.

He had flown over other jungles, in Central America and the South Pacific and Africa, but he'd never seen anything like this. For minute after minute the flat, gray-green mat stretched to the horizon in every direction, broken only by meandering loops of brown river the color of coffee with cream. What was especially strange was that the landscape looked almost the same from five thousand feet as it had from twenty-five thousand feet: like a huge green sponge, evenly pimpled and almost perfectly level, with no visible open spaces, even small ones, other than the river itself.

At five thousand feet visibility was cut off due to the misting of the windows, an ominous indicator of the heat and humidity to come. Gideon, who had long ago grown to love the cool, crisp air of the Pacific Northwest, valiantly prepared himself to suffer.

"HEY, look at this, this is cool," John said with unintended irony as he came down the steel steps that had been rolled up to the Airbus. "It's like being in an Indiana Jones movie."

Gideon nodded his agreement. The Iquitos Airport consisted of two crisscrossed runways sitting in a sharp-cornered rectangle carved out of the jungle. No other planes there. No sign of a city or anything like it, and no sign of the twenty-first century, either, for that matter. Except for the jet airliner they had just left, they might have been in the 1930s. There was a long, low, one-story terminal awaiting them, and a few thatch-roofed huts around the perimeter of the field. At the very edge of the clearing, up to their bellies in weeds, were two rotting, doorless, windowless passenger planes of indeterminate age that had obviously made it to Iquitos once upon a time but hadn't managed to make it back out.

The air was everything Gideon had dreaded, as thick and hot as soup. Before he reached the bottom of the stairs, his shirt was wet with sweat and his unshaven face was greasy. He felt like a turkey basting in the oven.

"A little hot," he said mildly.

"You think this is hot?" Phil said. "Ho, ho, this is only the morning. Wait till the afternoon!"

THE ride into town was by means of a couple of two-passenger "motokars"—open-sided, surrey-like conveyances (including the fringe on top) perched on three-wheeled motorcycles driven at breakneck speed that forced the riders to hang on for dear life at every curve. These were the only taxis to be found in Iquitos, and the streets were full of them, all skidding and scooting around each other (and around the occasional hapless pedestrian trying to cross a street) with a reckless élan that would have earned the admiration of a London bicycle courier.

The liveliness and bustle of the city came as a surprise. Gideon had known that it was the second largest settlement on the Amazon, with a population of over a quarter million, but all the same he'd anticipated a languid, heat-frazzled sort of place, where nobody moved very fast and everybody got out of the sun at midday. Instead, careening down Calle Próspero toward their hotel, he found a tacky, colorful, hardworking town that was anything but languid. There were block after block of surplus stores, off-brand clothing shops, luggage stores, check-cashing services, hole-in-the-wall restaurants, and tobacco and liquor stores, most of them with bars on their windows but their doors wide open. Many of the merchants seemed to be out on the street arguing or chatting with passersby. If not for the absence of anything taller than three stories, he might have been on Canal Street in lower Manhattan.

Still, there was an unmistakable frontier quality to it, perhaps from the musty, jungly smell of the great river only a few blocks away, perhaps from the people themselves, an extraordinarily diverse mix of tall, blond, blue-eyed Europeans, short, black-haired, wary-eyed Indians, and absolutely every possible variant between the two. The whole scene, Gideon thought, could have come straight out of a Joseph Conrad novel.

The motokars screeched to a stop in front of a grand, multicolumned hotel, with nothing at all tacky about it, that fronted a pretty square with fountains and neat green lawns. Phil made a show of paying all their fares—a total of four *nuevos soles* for the four-mile ride: a little over a dollar. The drivers seemed happy with their two *soles* each.

"This is the Plaza de Armas, the main square," Phil told them after they'd pulled their luggage down from the racks at the backs of the taxis, "and that monstrosity is your hotel, the Dorado Plaza. Go freshen up, take a nap or something, and I'll meet you right out here at, say, four o'clock, after things have cooled down. I'll give you a quickie tour. I'd go inside with you in case there's any problem at the desk, but they'd never let me through the door."

At this stage of their journey, none of them looked very appetizing, but Phil was in a class of his own. He was, to put it mildly, not a man greatly concerned with outward appearances. His come-again, go-again, pepper-and-salt beard was three weeks on its way in, and his lank, thinning gray hair looked as if it had seen its last pair of clippers six months ago. In addition, he was dressed in his standard travel apparel: a tired T-shirt with a sagging neckline, baggy, multipocketed, knee-length khaki shorts, scuffed, sockless tennis shoes that did nothing to enhance his skinny legs, and a faded On the Cheap baseball cap with a sweat-stained, curling bill. Gideon knew that in his backpack—Phil's first rule of travel was never to take anything that couldn't fit into a backpack—were duplicates of each item of clothing that he wore and a few necessities such as toilet paper (you never knew), toothpaste, insect repellent, and a pair of flip-flops. That was it. He would be dressed exactly the same every day of the trip. And he would spend a lot of time washing clothes in his bathroom sink.

"You know," he said, shrugging into the backpack for the short walk to his own hotel, but hesitating before starting, "it's not too late to cancel your reservations here. You can still get a couple of rooms at the Alfert with the rest of us."

"Why would we want to do that?" Gideon asked.

"Because it's sixty bucks cheaper, and also because almost everyone else on the cruise is there, but mainly because it doesn't have air-conditioning, and minifridges, and TV, and all that crap that you tourist types go for. What's the point of coming down here at all if you're going to live the way you would in Seattle or New York? The Alfert is a real Iquitos hotel. It's the kind of place the *real* people stay."

"Phil," Gideon said with a sigh, "I am a real person. Even John is a real person."

"Damn right," agreed John. "Wait a minute—"

"To appreciate a certain amount of material comfort," Gideon continued, "does not mean you are not a real person."

Phil shook his head sadly. "And you call yourself an anthropologist," he said, dripping contempt, as he had on similar occasions in the past and was sure to do again in the future.

PHIL was right about the afternoon heat. Even at four o'clock, supposedly after things had "cooled down," the thermometer in the lobby of the Dorado Plaza read thirty-seven degrees centigrade. Approximately ninety-nine degrees Fahrenheit. And the relative humidity was even higher, according to the humidity sensor: 100 percent. The air couldn't hold any more moisture if it tried.

Gideon's crisp, fresh shirt went limp even before he and John were all the way through the revolving door to the plaza, where Phil, also apparently in fresh clothes (although, who could tell for sure?) was waiting. From there he led them on a walking tour of the highlights of Iquitos: the moldering once-grand, porcelain-tiled houses of nineteenth-century rubber barons on the Malecón Tarapacá; the strange Iron House, made entirely of engraved iron plates (it looked like a house made of tinfoil), designed by Gustav Eiffel for the Paris exhibition of 1889 and shipped to Peru by one of the barons; and the floating "village" of Belén, a swarming, astonishing, malodorous marketplace hawking everything from native medicines to capybara haunches, smoked monkey arms, and fresh turtle eggs.

By five-thirty even John was drooping from the heat, and they were all ready for a cold beer and something to eat. Gideon suggested the Gran Maloca, a nice-looking restaurant they'd passed, with white-shirted waiters visible through the windows and Visa, MasterCard, and *aire acondicionado* stickers on the door. But he was outvoted, as he knew he would be, by Phil and John, who opted for the open-air Aris Burgers; John because of the word *burgers* and Phil because it was where the motokar drivers and other "real" people ate.

The food was good enough, however—there were Peruvian dishes as well as burgers—the beers were cold, and the real people were colorful. By the time they finished they were relaxed and contented, and very much ready to call it a day. Phil headed for the Alfert and John and Gideon walked back to the Dorado Plaza. On the square, they found a crowd of at least a hundred people watching a remarkably good Michael Jackson imitator go through his routines to the accompaniment of a boom box. Gideon and John watched too, for a good twenty minutes, while the young man with fedora and single sequined glove gyrated and tapped and moonwalked.

"How does he do it in this heat?" Gideon said, shaking his head.

"I guess you can get used to anything," said John.

They each left a dollar in the can he was using for donations and went up to their rooms.

Thirty minutes later, exhausted, lying in his bed with the air-conditioning turned up to high, Gideon could still hear the boom box going.

SIX

THERE are no roads into or out of Iquitos. A few supplies come in by air, but the great majority of its goods come and go via the river. As with almost every settlement on the Amazon, however, it has nothing resembling a working port or pier or dock. This is because every year the river rises forty to sixty feet in flood season, and then, of course, sinks again six months later. To build a commercial pier able to handle that kind of elevation change is beyond the resources of these jungle communities.

Thus, this being what is laughably called the dry season on the Amazon, John and Gideon got their first look at the *Adelita* the next morning from the crest of a long, unpaved, muddy, slippery incline that dropped from the level of the town down to the current shoreline.

"There she is," Phil said as proudly as if he owned her.

"Jesus," said John, staring. "That's the *Adelita*?"

Phil looked offended. "What's wrong with her?"

"Nothing, except it looks about a hundred years old."

"It *is* a hundred years old. More."

It had been built in the boom times of the 1890s, he explained, to carry supplies and company VIPs to and from the rubber plantations. In the 1920s and '30s it had spent a decade as a prison ship to transport criminals to hellhole prisons in the jungle. Very few had made the return trip. When Captain Vargas had rescued it from the river five years ago it had been a half-sunk hulk, rusting away on the shore, like quite a few of the other derelicts that were still to be seen along the riverbank. He'd installed twin diesel engines in place of steam power, gotten the boat into reasonable shape mostly with his own two hands, and had been hauling cargo and mail up and down the river ever since. Now he was eager to convert to the burgeoning eco-tourism trade—to what he *hoped* would be a burgeoning eco-tourism trade. This would be his first try at it.

"So we're his guinea pigs," John said. "What the hell, as long as it floats." He eyed Phil. "It *does* float, doesn't it?"

"It floats, all right, but just don't expect too much," Phil said. "The accommodations are pretty, um, basic. Don't expect a basket of goodies in the bathroom."

"Uh-oh," Gideon said. "Sounds like the real people are going to love it, but we fake people may have a few reservations."

But in fact he did love it at first sight. A peeling, white-painted, metal-hulled, much-dinged old bucket of a two-decker about the length of a Greyhound bus, it was everyone's idea of an old jungle steamer: tubby and experienced and just a little raffish.

Negotiating the slick incline down to it was tricky, but they managed it without falling. Waiting on deck to greet them, effusively and somewhat anxiously, was an overweight, bespectacled, heavily perspiring man in jeans, T-shirt, and a bright new captain's cap complete with woven gold-oak-leaf filigree. "Felipe, you're here! Welcome, welcome. I was worried! You are the last to come." He turned for a second to signal someone in the wheelhouse and at once the engines revved up and someone ran to untie the mooring lines from their cleats and haul them in.

"Captain, these are my good friends Professor Gideon Oliver and Mr. John Lau," Phil said. "John and Gideon, *Capitán* Alfredo Vargas."

"Welcome to the *Adelita*." Vargas pumped hands all around. "Welcome, welcome, welcome."

"Me llamo Juan," said John.

"In thirty minutes we have a nice meeting for everyone, yes? In the ship's salon. Until then, perhaps you would like to see your cabins? Chato will show you."

Chato, slim, silent, and about five feet, two inches tall, took them to the upper deck, where there were ten cabins, set back to back, five to a side, with doors and single windows opening out onto the deck. He opened their doors—there were no locks—and left without having said a word or once having met their eyes. The boat began to slip away from the shore.

BASIC was the right word. Gideon's cabin, the rearmost one on the starboard side, consisted of a cot-sized bed with a thin kapok mattress under the single window, an open alcove with two shelves and hooks for hanging things—no closet, no drawers—and a bathroom with a sink about as big as a medium-sized mixing bowl, a toilet, and a claustrophobia-inducing shower. Both rooms were in a total of what couldn't have been even a hundred square feet. Not places to spend a lot of time, but perfectly fine for sleeping. And the barred window over the bed—a leftover from the *Adelita*'s days as a prison ship—opened, which was good, because the heralded air-conditioning, a clanking, groaning unit on the ceiling, while it was trying its best, wasn't quite up to the task. He guessed the temperature in the room was about eighty-five degrees, maybe ten degrees cooler than outside. The humidity was considerably less oppressive, though. It was bearable. It would do.

Fortunately, Vargas had made available two unoccupied aft cabins for the botanists to store their equipment and for everyone to leave their luggage. If not for that, they would all have been climbing over their bags to get into and out of their rooms.

In the bathroom, atop the toilet tank, were a plastic liter-bottle of Cristalina water, a squat, heavy tumbler, a cleanly cut half of a new bar of Ivory soap, and a roll of toilet paper. No toilet-paper holder, no towel rack, no washcloth, and most definitely no basket of goodies. A single thin towel the size of a moderately large dish towel lay neatly folded on the blanketless bed. But everything looked clean and shipshape. The wood-plank walls were gummy with multiple coats of paint, the latest a glossy off-white that had been applied recently enough so that it still gave off a painty smell. Gideon didn't doubt that under all the dried goop were the original cabin walls that the ship had come with. Except for the air-conditioning, the shower, and the window bars, in fact, he guessed that what he was looking at was pretty much what an 1890s VIP traveler would have found as well.

When he went to the sink to wash his hands and face, he found that there was no hot water. The same cloudy, luke-warm fluid came out of both taps. Well, no problem there, either. There wasn't going to be much demand for piping hot water on this particular cruise. He washed up as well as he could in the tiny sink, got into a fresh shirt, and went downstairs to join the others. He was surprised to see that the *Adelita* was already to the outskirts of Iquitos. Ahead lay an unmarred vista of brown river and green jungle.

SEVEN

"WELCOME, welcome, my dear friends, my good friends, welcome," enthused the overexcited Captain Vargas. "Or as we say in Peru, *bienvenidos amigos*! It is my great pleasure to welcome you to the *Adelita* with pisco sours, the national drink of Peru. Or you can have Inca Kola, the *other* national drink of Peru, both completely without any necessity of payment. Only for this one time, of course. Afterward, payment will be gratefully accepted, ha-ha. Please, help yourselves, all you wish, go ahead." He motioned them into action with his hands.

The "ship's salon" had turned out to be a small open area on the lower deck, bounded by the dining room on the forward side and a storage room to the rear. Projecting into this area from the dining room wall, on the left side of the entrance, was a small, glassed-in bar fitted with a Dutch door, the upper half of which folded outward to make a serving counter. There were four white plastic tables with a few green plastic garden chairs around them. Two of the tables were empty. One was fully occupied, with four people around it. The last had only one person at it, and it was there that Phil, John, and Gideon had sat down. Their companion was a quiet, lost-looking individual who had introduced himself as Duayne V. Osterhout and who looked like a cartoonist's version of John Q. Public, right down to the toothbrush mustache, the horn-rimmed glasses, and the air of timid, put-upon uncertainty.

There was a breeze wafting through the open space, created by the vessel's movement, that would hardly have qualified as "cool" in the Northwest, but that felt wonderful here. On each table was a small pitcher of foamy white liquid—those would be the sours—several dark green bottles of Inca Kola, and some bottled water. John and Phil twisted the caps off water bottles, Gideon tried the Inca Kola, and their tablemate reached for the pitcher. "Never had one of these," he murmured, pouring himself a brimming glassful. He took a tentative sip, cocked his head, and swallowed. "Say, this isn't bad!" He tried another sip and obviously enjoyed that one too. "Salty, sweet, and bitter at the same time." He smacked his lips. "And sour too. It engages all the taste receptors. Well, except for umami, of course, inasmuch as there wouldn't be any glutamic acid in it."

"You a professor, by any chance?" John said.

"Ah . . . no," said Osterhout, returning to his enthusiastic sampling of the sour.

"So what's the Inca Kola like?" John asked Gideon.

Gideon rolled the liquid around his mouth and swallowed. "Mmm, something like a Vanilla Coke, but with some kind of, I don't know—"

"Try to guess!" Vargas boomed, overhearing. "No? It's lemongrass! The secret ingredient. No lemongrass in Coke! Hey, you know Peru is the only country in the world where we got our own drink that sells better than Coca-Cola? It's a known fact. Tastes pretty good, huh?"

"It's delicious," said Gideon, who thought it might conceivably have been passable if the sugar content had been cut by 60 percent or so.

Vargas then provided a general introduction to the ship and the cruise. They would cruise for the remainder of today and the next along the southern bank of the Peruvian Amazon. At the Colombian border they would take a northern, more remote branch of the Amazon known as the Javaro River, on which they would travel for several more days, until they rejoined the main body of the Amazon at Leticia, Colombia, at the end of their journey.

"You mean we don't even spend two days on the Amazon?" their tablemate Duayne Osterhout asked, plainly disappointed. "I thought—"

"Let me explain," interrupted a stocky man of forty-five, with a tanned, ruddy face, a reddish crewcut just beginning to go gray, and small, bright, intelligent eyes. "You see, the Amazon River itself, as you get anywhere near Leticia, is pretty broad and well-traveled . . . crowded, you might almost say. But the Javaro is much smaller, a dark, serpentine, little-known stream through an almost totally unpopulated area. Hardly anyone uses it as a thoroughfare because, with all its S-curves and its looping back on itself, it takes forever to get anywhere."

"Still, the *Amazon* . . . !"

"You won't regret it, I assure you. Because of its remoteness, you see, the Javaro is an absolute treasure-house of exotic plants and wildlife. Like the Amazon was forty years ago."

"If you say so," said Osterhout with a pallid little sigh.

"I guarantee it."

Vargas waited politely until, with a wave of his unlit pipe, the man signaled him to continue. In addition to the passengers, they were carrying a cargo of coffee, along with a few miscellaneous items—a generator, a few dozen pairs of rubber boots for a jungle store, a dining room table and chairs, a wooden door, and some miscellaneous lumber. The coffee was bound for a warehouse on the Javaro; the other items would be dropped off along the way. All other stops would be at the discretion of the expedition guide, and of Dr. Scofield—he nodded at the stocky man, who returned it with another wave of his pipe, by now lit and smoking and emanating a sweet, coconutty aroma.

"Speaking of our expedition guide," Scofield said genially, "the famous Cisco. I don't believe I see him among us. He *is* aboard, I hope?"

"Aboard?" Vargas said as if the question were laughable in the extreme. "Of course he's aboard. He's, ah . . . resting at present. Yes." Gideon could practically see the sweat popping out on his forehead. "You'll meet him soon, don't worry."

He hurried on before Scofield could pursue the matter. The *Adelita*, the group was told, would provide them with many amenities. Their cabins would be cleaned each day, their linens replaced two times during the week. A fresh liter of drinking water would be placed in their rooms every morning. There would be three healthful meals a day, the precise timing to depend on the day's excursions. Today's dinner would be at six-thirty. Coffee, fruit, and more drinking water would be available twenty-four hours a day on the buffet table in the dining room. The bar would open for an hour before dinner each day, and drinks could be signed for and accounts settled at the end of the cruise.

The list of nonamenities was shorter but more striking. Between Iquitos and Leticia, there was no TV reception, no e-mail, no Internet, no cell phone transmission. Here in the nearly unpopulated jungle there were no communication satellites zipping overhead for such things. Unless any of the passengers happened to be carrying a shortwave radio, the sole communication with the outside world would be the captain's shortwave in the wheelhouse.

Were there any questions?

"Yeah, I'd like to organize my notes on my laptop in the evenings," said a man with a Neanderthal jaw and a tree trunk of a neck, but a friendly, open face, "but there aren't any outlets in my room. How do I recharge?"

"Unfortunately," Vargas said sadly, "the cabins don't have electrical outlets yet. This will be repaired in the future. But there is an outlet in the dining room that is available to you at any time. Other questions?"

"I notice the rooms don't have locks either," Scofield said. "Also to be repaired in the future, I assume?"

"Yes, of course, everything in due time. I can't do everything at once, ha-ha. There used to be great, big locks, enormous locks, from the prison days, but I had them taken off. They made such a bad impression. But I still have them, so if you don't trust each other," he said archly, "I can have them put on again."

"That won't be necessary," Scofield said drily.

Were there other questions?

Yes, Duayne V. Osterhout had one too. He had noticed that the water coming out of both taps was the same lukewarm temperature. And a definite greenish cast could be seen in the water in the toilet. Was that *river* water in their bathrooms?

"Ye-es," said Vargas, as if to say, "What else would it be?"

"Do you mean untreated water? Straight out of the Amazon? And when we flush the toilets it goes—"

"Straight back. Out of the Amazon, back into the Amazon." Vargas chuckled. "That's recycling, my friend."

A mild tremor passed through the ship, and then a more pronounced juddering, along with a scraping noise. "Don't worry, this is not a problem," Vargas said, glancing nervously over his shoulder toward the bow of the boat, "but it is best perhaps that I attend to it."

"I knew it," John muttered. "Didn't I say the damn thing wouldn't float?"

With Vargas gone, having promised to return shortly, Arden Scofield took over. He stood, placed a foot on the seat of his chair, leaned one elbow on his knee, and inhaled a long breath. In his hand was his unlit pipe. Behind him the jungle slid smoothly by on the far bank.

"To those who know nothing of botany," he began dreamily, "a great rain forest can only be a jumble of colors, forms, and sounds, unintelligible and mysterious." He had a nice voice, chuckly and avuncular, well suited to his lively eyes. "Beautiful, yes; treacherous, certainly; awe-inspiring, perhaps; but in the end without meaning or co-herence. Only for the botanist does the jumble resolve itself into a precise and harmonious whole of many parts, a mosaic, if you will, of discrete components, each play-ing its prescribed part in the natural order. And only for the *ethno*botanist do these components present themselves as a cornucopia of almost untapped gifts that can heal and nourish and protect, gifts the uses of which it is our great good fortune to study and make known to the world at large."

He paused to gaze out over their heads and to contem-platively put the pipe in his mouth and chew at it, as if thinking hard about what to say next, but Gideon, who had plenty of experience delivering "spontaneous" lectures of his own, knew a fellow fake when he saw one. He had to hand it to him, though; it was well prepared and mellifu-ously delivered—well, maybe a little bombastic (Gideon could have done without the "if you will" and the "cornu-copia"), but effective all the same.

Scofield judged that his pause had been long enough. The pipe was taken from his mouth. "The isolated, little-known rain forest into which we now sail is not only the greatest, the least discovered, and the most prolific forest on earth, it is one of the very most ancient. When we enter it, we go back in time to a primeval jungle hardly changed, hardly disturbed, in a hundred million years. The temper-ate European and North American forests that are more familiar to us are only as old as the end of the last ice age, eleven thousand years ago—*one ten-thousandth*"—the words were drawn-out and caressed by his tongue—"of the age of the Amazon Basin. In this rich, nurturing . . ."

Gideon had been marginally aware that something was bothering him about the people at Scofield's table. Some-thing wasn't right, something about their postures, or the way they toyed with their drinks, or what they chose to rest their eyes on. Something.

He suddenly realized what it was. *Why, they don't like him. Not one of the people at his table likes him, or at any rate they sure don't like listening to him.* There was a long, gangly, beak-nosed guy in his late twenties—a graduate student, probably, or maybe post-grad—who was following every word with avid fascination plastered all over his face, but any experienced professor (including Scofield, you would think) could recognize the grim, deeply resented necessity to suck up that was in those glazed, rigid eyes. *Scofield's probably his major prof*, Gideon thought. *Poor guy*. Gideon himself had no doubt worn that sorry look on his own face many a time during his graduate years at Wisconsin under Dr. Campbell.

The other two people at the table weren't being quite as obvious. There was a tall, bemused-looking woman of forty with a decades-out-of-date Laura Petrie hairstyle— a flip, was it called?—whose expression was opaque enough, but Gideon could see an impatient, sneaker-clad foot jiggling away under the table at supersonic speed. Next to her was the big guy who had asked about outlets. Thick-chested but showing the usual middle-age signs of losing the battle against weight and gravity, he looked plain bored out of his mind, as if he'd heard Scofield speak two or three hundred times too often, and it took every ounce of his willpower simply to sit still and listen. His eyes had been tightly closed for a while, as if he had a headache.

This is going to be one interesting trip, Gideon thought.

"This confluence of land and water is also the most biologically diverse reservoir of life on earth," Scofield was saying. Lost in his own presentation, he appeared to be oblivious to the cloud of aversion that enveloped him. Either that, or he just didn't give a damn. "There are at least a hundred thousand plant species here, only a fraction of them known in the scientific literature," he said, "and only a fraction of *those* whose potential attributes are understood. There are two million species of insects—five thousand species of butterflies alone and—"

There was a gentle throat-clearing sound to Gideon's right. Duayne Osterhout's left forefinger rose tentatively.

Scofield pretended not to notice. "—and almost two thousand species of birds. The river itself is home to two thousand species of fish—compare that to the hundred and fifty that are found in all the rivers of Europe combined."

Osterhout's finger remained in place, gently waggling. Scofield's lips compressed. He nodded—at the finger, not the man. "Did you want to say something?"

"Only a minor correction, professor," Osterhout said. "I believe that four thousand butterfly species would probably be a safer estimate if it's generally accepted classified species that we're referring to." He was being very deferential, very unassuming. Uneasy under Scofield's cool glare, he cleared his throat a couple of times more. "Of course, there's little doubt that five thousand species, perhaps even more, do exist here but are not as yet all identified. Perhaps that's what you meant?"

"Thank you," Scofield said sourly. "Four thousand, then. We certainly wouldn't want to exaggerate the butterfly population. In any case, that's enough blather from me. Let's go on to something else." This was not a man who appreciated being interrupted, Gideon saw. Throw off his timing and the show was over. Glowering, he looked down at his pipe and plucked an offending shred of tobacco from the bowl. When he raised his face a moment later he was back in his twinkly, avuncular mode—an instantaneous, apparently effortless switch.

"Not everyone here knows everyone else," he said pleasantly. "In fact, there isn't anyone here who knows *every*one else—so I guess we'd better introduce ourselves before we go any further. My name is Arden Scofield, I'm an ethnobotanist, and I'm lucky enough to teach at the University of Iowa and at a wonderful little college called the Universidad Nacional Agraria de la Selva down here in

Peru, in a little town called Tingo Maria. Which is enough about me."

He sat down and reinserted the pipe between his teeth. "Tim, you take it from there," he said to the tall young man sitting with him, the one with the beaky nose.

Tim started, as if he'd just come out of a trance, which was probably not that far from the truth. "I'm, uh, Tim Loeffler," he said, almost knocking over his drink when he unfolded what seemed like more arms and legs than he strictly needed. "I'm a student of Professor Scofield's at UI, and I'm here hoping to learn more about, uh, the ethnobotanical practices and, um, resources of the Amazonian Basin, and, uh—" At a subtly impatient jiggle of the lighter that Scofield was using to relight his pipe, Tim skidded to an abrupt halt. "And, um, I guess that's about it."

"Thank you, Tim," Scofield said around the bit of his pipe. He clicked the lighter closed, turned to his left, and tipped his head benignly at the woman with the Laura Petrie hairdo. "Maggie?"

She stopped jiggling her foot, uncrossed her jeans-clad legs, and turned to face Gideon's table, the table of strangers. "My name's Maggie Gray—"

"Oh, I forgot," Tim blurted. "I should have said—I'm also a student of Maggie's—of Professor Gray's."

"—and, as Tim indicates, I also teach in the ethnobotany program at the University of Iowa." She paused. "At the moment, anyway. My primary interests are in the area of ethnopharmacology with a concentration on anaesthetics, hypnotics, and opiates." She had an unusual, not unattractive manner of speaking, biting and humorously ironic, as if everything she said was half taunting—self-taunting as much as anything else. The set of her face, with its wide, sardonic mouth, and with one eyebrow slightly raised—much practiced, Gideon suspected—added to the general impression of barbed, above-it-all skepticism.

"Mel?" said Scofield.

Beside Maggie, the fourth person at the table, the big guy with the bull neck, now smiled affably. "Hi all, I'm Mel

Pulaski and I'm not a botanist, I'm a writer, so in a way I'm kind of just along for the ride—"

"Wait a minute," Phil said. "I know you. Didn't you used to play for the Dallas Cowboys?"

"Minnesota," Mel said, pleased. "You got a good memory."

"Running back, right?"

"Linebacker. But that was a few years and a few pounds back. I'm a freelance writer now. I'm writing up an article on the cruise for EcoAdventure Travel. I also worked with Dr. Scofield on his latest book—"

"Indeed you did, and we'll come to that in just a few minutes, Mel," Scofield said, talking over him. "But there at that table are four gentlemen whom I haven't met." He leaned forward, smiling at Osterhout and radiating cordiality. "I think I can guess, however, who *that* particular gentleman, our butterfly expert, is."

"Well, I'm Duayne Osterhout. Yes, I'm an entomologist, an *ethno*entomologist, I suppose I should say in this august company, and I'm with the Department of Agriculture." He was still on his first pisco sour, but obviously he wasn't much used to drinking, because it had gone to his head. He was speaking a little too carefully, almost visibly preforming the words before trying them out. "In other words, I'm a bug man."

"Dr. Osterhout is being unduly modest," Scofield said. "He is not just *any* bug man, he is one of the world's *leading* bug men, and an internationally recognized authority on the order *Blattaria*."

Visibly pleased, Osterhout simpered and waved a dismissive hand. "Oh now, really, I don't know that I'd say . . ."

"What's *Blattaria*?" John whispered to Gideon.

"Cockroaches."

John inconspicuously shifted his chair a few inches further away from Osterhout.

"Surely this isn't your first trip to the Amazon, Dr. Osterhout?" Scofield asked. "I imagine your studies must have taken you here many times."

"Not really. I can assure you that if it's cockroaches one is interested in, one has no trouble studying them in the Washington, DC, area, so as a matter of fact, yes, it is my first visit. You see, my work at Agriculture has been so time-consuming, and then my wife was never in favor of my going, but since she left . . ." He clamped his mouth shut. Apparently it had struck him that the potent drink had made him a little too forthcoming. "Well, anyway, here I am."

"And we're delighted to have you as part of our merry band," Scofield said smoothly. "I'm sure we'll have a lot to learn from you. I should add, by the way, that I had the great pleasure of having Dr. Osterhout's charming daughter Beth as a member of last year's expedition in the Huallaga Valley. That lovely young woman is someone you can really be proud of, Dr. Osterhout; she'll be a real credit to the field. If I can ever be of help to her, I hope she'll feel free to call on me."

These generous if overdone remarks of Scofield's obviously called for an appreciative response from Osterhout, but they were met instead with a searing, squint-eyed look of what Gideon took to be pure malignity. *Somebody else who has some kind of a grudge against Scofield?* he thought. Osterhout's ferocious glower lasted but a second, however, before lapsing back into mildly intoxicated passivity. "Thank you, sir," he said tightly, through a barely opened mouth.

If Scofield was disturbed, he didn't show it. He moved his glance to Phil. "Sir?"

Phil offered a casual salute to all. "Hiya. I'm Phil Boyajian. I guess I'm just along for the ride too. I'm with On the Cheap, and I'm reviewing the *Adelita* for possible inclusion in our Amazon guidebook."

"Happy to have you with us, Phil," Scofield said. "I hope you'll feel free to join our little excursions whenever you like." He pointed the bit of his pipe at Gideon. "Sir."

"My name is Gideon Oliver. I'm a prof too, at the University of Washington, but I'm afraid the last time I studied botany was in high school. I'm here to help Phil out, basically, but I'm looking forward to learning a little about what all of you do too, if you'll let me."

Scofield was looking keenly at him, his clear blue eyes narrowed. He placed the bit of the pipe against his temple. "Am I wrong, or do we have yet another celebrity among us? Would you be a physical anthropologist, Dr. Oliver?"

"Well, yes—"

"Hey, right, the Bone Detective!" Mel Pulaski exclaimed, jabbing a thick finger at him.

"*Skeleton* Detective," John corrected helpfully.

"Yeah, right, Skeleton Detective. I knew you looked familiar. You were on the Discovery Channel or the Learning Channel or something, just a few weeks ago. All about—what was it—identifying people from their skulls, I think, or figuring out how old they were, or something like that. That was you, wasn't it?"

"Yes, it probably was," Gideon said, repressing a sigh. He didn't mind being identified as a forensic anthropologist, but he'd been looking forward to going a whole week without being the Skeleton Detective.

"Son of a gun," said Mel, visibly impressed.

"Well, we're certainly happy to have you aboard, professor," Scofield said. "I think we'd all love to learn a little about what *you* do, so shall we assume we have a quid pro quo to that effect? That leaves you, sir," he said to John.

"John Lau here. I'm also with Phil."

"You're a writer? You work for On the Cheap?"

"No, I'm just helping out too, so I guess you could say I'm along for the ride also. Actually I'm a special agent for the FBI."

"FBI?" Scofield cried, twinkling away. "Good heavens, are we under investigation?"

"Nope," said John. "Well, not yet, anyway."

Scofield chuckled, the others smiled civilly, and Scofield got to his feet again. "Well, now that we're all friends, I hope you'll let me present you with a little welcoming gift and do a little bragging at the same time. As most of you know, I have a few publications to my credit—"

"A lot more than a *few*, sir!" Tim enthused a little too ardently, then blushed bright pink.

"Well, thank you, Tim, but be that as it may, until now I've never written anything for the general public. So when Javelin Press asked me to put together something of an autobiographical nature, something that wasn't full of technical jargon, I didn't know where to turn for help. Fortunately, they were able to recommend a first-rate writer to assist me." He smiled at Mel Pulaski, who grinned back. "I want to thank you for all your help, Mel. I couldn't have done it without you."

"Hell, you did all the work, Arden," Mel said. "I just tweaked a word or two here and there. I was ashamed to take any money for it."

"Not true at all. Don't you listen to him. I would have been helpless without his guidance."

John made a rumbling noise low in his throat. He was getting tired of the bowing and scraping, the kowtowing, and the self-inflating modesty. As was Gideon.

"And here are the fruits of our joint venture," Scofield said. Reaching into a backpack, he took out a stack of four brand-new-looking books in their wrappers. "Hot off the press, ladies and gentlemen, and soon to be available at fine bookstores everywhere, I give you *Potions, Poisons, and Piranhas: A Plant-hunter's Odyssey*." He handed out the handsomely embossed, silver-and-green books to Maggie, Mel, and Tim, and walked the few steps necessary to give one to Duayne.

"I fear I brought only enough with me for our formal expedition members," he said apologetically, "so John, and Gideon, and, ah—"

"Phil," Phil said.

"—and Phil, I'm afraid I don't have copies for you, but if you'll give me your addresses at some point, I'd be pleased to send them to you."

There was a chorus of thanks all around and Scofield took his seat again. Gideon peeked at Osterhout's copy, opened to the title page, and saw that there was an inscription: "To Duayne V. Osterhout, with admiration, Arden Scofield. November 26, 2006, somewhere on the Amazon." Osterhout looked pleased.

"Of course," Scofield was saying jocularly, "this means that you three will be excused from the quiz on chapters one through five tomorrow morning, but I'll be glad to arrange—"

"What the hell," Mel Pulaski said under his breath.

"Is something wrong, Mel?" Scofield asked.

Mel was leafing—roughly pawing was more like it—through the opening pages of the book. Paper crumpled under his heavy hand. "I thought . . ."

"You thought what?"

"Nothing," Mel said grimly.

Scofield looked perplexed and a little unsure of himself. "If you'll notice, I did acknowledge your help. On page two of the acknowledgments, about midway down, you'll find—"

"I said 'nothing,' all right?" Mel slammed the book shut without bothering to check page two of the acknowledgments. Whatever was eating him, he was done kowtowing for the day.

The two were still staring at each other—Mel sullen, Arden with a concerned frown—when Captain Vargas appeared from the forward passageway, closely trailed by a man Gideon hadn't seen before.

"I am sorry about the interruption earlier," Vargas said. "A few trees in the water from the timber plantations. No damage was done. As I said, there is nothing to worry about. And now I have the pleasure to present to you the gentleman who will be your guide on this excursion. He has guided expeditions in this region for more than ten years, including many scientific expeditions like this one, and I am sure he will meet every expectation. I assure you, there is no one who knows the Loreto jungle and its inhabitants better. He is a true professional in every respect. And a man who knows so much about the ancient teachings of the jungle shamans that he himself is known by many as"—a dramatic pause—"the White Shaman—*el Curandero Blanco*."

He stepped aside to give the stage to his companion, whose appearance didn't live up to the introduction.

Gaunt, gray-bearded, and hollow-cheeked, he was bizarrely dressed in baggy, bulgy camouflage pants, new faux combat boots with peppermint-striped shoelaces, and a grimy Chicago White Sox baseball cap worn backward. A loose red tank top with *Maui Rules* on it bared stringy, leathery arms with a multitude of pale scars. Down the back of his neck ran a dingy gray ponytail tied with a knotted blue rubber band. All he needed was three coats and a supermarket cart stuffed with plastic garbage bags and he would have fit right in mumbling at the tourists from a park bench in Seattle's Pioneer Square.

Several crew members were standing off to the side watching, and Gideon heard one of them speak to another. *"El Curandero Blanco,"* he repeated with a derisive laugh. It was Chato, the one who had taken them to their rooms. *"El Lechero Blanco."* The White *Milkman.* The other one laughed as well.

Swaying slightly, the White Whatever-he-was looked vaguely at his charges. His head was held slightly to one side at a rigid, upright, unnatural angle that immediately engaged Gideon's interest. (*Fused cervical vertebrae?* he wondered.)

"Okay, I'm Cisco." He spoke in a mushy, moderately accented English that wasn't easy to follow. His teeth, as many of them as could be seen, were gray-brown, in terrible shape, which didn't help in understanding him. Visibly thinking hard about what else to say, he came up with: "So, like, does anybody want to ask anything?" He spoke in a thin, strained voice, as if he'd been shouting for the last two hours. His Ahab-style beard had been trimmed a week or so ago, but it looked as if he hadn't shaved around the edges since. Silvery stubble glinted down his throat, across his upper lip, and on his dark, starved cheeks.

"Yes, tell us about your plans," Scofield said.

"My plans. Well, we'll take a few treks, you know? I know some cool places, great botanicals, weird pharmaceuticals. It'll be fun, you'll be able to collect some stuff you never saw before, never heard of before." He dug at his bristly cheek with a ragged fingernail and yawned. "You know?" His mind was very obviously elsewhere, or possibly nowhere. Not there with them on the *Adelita*, at any rate.

Understandably, his audience was less than overwhelmed. "And when exactly is our first trek planned?" Maggie Gray demanded, sounding like a schoolteacher wanting to know what had happened to some miscreant's homework, but with no expectation of a satisfactory answer.

"Tomorrow, probably. I mean, yeah, tomorrow, sure." Gideon sensed a ripple of unease go through the group. It was clear to everyone that Cisco was making this up as he went along.

"And you'll be able to get us audiences with working *curanderos*, is that correct?" Maggie's doubt increased with every word.

"Oh, yeah, I think so. I don't know about tomorrow, though. Weather. Conditions. Maybe. Prob'ly." *He's spent time in the States*, Gideon thought. The accent was Spanish, but the speech rhythms and intonations when he spoke English were American.

Maggie wasn't about to let him off the hook yet. "From which groups?" she wanted to know.

"Which groups?" Cisco took a few seconds to reconnect. "I don't know yet. I mean, how can I know? We have to see how it goes. Depends on which side of the river we go along."

"Captain Vargas has already said we'll be on the south bank through tomorrow."

"He did? Okay, then the Huitoto, or maybe the Mochila, or even the Chayacuro if you want to see some really—"

"Oh, I rather doubt that Arden's going to want to meet with any Chayacuro," Maggie said archly. Mel and Tim grinned, although Tim quickly covered his mouth with a hand.

"You're right enough about that," Scofield said with an affable roll of his eyes. "Let's leave the Chayacuro out of this, if you please."

Now what's that about, I wonder? Gideon thought, intrigued. The Chayacuro were a famously fierce Amazonian Indian group, notorious as headhunters and headshrinkers. They and the equally feared Jivaro, to whom they were related, were the only South American Indians whom the Spaniards had never been able to subdue. Neither had anyone else. Even now, they were as free and dangerous as ever, occasionally linked to the murder of a missionary or a traveler. A couple of years earlier they had hacked a doctor and his assistant to death when the two had unknowingly violated their rules of proper behavior in their examination of a Chayacuro girl. As far as Gideon knew they had never been prosecuted for these things. An isolated and seminomadic people, they were hard to find when they didn't want to be found. Besides, the authorities, perhaps wisely, preferred to stay out of Chayacuro territory.

So what was Scofield's connection to them? Had he had a run-in with them? When he got to know them all a little better, he'd ask.

Cisco shrugged. "Okey-dokey, no Chayacuro. Anybody got anything else?"

"Do you have a schedule for us?" Mel asked. "I could use a copy."

"A what?"

"A schedule."

Cisco looked at him as if he was having trouble understanding the word. "Schedule," he repeated with a whinnying laugh. "Hey, I don' got to show you no steenkin' schedule."

Scofield managed a polite chuckle. "That's funny, Cisco—that was your name, Cisco?—but I think all of us would appreciate having some idea—"

"I don't use schedules, man. Schedules don't work in the jungle."

"You could be right about that, but they do work aboard a ship. It would help me—help all of us—to plan our other activities—pressing, drying, and so on—if we knew, for example, that on Monday at two there was a plant-collecting expedition, and on Tuesday at nine we were to meet with—"

Cisco interrupted. "What's your name, buddy?"

"Arden Scofield."

"Well, Arden"—Gideon saw Scofield's jaw muscles stiffen—"let me let you in on something. Last time I knew what *day* it was, or even gave a shit, was probably about 1992. And I don't wear a watch, so don't talk to me about Tuesday at nine o'clock, man. And I got news for you. The *curanderos* don't wear wristwatches either, so Tuesday at nine don't mean anything to them either. When it's time to go, I'll come get you. Let me worry about it, okay? I mean, it's not exactly like you're going to be hard to find, is it?"

Scofield's face had revealed a momentary flare of anger, but he decided to let it go and held up his hands, palms out. "It's your show," he said coldly. "Man."

"Okay." Cisco suddenly shuddered, put a hand to his face, and massaged his temples. "Hey, look, Arden, I'm sorry, I didn't mean to start off on the wrong foot. I'm not feeling that great today, that's all. I get these frigging headaches, and this new stuff I'm taking for them, it didn't agree with me—look, I didn't mean no offense, okay?"

"None taken, my friend," said the wonderfully change-able Scofield, now all ruddy cordiality.

"I have a question, Cisco," Duayne said. "Or rather a re-quest. I'm primarily interested in insect life, especially un-usual or rare insect life. So if there are opportunities to see some on some of our treks, I'd appreciate it—"

"You want to see bugs?"

"Well . . . yes."

Another whinny from Cisco. "Well, you sure as hell picked the right place to come, Chief. We got bugs up the wazoo."

EIGHT

A surprisingly good buffet lunch, its service genially overseen and described course by course by the captain, was set out for them in the dining room: Amazon River codfish in tomato sauce (a Peruvian national delicacy, according to Vargas), fried plantains, rice, beans, and cucumber-and-onion salad. There was a bowl of watermelon slices for dessert. Only the coffee service—open jars of Nescafé instant and powdered creamer, each with a crusted teaspoon stuck in it—left something to be desired. Still, considering where they were, thought Gideon, there was nothing to complain about.

Cisco had shakily disappeared down the corridor from which he'd come, but the rest ate at three trestle tables that had been pulled together. The tensions that had shown themselves earlier were no longer apparent, except in the case of Mel Pulaski, who sat as far as possible from Scofield, wolfed down his food without conversation, and left early. Everyone else, in good spirits, made an hourlong meal of it, most, including Gideon, even going back for more of the coffee.

Toward the end, when the general talk had broken down to conversations between two or three people, Maggie Gray and Scofield found themselves quibbling over the biochemical properties of *Tynanthus panurensis*, a rain forest vine used to treat fevers and rheumatism.

"I have a copy of Duke and Vasquez in my duffel bag," Scofield said, rising. "If that doesn't convince you, I don't know what will. It's in that first storage room."

Tim Loeffler, sitting nearby, leaped to his feet before Scofield was all the way up. "I'll get it, Professor."

"Thank you, Tim," Scofield said, sinking to his seat again. "It's a blue bag with something about Peru on it. '*Perú: un destino privilegiado*,' or something. It's stuck way in a corner by the back wall."

Tim returned shortly with the bag and set it on the table in front of Scofield, who unzipped it, reached in, and jumped back with something between a yelp and squeak, a colossal, hairy, brown spider clamped around his hand and halfway up his forearm. When he reacted with a shudder, the thing flopped down to the table with an audible *thwack*, unharmed, its body held a good three inches off the surface by its jointed, yellow-banded legs. It glared at Scofield with two highly visible red eyes (and probably with the other six as well, Gideon supposed) and reared malevolently up onto its four back legs like a crab ready to do battle.

By now they were all on their own legs, well away from the table. Three of the chairs lay on their backs.

"*Jesus!*" a pallid Tim said. "What *is* that?"

"Whoa," Phil marveled, "look at that thing. It's the size of a medium pizza. That's got to weigh three pounds."

Duayne, staring at it with something like ecstasy on his face, responded in an awed whisper. "It's *Theraphosa blondi*, the Goliath spider. A male, if I'm not mistaken." He turned to the others. "It's the biggest spider in the world. It eats birds." Tears of happiness had formed at the corners of his eyes.

"Did you hear that? The damn thing just *hissed* at me!" Scofield cried. As, inarguably, it had.

"No, no," Duayne said, "not really. It's not a hiss. He does that by rubbing the bristles on his legs together." He pointed. "See? He's doing it now. He does that when he feels threatened."

"*He* feels threatened! How do you think I feel?" Like everyone else, Scofield had his eyes fastened on the creature, which was still in its reared-up position, its upper body swaying slightly. "Tim, go get a broom and mash the damn thing."

"Yuck," said John.

"Me?" Tim asked woefully.

He was saved by Duayne, "No, you don't want to frighten him any more than he already is."

"The hell I don't," Scofield growled.

"Believe me, you don't," Duayne said, asserting himself. "He's not particularly poisonous, but he defends himself by using his legs to flick off the hairs on his abdomen. He can send them five or six feet through the air"—everyone other than Duayne moved back another step—"and they're barbed, you see, more like thorns than hairs, so they're very irritating, like a nettle rash. And if they happen to get in your nose or mouth, they can swell the mucous membranes enough to choke you. Look, you can see the way his hair is standing on end right now."

"He's not the only one," John muttered.

Osterhout, clearly enchanted, moved gingerly forward for a better look. The spider dropped down on all eight legs and ran with amazing rapidity to the far end of the table, its feet making an unsettling skittering sound. There it turned to face them again.

"Jesus, it's fast," marveled Phil.

"It certainly is," affirmed Duayne. "It eats birds, you know. Did I tell you that? And it doesn't need a web to catch them. It sneaks up on them, and then . . . *bam!* It's got them."

"That's all very fascinating, doctor," Scofield said. He was beginning to take command again, having largely collected himself by this time. "Now, perhaps you'd like to tell us how we get rid of the thing?"

"Oh, I'll take care of it. I have to get some equipment. It'll take just a minute." He trotted to the door. "Don't let it get away," he called over his shoulder.

"Right," John said to Gideon. "And how are we supposed to stop it again?"

"I didn't hear that part," Gideon said.

But the creature cooperated, remaining at the very edge of the table, immobile except for its moving mouth parts. (Were they slavering, or was that just Gideon's imagination?) Duayne returned with a large, open, plastic jar—it looked like the sort of thing you'd get five gallons of peanut butter in at Costco—which he slowly set down a foot behind the spider.

"If someone would come *very slowly* back here and hold the jar steady . . . ?"

Gideon volunteered, holding it with both hands and leaning as far as possible away from the spider, while Duayne, who had slipped on a long-sleeved shirt, had put on thick work gloves, and had gotten a dust mop somewhere, went around the table to the spider's other side. The spider turned with him, presumably to keep its two rows of eyes on him, and began to hiss again.

"He can't really see me, you know," Duayne said softly. "Even with all those eyes it only sees differences in light levels. It relies on those hairs to feel the slightest vibration. . . ."

While he spoke he very slowly slid the working end of the mop toward the spider, then, tongue between his teeth, very gently nudged it. The spider obliged by immediately leaping backward directly into the jar. It seemed to Gideon he saw a few of its eyes widen in surprise, but he put that down to his imagination as well. In the meantime, with more speed than he would have judged possible, Duayne rammed a large rubber stopper into the neck of the jar, sealing it. Everybody, Gideon included, heaved a sigh.

"Now what?" Maggie said. "Don't tell me you're going to keep it."

"Of course, I'm going to keep it. It's a *Theraphosa blondi*, for God's sake!"

"Alive?" John asked.

"Ah, no, unfortunately. They can live for twenty-five years in the wild, but they don't do well in captivity, and, sad to say, they tend to be a little aggressive. They don't make very good pets."

"Oh dear," Maggie said. "That *must* be sad for you."

But Duayne was impervious to sarcasm at this point. He was holding the jar proudly aloft for all to see, at the same time slowly rotating it in front of his face. The spider turned in reverse as the jar turned, looking steadily back at him from six inches away. "I brought along some alcohol, of course," Duayne said dreamily, "and this will do for a killing jar."

"Duayne, are you sure the Peruvians will let you take something like that out of the country?" Phil asked.

"I would have thought the Peruvians would be more than glad to have it taken out of the country," Maggie said. "I'd think your problem would be with the United States letting it *in*."

"Not to worry, they don't much care about dead specimens. Anyway, I'll have filled-out copies of FWS 3-177 all ready for them, just in case. Will you just *look* at those pedipalpae go!"

He lowered the jar and looked at his fellow passengers, smiling. "I have an insect and arachnid collection that covers one whole wall of my living room. It's excellent, really, but what a showpiece this little fellow is going to make." He wrapped both arms around the jar to hold it to himself and left smiling.

Gideon turned to John and Phil. "You know, I think I just might have a clue," he said, "as to why his wife left him."

ONCE the excitement of the spider episode had died down, the regular passengers, all of whom except Scofield had spent the night in the Lima Airport, trudged off to their cabins to recuperate. Phil, who had had a good night's sleep in Iquitos, but who rarely passed up the chance for a snooze when he was traveling, did the same. Gideon and John went back to their cabins to unpack to the extent that the closet-less, drawerless accommodations allowed, then came back downstairs to the open-air salon at middeck, pulled a couple of chairs up to the boat's starboard railing, and, in the shade of the upper deck and the soft breeze from the ship's motion, settled back to watch the jungle go by.

There wasn't much to watch. In the middle of the afternoon, with a blazing sun hanging motionless overhead, the jungle was hazy and still, seemingly without inhabitants other than an occasional darting swift or flycatcher or swallow along the shore. The already slow-moving river seemed to have slowed down even more. The two men did a lot of yawning, maybe even dozing, for a pleasant half hour, and then their desultory, sporadic conversation, which had mostly concerned giant spiders, turned to their shipmates.

"So what do you think of our companions?" Gideon asked lazily. "Interesting bunch, wouldn't you say?"

"Not too bad, all in all. And yeah, this ethnobotany stuff could be interesting. I don't know about Scofield, though. I mean, maybe the guy's a big-time expert, but he's a phony right down to his toenails. All that chuckle-chuckle crap and that cutesy business with the pipe." He dug an imaginary pipe stem into his cheek. "The others can't stand him. I don't know if you noticed. Even Duayne's got something against him, and he never even met the guy."

As it often did, John's perspicacity caught Gideon by surprise. Not that he thought John was dumb—far from it—but the man didn't show much, and even when he seemingly wasn't paying attention he was taking things in.

"I noticed."

"And what about the Cisco Kid?" John asked. "Oh, that's gonna be great, following *him* into the jungle."

"Yes, he was a little . . . off, all right. Obviously, the guy has a problem."

"Yeah, the problem is, his brains are fried. He's put in a lot of years stuffing stuff up his nose, or however they do it down here."

He wrinkled his own nose. "I smell smoke."

Gideon pointed toward the shore. "There's a fire. Several fires."

Up ahead, atop a high bank, was what looked like the epicenter of a gigantic bomb blast, a huge wound in the jungle, a good three hundred feet across, littered with hundreds of felled trees and piles of burning, smoking, head-high debris. At least a hundred nearly naked men were scrambling through the hellish scene, trimming branches with machetes and chain saws and tossing them into the smoldering piles. An earthen ramp, red and raw, had been chopped into the bank, and on it lay some of the trunks, tilting down toward the river, where an old barge waited. Another group of workers toiled, their brown backs glistening, pulling and pushing one of the trunks down toward the barge with nothing but chains and ropes and rough posts used as levers. Shouted orders and cries could be dimly heard through the racket of the chain saws.

"It's like something out of the *Inferno,* isn't it?" a suddenly subdued Gideon said.

"Or the building of the pyramids," John said. "Not a machine in sight. Not a backhoe, not a crane."

"And how would they get a crane there?" said Vargas, who had strolled up behind them. "They could barge it down the river, yes, but how would they get it up the bank? Forty feet, almost vertical." He shook his head. "Impossible."

"What are they doing?" John asked. "Is it logging?"

"Oh, yes, logging. There are many such. Ugly, yes? And do you know what is the most amazing thing about it?"

They looked at him.

"It wasn't here at all two weeks ago," Vargas said. "The forest here was untouched. And two weeks from now, they will be gone, doing the same thing somewhere else along the river."

"It's controlled, though, isn't it?" Gideon asked. "I mean, there are regulations, oversight . . ."

Vargas smiled. "This is Peru, my friend. It's regulated by how much money changes hands."

"How long does it take to grow back?" John asked.

"Oh, it grows back quickly enough. A year from now, all will be green again. From here, it may look the same, but it will not be the same, it will no longer be, I forget the word, natural forest, first forest . . ."

"Virgin forest?" offered Gideon.

"Yes, professor, virgin forest. No, it will be all brambles, and thorns, and swamps, and mosquitoes. The big trees won't be back for a hundred, two hundred years."

Silently, the three men watched the gash disappear behind a wall of jungle as the boat moved on. All were glad to see it go.

"Well, well," said Vargas brightly, to introduce a change of subject. Had they spotted any of the Amazon's famous pink dolphins yet? No? Well, they must be sure to look for them, they were something that shouldn't be missed. Would they care for a drink from the bar? Technically, it wasn't yet open, but it would be no trouble at all—it would be a pleasure—to pour something for them. In their cases, of course, he whispered with a wink—an actual, literal wink—there would be no charges at the end of the voyage, and the same went for their excellent friend Phil. Their tabs would discreetly be made to disappear, poof. Only please— he looked around and leaned closer—don't tell the other passengers.

This offer they politely declined in their own and in Phil's behalf, and Gideon asked if it was possible for the boat to travel a little closer to the shore so that they might perhaps catch a glimpse of the rain forest wildlife. Vargas, as always, was anxious to oblige: as it happened, there was a sufficiently deep channel on the starboard side that ran along only a hundred feet from the southern bank, and he would be pleased to have the *Adelita* cruise in it for the next few hours. John and Gideon were to make certain to be on the lookout for monkeys and sloths in the trees, and down below for caimans and capybara, who liked to come down and lounge along the waterside when the heat of the day was on the wane.

Indeed, as dusk approached, and enormous, pink-tinged, end-of-the-world clouds began to build on the horizon, and the light turned from brassy to golden, the small, darting swifts and swallows were replaced by larger birds: white cattle egrets and brilliant toucans and macaws. The caimans did show up along the shore, as still and gnarly as old tree stumps, their eyes and nostrils poking out of the water. And life within the trees became visible. They saw a sloth making its lethargic, languorous upside-down way along the branch of a tree—it covered only three or four feet in the five minutes it was in view—and a spider monkey and a family of squirrel monkeys chittering among the leaves.

"This is what I was hoping it would be like," Gideon said happily.

"Yeah. Hey, is that a capybara?" John gestured at a pig-size animal wallowing in an eddy along the shore. "With the nose?"

"Tapir," Gideon said, as confidently as if it weren't the first one he'd set eyes on outside of a zoo.

"Well, whatever the hell it is, you don't see them in Seattle." He shook his head and considered. "We are really a long way from civilization here, you know?"

"Can't argue with that."

The local denizens, the ones aboard the ship, also began making their appearances as the air cooled. Arden Scofield, in gym shorts and with a towel draped around his neck, came out to circle the deck for exercise. "Hundred and ten feet per circuit," he informed them as he zipped by. "Forty-eight circuits to a mile." Apparently completely recovered from his earlier encounter with *Theraphosa blondi*, he merrily mimed exhaustion and panting. "Only forty-six to go, if I can last."

Fifteen minutes later, the *Adelita* slowed and Vargas returned with exciting news. There was a school of pink Amazon dolphins playing up ahead and if they cared to move back to the port side of the boat they could see these remarkable creatures for themselves.

They saw three of them slipping in and out of the water

in concert a few hundred yards ahead; gleaming, blubbery objects not as sleek or graceful as the more familiar dolphins of the north, but assuredly, indubitably pink.

"Aren't they marvelous?" Scofield called out from behind them. He had finished his walk and now stood leaning against the bar, mopping his face and watching the dolphins play.

"These fish," Vargas said, "in all the world are found only in the Amazon. On our future trips, there will be a, what do you call him, a naturist, a naturalist, aboard to—"

He was shocked into silence by a reverberating *thunk* that could be felt in the floorboards, and then a microsecond later a tremendous crashing and tinkling of glass. The racket had come from behind them, from the bar, which was basically a slightly modified eight-by-six-foot prefab storage shed, the back of which had been bolted to the outside of the dining room wall, beside the entrance. Glass shelves filled with bottles and glasses around three sides left just enough room for a bartender to fix drinks and serve them through the opening of the Dutch door. The walls on either side had been fitted with large, fixed glass panes so that the attractive array of bottles within could be seen from the outside.

At the moment, however, it was anything but attractive. The glass pane on the port side had been shattered—shards lay everywhere underfoot—and two of the glass shelves had come down in fragments, their bottles—those that hadn't been broken—rolling around on the floor. The air reeked of whiskey and beer. In front of this enclosure stood Scofield, openmouthed and frozen in place, his towel clutched to his chest with both hands. His eyes popping, he was staring at the shaft of a heavy, still-vibrating six-foot-long spear that had buried its point in a half-empty vodka carton inside the little room, nailing the carton to the floor. Given where the chalk-white Scofield was standing, it couldn't have missed him by more than a foot.

The three others ran up to him. "Arden, are you all right?" Gideon asked.

Scofield just stood there quaking; rippling shudders wrenched him all the way down to his legs.

John shook him roughly by the shoulder. "Are you hurt? What the hell happened?"

That brought him around, at least to the point at which he could speak, if not yet in full sentences, then in a torrent of disconnected chips and chunks of speech, from which at least some sense could be made. "Someone . . . I was just, just standing . . . that, that spear, it, it . . ."

It didn't take long for them to understand that the obvious had happened. Someone had hurled a spear at the *Adelita*. Scofield had been watching the dolphins, his back to the nearby shore. He had seen nothing, heard nothing, when suddenly, next to him, the window exploded and the spear came crashing through, showering him with glass shards. The wooden shaft had actually brushed him in passing. Look, you could see the abrasion on the back of his right hand. And see the little splinters of glass stuck in his arm? He had almost been killed! But miraculously the point had passed him by. If it had been even six inches to the left . . .

"Come along, now, Arden," Maggie Gray said in her teacherly, dismissive, *Our Miss Brooks* tone, taking his other arm. With some of the others, she had come to see what the clatter had been about. "Let's go and sit you down in the dining room. I'll get the splinters out of your arm. You've got some in your hair too."

"Don't patronize me, dammit," he snapped at her, shaking his arm loose, but then, mumbling, let himself be led away, "Oh, hell, I'm sorry, Maggie. . . . It was just so . . . I mean, if I'd been standing . . ."

John had been peering keenly at the shore, seeking out some movement, some glimpse of the thrower, but there was nothing; no stirring fronds, no flash of a brown body retreating into the undergrowth. He sighed and turned to Gideon. "So there aren't any more headhunters, huh? Well, that's sure a relief. They just spear you now."

Gideon shrugged. "What do I know?"

Vargas, looking about as distraught as a human being

could possibly be, waved helplessly at the mess in the bar and shook his fist at the shore. "Goddamn Indians, what have they got against my poor *Adelita*? Did I ever hurt them?"

"You mean this kind of thing has happened to you before?" John asked. "They throw spears at passing boats? It's just something that happens?"

"No, no, it never happen to me before. I never hear that it happen to anyone." He shook his head in distress. "Chato, where the hell are you? Bring a mop! Look at that window! Look at that bottles! What I'm supposed to do now?" The excitement was playing havoc with his English.

The question was presumably moot, but John answered anyway. "Well, first off, Captain," he said mildly, "I'd suggest you get us a little farther away from the shore."

The suggestion snapped Vargas out of mourning his lost supplies and he ran clumsily toward the wheelhouse, shouting in Spanish. "Hulbert, quick, put us in the central channel, what are you waiting for? Hurry up, don't waste any time . . . mother of God . . ."

NINE

ALTHOUGH the tip of the spear was still hidden from sight in the vodka carton, Gideon knew what it was. He had seen a pair of them in the South American collection of Harvard's Peabody Museum of Archaeology and Ethnology. It was called a shotgun lance, used by several Indian groups in the Amazon basin. It was made by taking the barrel from a worn-out rifle or shotgun, pounding its base into a point, and then sticking a wooden shaft, honed to the diameter needed for a snug fit, into the muzzle end. It was, he knew, a man-killing spear (as opposed to the lighter ones used for hunting animals). But he thought he'd read somewhere that they had gone out of use by the 1950s, by which time new firearms had become more freely available. So how did . . . ?

Maggie stuck her head out of the dining room. "Arden could really use a drink. Scotch." The door popped briefly open again almost before she'd closed it, and once again her head poked out, one eyebrow raised. "For that matter, my dears, so could I."

"I'll get them," Gideon said, stepping gingerly through the space where the window had been. "Looks like the bar's open early today, anyway."

IN the dining room he found Maggie standing over Scofield and meticulously plucking bits of glass from his crew cut, which she then laid on some paper towels that had been spread out on the table. Scofield grabbed for his drink so convulsively that he spilled half of it. The other half went down his gullet in a single swallow, followed by a grateful sigh. Maggie, on the other hand, sipped primly, then went back to exploring Scofield's scalp while Scofield, passive and docile, sat motionless. Gideon felt a highly inappropriate bubble of laughter trying to work its way up his throat. The thing was, it was like watching a pair of rhesus monkeys at grooming time.

He managed to stifle the thought, however. "Can I do anything else for you?" he asked.

"No thanks, I'm fine," Scofield said, and indeed the Scotch seemed to have gone a long way toward restoring him. The ruddy little disks that were natural in his cheeks were coming back. He even tried a feeble little joke. "But I'm beginning to think that becoming an ethnobotanist might not have been such a great career move after all."

Gideon smiled. "I'll admit, you're not having much of a day so far."

"And it's not even six o'clock yet," Maggie dryly observed.

"Say, Doc?" John had opened the dining room door. "Could you come on out when you have a minute?"

His overdone nonchalance (John wasn't much of a dissembler) made it clear that it was something important, and Gideon went out to join him. Most if not all the others were there now, gathered around the smashed bar, gabbling away and gesturing at the spear, which had been pulled from the floor and laid on one of the salon tables.

John pointed at its front end, which had formerly been

hidden by the vodka carton. "Is that thing what I think it is?" he asked soberly.

Gideon bent to examine it. The others quieted down, watching. Attached to the base of the metal spear point by a length of twisted fiber was a sinister, misshapen object a little bigger than his fist.

"Ugh," he said. "I hate these."

Looking up at him was a distorted, monkeylike, yellowish-brown face made even creepier by the rim of beautiful, combed chestnut hair that framed it. A dangling length of string had sewn each eye shut, and three more knotted strands threaded through the grotesquely distorted lips. The nose too had been stretched to impossible proportions.

Gideon gingerly turned it to peer into the nostrils. He pressed a finger against the closed eyes. He moved the long hair aside to study the ears. Finally, he put it down.

"No," he said.

It had been several minutes since John had asked the question and people looked confused.

Phil spoke for them. "No, what?"

"No, it's not what John thinks it is."

John's eyebrows shot up. "It's not a shrunken head?"

"It's not a shrunken *human* head, which is what I presume you meant."

"What the hell is it, then? A monkey head?" He frowned. "Do monkeys have eyebrows?"

"Not so to speak, no, but it's not even that. It's not a head at all. This is a tourist item. They make them from monkey skin or goatskin, and carve them and mold them to look like this, and add a little hair where they need to."

"It's true," Vargas said. "You can buy such things in Iquitos."

"You can buy them on eBay," Gideon said.

All the same, Duayne Osterhout was intrigued. "But it looks so . . . Why are you so sure it isn't human?"

"Oh, a lot of things," Gideon said. "This is a pretty good one, as they go, but there are some things that are almost impossible to duplicate in a fake head." He turned the head upside down. "For one thing, as you see, where's the neck opening? But, more important—there's no nasal hair."

"If it was real, it would have nose hair?"

"Oh yes. I'm talking about the bristly little things in the nostrils—they act as filters—that everybody has. They stay right there even when a head has been shrunk. To fake them, you'd have to plant each one separately, which would take a long time, and even then it'd be hard to make them look authentic. But since just about nobody knows to look for them, they don't bother with it. And then, these threads from the eyes, from the lips—they're obviously commercial twine, the kind you can buy at the local hardware store, not the kind you get from slicing palm fronds into narrow slivers and twirling them into a cord. And the ears . . ." He pushed back the hair. "Human ears are very intricately shaped, very difficult to reproduce convincingly. You can see how crude these are. That's why these things always have so much hair hiding them."

"Yes, yes, I do see," Duayne said, nodding.

"And then the skin itself. There are tool marks on it, see? Burn marks too, right under—"

"Okay, enough already, Doc," John said. "Now the next time we're in the market for a shrunken head, we'll know if we're getting ripped off. But what's it supposed to mean? Is it some kind of curse or something?"

"A warning?" Tim suggested. "Are they threatening us?" His eyes slid sideways to the slowly passing shore, now a safe three miles away.

Gideon put the head down and straightened up. "Beats the hell out of me. I'm reasonably sure it's not meant as a gesture of welcome, but I've never run into this custom before: tying a head to a spear. On the other hand, I'm not exactly up on South American ethnography."

They all stood staring down at the head as if expecting it to open its sewn-together lips and provide answers on its own.

"Chato says he knows what it is," Vargas announced into

the silence. Chato, the Indian crewman who had mutely conducted Gideon, John, and Phil to their cabins earlier, had appeared a few minutes before to begin mopping up broken glass and spilled liquor. But now he was standing on tiptoe, whispering excitedly into Vargas's ear.

"*¿Qué quieres decir, Chato?*" Vargas asked impatiently.

The Indian began to whisper again.

"Speak up so everyone can hear," Vargas ordered.

Chato, looking uneasy at the attention, raised his voice to just barely above a whisper. Not only was he almost inaudible, but he spoke in a Spanish-English-Indian patois with which even Phil had a hard time.

"Translate, will you, Captain?" Phil said.

Vargas accommodated him, translating after every couple of phrases. "He has heard of it before, this custom. . . . In olden days, one of the native groups used it as a—a what, Chato? . . . ah, a death-warning, a revenge warning, to an enemy tribe. . . . They would use . . . no, they would take . . . no, they would shrink the head of a killer, someone who had killed one of their own people, and they would attach it to a spear . . . and they would, they would throw the spear into the hut, into the wall of the hut, of the family of this killer . . . to tell them that one of them would soon die too . . . for the purpose of . . ." He searched for the English word.

"In retaliation?" Gideon suggested.

"Yes, professor, that's correct, in retaliation." He thought Chato was done and began to say something else, but Chato hadn't finished. Vargas listened some more.

"Ah. You see, the fact that the victims received the shrunken head of their own kinsman back, that was to show the contempt that the attackers had for them . . . that the head wasn't even worth keeping. And sometimes it would not be the head of the actual killer, but the head of another member of the enemy tribe. Sometimes *two* heads would be—"

"So . . . what's this got to do with us?" Tim asked. "Why would they . . . I mean, what reason would they . . . ?"

"Ask him what tribe," Scofield said hoarsely. He had emerged from the dining room while Vargas was translating.

Vargas put the question to Chato.

"Los Chayacuros," Chato said.

"The Chayacuro," Scofield said in a dead voice and then, as he sagged back against the dining room wall, laughter started gurgling out of him, limp, helpless laughter that built until it convulsed his whole body, so that he slid slowly down the wall into a sitting position on the deck.

The others stared at him, appalled. Vargas hurried toward him with his arms out, but Scofield, still shaking with deep but silent laughter, waved him off. "I'm all right, I'm all right," he said when he finally stopped and sucked in a deep, shuddering breath. "Oo, ow, that hurt."

But he wasn't all right. There were oily tears running down his cheeks and he was still giggling. "They want to kill me . . . they remember, don't you see? They've waited for me all these years . . . can you believe it? All these years . . . They want to finish the job, they—"

Mel Pulaski stepped forward and reached down to grasp his hand. "Come on, Arden, get up," he said disgustedly. "This isn't doing anybody any good. Okay, you've had a hell of a scare, but it missed you. You're okay, you're fine. A couple of little nicks."

"A hell of a scare," Scofield echoed woodenly. "Yes, yes, it was certainly that." Another little hiccup of laughter.

The big ex-linebacker pulled him unresisting to his feet. "Come on, let's get you to your cabin."

"I'll do it," Tim said, running up. "Come on, Professor, you want to lie down for a while. Easy does it now. . . ." He took Scofield's elbow and began to shuffle him tenderly forward the way a nurse would shuffle an aged patient down a hospital corridor to get a blood test.

That brought Scofield to sudden life. With a violent twist of his arm he shook the young man off. "Dammit, Loeffler, don't treat me like a child! I'm a little shaky, yes—who wouldn't be?—but I can damn well get to my cabin without your help!"

Tim's face turned redder than Scofield's. "But I wasn't— I was only—"

"Oh, forget it, never mind," Scofield muttered and strode off, steadily enough after the first tottery step or two, to the flight of stairs that led up to the cabins.

When he was gone, most of the others sank into the plastic chairs at the various tables, sighing, or shaking their heads, or otherwise expressing shock and discomfort. Tim was flushed and sullen. Gideon and John remained standing, leaning against the deck railing.

"My Lord, I wonder what that was all about," Duayne said. "Why should he think these people, these . . . Chayacuro, would be trying to kill him?"

"Oh, I know what it was about," Maggie said. "Most of us do, actually. Or at least the ones that know Arden."

"So how about enlightening the rest of us?" John suggested.

Maggie shrugged. "Why not? Well, you see, it goes back quite a way. When Arden—" She stopped and turned to Mel. "Mel, why don't you tell it? You're the man who just wrote his life story."

Mel made a face. "I didn't write his life story. I wrote what he *told* me his life story was, which is a different thing. That old story about the Chayacuro that he's been dining out on for thirty years? Who knows if it really happened? There's nobody around to check it out with."

"Well, obviously, *something* happened," Gideon said. "He was pretty shaken up there."

"Yes," Maggie agreed. "I've known Arden a long time, and I've never seen him like that. Not even close. Arden is usually—always, really—one of the most in-control people you'll ever . . ." Shaking her head, she didn't finish the sentence. "Just go ahead and tell it, Mel."

"Okay, why not? Here's the story." Mel lounged back in his chair, his massive brown legs stretched out and crossed at the ankles, his hands in the pockets of his shorts.

Thirty years earlier, he told them, Scofield, as a twentysomething-year-old graduate student, had been on a rubber-seed-hunting expedition in the Amazon with his two best friends, fellow students at Harvard.

"They were on assignment for a big Malaysian rubber plantation," Maggie put in. "They made a lot of money from it. Arden did, at any rate. The other two never made it out."

"You want to tell the story, be my guest," Mel said grumpily. No less than Scofield, he didn't care for having his narrative flow disrupted or his punch lines telegraphed. But with this Gideon could easily sympathize.

Maggie threw up her hands. "Well, please excuse me. I was just trying to fill in a few details. You go ahead, you're the professional storyteller, after all."

"Okay, then," Mel said uncertainly, not sure whether or not he'd just been insulted. "So while they were coming back through the jungle to their boat, they were attacked by this band of Chayacuro Indians. First one of his pals gets it—a poison dart through the neck. So Arden and his other buddy drag him along, trying to stay ahead of the Indians, but in a few minutes they could see he was dead, and they have to leave him there. Then the second guy gets hit—"

"Wait, before that happened," Tim said, "they actually heard the sound of them chopping off the first guy's head, *chonk!* And the first guy was the second guy's brother!"

"His brother!" Vargas exclaimed with a shudder. *"Ay, qué asco!"*

Mel sighed, seeing how it was going to be, but he took it in good stride and continued: "When the second brother was hit by a dart he went sort of crazy—"

"Arden went crazy?" This time it was Phil. "Or the brother?"

"No the *brother*, for Christ's sake. He ran off in a panic, into the jungle, and Arden chased after him, trying to get him back to the path."

"Which was pretty brave, when you think about it," Gideon said. "He could easily just have taken off, trying to save himself."

"Yeah," said Mel, "assuming that the way he tells it is the way it happened."

It was the second time Mel had expressed doubt. "And you don't think it is?" Gideon asked.

Mel thought before answering. "No, I didn't say that. Look, I'm a careful writer. I'm serious about fact-checking, that's all, and I get uncomfortable when there's no way to check something out, especially when it happened a long time ago, and it's a story that makes somebody out to be a hero—or a coward, for that matter. People forget, they embellish, they like to look good, you know? I'm not talking about lying, just about maybe remembering something the way they *want* to remember it. But no, I don't have any real reason to doubt him, just . . ."

"Come, come, tell us what happened," an engrossed Vargas urged. "The other brother, he died also?"

"Yes, but not before one of the Chayacuro, a big guy for an Indian, catches up with them. As Arden tells it, the guy has his blowgun to his lips, aiming it right at his throat from only fifteen feet away, and Arden shoots him just in time.

"Whoa," said Phil, shaking his head. "That's hairy."

"Yeah. Anyhow, then the second brother dies too, right in his arms. Arden leaves him for the headhunters too—in all fairness, what else could he do?—and runs for the boat they'd stashed at the river, and he gets away. And that's it, that's the story."

But he couldn't resist a final aside. "As Arden tells it."

A thoughtful silence now settled down over the group, moderated only by the soft, steady *swish* of water against the hull and the clinking of broken glass as Chato quietly finished sweeping the last of the shards into a dustpan.

After a time, Duayne spoke. "I guess I don't understand. Does he think these Chayacuro are still after him? Why would they be?"

"Presumably because he killed one of them," Mel said.

Duayne shook his head. "But that doesn't make sense. It was kill or be killed. He had no choice. They were chasing *him*; he was defending himself. It was completely justified. What else could he do?"

"No, you don't get it; that's not the way their minds work." The speaker was Cisco, making his first appearance since the introductions that morning. He had returned to take a chair against the dining room wall, a little away from the others, where he sat. Looking not quite so much on his last legs as he had earlier, he had changed to shorts and flip-flops that revealed knobby, hairy knees and bony, callused, misshapen feet that looked like illustrations from a podiatric pathology textbook.

"See," he said, "to them, there's no such thing as 'self-defense' or 'completely justified.' They just don't think that way. A dead guy is a dead guy." He paused to take a shaky pull on the cigarette he'd brought with him, an action made more difficult by the stiff, uncomfortable way he held his head. "If it's caused by somebody else, it has to be avenged. Period. Hell, even if it's not caused by somebody else, they find somebody to take it out on; in their world, nobody except the old folks dies because he just plain got sick and croaked; it's always a murder, a curse, you name it. Booga-booga. Somebody *did* it to him. Witchcraft, poisoning, whatever. These people, they got a very fixed, well-integrated belief system regarding causality."

Gideon nodded. It was a common enough worldview among nonliterate peoples, especially fierce groups like the Chayacuro. Cisco seemed to be a bit more on the ball than he'd given him credit for. He was considerably sharper than he'd been earlier. Apparently he'd had more education than his manner suggested too. "A very fixed, well-integrated belief system regarding causality"—that was hardly the language of your typical dope-addled drifter or dropout or whatever he was, especially considering that English wasn't his first language. Gideon was even beginning to have an easier time understanding his mush-mouthed speech. Still, there was always a sense of something being "off" about him. When you spoke to him, it was as if your words were going by about two feet to the left of his head, and his were missing yours by about the same distance.

"But it was so long ago," Tim said. "How could they remember? Would anybody still care?"

"They don't see time like you do," Cisco said. "They see connected events: killing, revenge. The first, like, requires the other, you know? The time in between doesn't have anything to do with it. It doesn't compute, you know?"

"And what do *you* think about it, Cisco?" Maggie asked. "Was it really them? Were they really trying to kill him?"

Cisco shrugged. "Don't ask me." Thin ribbons of smoke trailed from his nostrils as he spoke. "All I'm saying is, look around, look where we are." He waved, without turning, at the darkening jungle behind him. "This ain't Kansas, Toto. It's a different world, it's got different laws you and me can never understand in a million years."

"Wow," murmured a thrilled Tim. "Damn." Others murmured similarly.

"Hold on a minute, folks, this doesn't hold water," said Gideon, for whom things were veering too close to the occult to be comfortable. "What Cisco says is true enough, generally speaking, but it doesn't apply in this case. How could they recognize Arden after so many years? How would they know he'd be aboard the *Adelita*?"

Phil backed him up. "And how could they know that he'd be standing there in plain sight right at that moment? They couldn't, it's impossible."

John chimed in too. "Yeah, and how would they know exactly where the boat would be passing at that exact time? How would they know to station somebody right there with a spear?"

"Yes," said Duayne, throwing in his sensible two cents' worth as well. "How could they possibly know we'd be close enough to shore for a spear to reach the boat? For most of the time, we would have been way out of range."

"That's right," Gideon said. "The only reason we *were* that close is that I asked Captain Vargas to move us in so that we could see some wildlife."

"Yes, that's so," Vargas concurred.

"So whatever the hell it was about," John said, "it wasn't because anybody was laying in wait, specifically trying to get Scofield."

"Yeah, yeah," Cisco said, unimpressed, and coming within a millimeter of burning himself as he scratched one bare leg with the hand that held the cigarette. "I'm not saying they did or they didn't, but I tell you this: I been here a long time now, and I spent a lot of time in the jungle, and I seen a lot weirder stuff than this. These people—I don't just mean the Chayacuro, I mean, you know, a lot of the indigenous jungle people—well, our laws of physics, and motion, and even the material world, they don't apply. We think there's no way they could know he'd be coming back, but they have ways of knowing things that science doesn't even begin to understand. Let me ask you . . . um . . . ?" With his chin he gestured questioningly at Gideon.

"Gideon," Gideon told him.

"Okay, let me ask you, Gideon. You want to know, how could they know you would ask Vargas to bring the boat close at that exact point, right?"

Gideon nodded. "I sure do."

"But I see the question a different way. *Why* did you ask him to bring the boat close at that exact point? Where did the idea come from? Ideas don't come from nowhere. What was it that made you do it right then and not some other time? What made the other guy, Scofield, stand right there, out in the open, in full view, at that exact second? Isn't it possible that forces beyond anything we—"

"Nothing *made* me do it," Gideon retorted with heat. "Look, Cisco, I have a pretty well-integrated belief system regarding causality myself, and in this case you can take it from me that no jungle witch doctor"—he winced at his own highly unanthropological choice of words, but phrases like "ways of knowing things that science doesn't begin to understand" tended to buzz irritatingly in his ear, like a cloud of little mosquitoes, and made him cranky and argumentative—"put the idea in my head. I assure you, I'm quite capable of coming up with it all by myself."

Before the words had left his mouth he was ashamed of himself. Snapping so pompously at a human wreck like Cisco was contemptible. "On the other hand," he said in a lame attempt at making amends, "of course you're right: nobody really can say where his ideas come from."

Cisco's reaction only made him feel worse. He'd hurt the poor guy's feelings. The gaunt, gray-bearded man dropped his eyes and held up his hands in submission. "I'm just saying," he mumbled around the half-inch, burning butt still in his mouth. "No offense, buddy."

At that point, one of Vargas's Indian crew—the cook, obviously, inasmuch as he was carrying a wooden ladle and wearing a gravy-stained apron tied at the waist, an equally grubby white undershirt, and a villainous black bandanna tied around his head—came out of the kitchen with fire in his eyes.

"*Se va a enfriar la cena,*" he told Vargas sourly.

Dinner was getting cold.

TEN

ANOTHER unexpectedly tasty meal was waiting for them on the buffet table: warm potato and carrot salad, white rice, stewed bananas, chicken and vegetables over spaghetti, and beans, with caramelized bread pudding for dessert. As with lunch, there was no wine served, only water. Everyone seemed hungry, going at the food with gusto. And with rice, potatoes, and spaghetti all in the same meal, the carbohydrate-deprived John looked like a man who'd died and gone to heaven.

But conversation was subdued. Some people feared that the trip was over and done, that Arden might call it off and have Vargas turn the boat around. Those who knew Arden best, however—Maggie, Tim, and Mel—were confident that with a night to sleep on it he would see things as they now did; that is, that the spear attack, whatever its cause, could not have had anything to do with him personally. Despite Cisco's metaphysical mumblings, the evidence against it was inarguable, and Arden, a scientist through and through, would understand that once he'd gotten over his initial shock.

So what, then, *was* the attack about? Vargas, at his station behind the buffet, professed to have no idea. In his six years on the river he'd never heard of anything like it.

"This is your first passenger trip, isn't it?" Mel asked him between forkloads of spaghetti. "You usually ship cargo, right? So is it possible that the Chayacuro, or whoever, don't want you bringing people—tourists—in? That this is a warning to *you*? You know, 'Don't screw up our pristine rainforest'?"

No, it wasn't possible, Vargas told him. There were two other ships out of Iquitos already in the tourist trade. The *Dorado* and the *Principe de Loreto* both had every-other-week cruises to Leticia and back, and such a thing had never happened to them. So why pick on his poor *Adelita*? What was special about this trip? No, no, there was nothing— He frowned momentarily, as if an answer, and not a very welcome answer, had crossed his mind, but he only opened his mouth, shut it, and shook his head. No.

Tim, like everyone else, had seen the shadow cross his face. "Captain, you don't think we'll be attacked *again*?"

"Again? No, no, of course not. Well, I don't think so . . ."

The answer, half-baked at best, didn't appear to do much to ease Tim's mind. He cleared his throat. "I know it's not up to me, everybody, but I think that if there's any possibility of future attacks, well, it might be better to call the whole thing off and go back. Who needs this?"

"I think Tim has a point," Duayne said. "It grieves me to say it, but perhaps we'd better call it a day. We're agreed that we have no idea what this is all about, so how can we know they won't try again? Maybe next time we won't all be so lucky."

"Oh, that's totally ridiculous," Maggie barked. "Whoever it was, we've already left him forty miles behind. There are no roads out there. How is he supposed to keep up with us? In a dugout canoe?"

"But we don't know that there's only one of them. He was waiting for us, wasn't he? How do we know there won't be others waiting for us?"

"Well, for Christ's sake, we're traveling down the middle of the river, aren't we?" Maggie said. "We're miles from shore. What's some Indian with a spear going to do, shoot it out of a shoulder-mounted missile launcher?"

"And how do we know it'll just be some guy with a spear?" Duayne demanded. "Somebody obviously doesn't want us here, that's the only thing we know for sure. Maybe it *will* be a missile-launcher next time. Maybe—"

"Oh, ridiculous," Maggie said again, this time with a snort. "Don't get carried away, take a deep breath."

"It is not ridiculous," Duayne said, flaring up. "I've done my research on the area, Dr. Gray. We're quite near the Colombian border. This region of the jungle is a well-known route for getting coca paste out of Peru into—"

He was interrupted by a crash from the buffet table. "Sorry, sorry," croaked Vargas, bending to pick up the plates he'd knocked onto the floor.

"Into Colombia," Duayne continued. "There are drug lords out there, and they have all *kinds* of weapons. Isn't it possible that we've accidentally gotten in the middle of some kind of drug war? That they're warning us . . . that they think . . . well, I don't know what they think, but—"

"Not likely, Duayne," John said. "If some drug lord wanted to send us a message, trust me, he wouldn't get some Indian to do it with a spear. Besides, when those types give you a warning, they don't want you guessing as to where it came from or what it means. They want you to *know*."

"All right then, John, you tell us: what was it all about?" Duayne said.

John, sipping on his Nescafé and powdered milk, shrugged. "Beats the hell out of me."

"We may be reading way too much into this," Gideon said. "For all we know, some crazy kid might have done it, maybe not an Indian at all, just some teenager out for a thrill."

This feeble try at an explanation was received with the dubious expressions it deserved, not that anybody could come up with anything better. After a moment, Duayne spoke up again, more mildly than before:

"Anyway, it's not just the cruising part we have to worry about. What about when we're out there in the jungle, botanizing and so forth? How do we know who might be watching us, waiting for us, following us? How do we know—"

"Okay, I got a suggestion," said Mel, who hadn't participated thus far. He twisted around to see Cisco, who was sitting apart from the others, his chair pushed so far away that it was backed up against another table. He had passed on the main courses, eating nothing but the bread pudding, a second large helping of which was being spooned from the soup bowl he held on his lap. "Cisco, if I remember right, you said our treks the next couple of days would be on the south side of the river, is that right?"

Cisco, working hard on the pudding, looked reluctantly up from it. "What?"

"These hikes and things, we're supposed to be taking them on the south bank, right?"

It was dishearteningly obvious that Cisco had no idea what Mel was talking about, no memory of what he himself had told them a few hours ago. "Yeah, that's the plan, you got it," he said.

"Well, what's so special about the south side? I mean, aren't the plants and things pretty much the same on either side?"

A shrug. "Pretty much. Same microclimate."

"Okay, so why don't we just stay away from the south side? That's where the damn spear came from, and if people are really worried that somebody else might be waiting farther down, we can do our treks on the other side. That'd put seven miles of open water between us and them."

"I guess we could do that," Cisco agreed. "Hell, I don't care. Whatever you want."

"Are there any Chayacuro on that side?" Tim asked.

Cisco, seeing that he wasn't going to be able to devote his full attention to the pudding for a while, sighed and put it on the table behind him. "No one knows where the Chayacuro are, buddy. See, they're not a tribe, like you're thinking of a tribe, with a chief and a village and everything. They're a bunch of small bands, maybe three or four families in each one, and they don't stay any one place more than a couple of seasons. They say there used to be bands on both sides fifty years ago, but who knows anymore? My guess is no."

"What about other groups?" Maggie asked. "Friendly groups, I mean. Remember, we want to meet with some *curanderos*. Do you have any contacts on that side?"

"Lady, I got them everywhere. The Orejón, the Boruna. I can dig you up a couple of old-school shamans, the real thing, pals of mine."

"Good. Captain, would you have any problem with the change in route?"

Vargas, still at his station behind the buffet table, shook his head. "No, no trouble. It would only be for tomorrow anyway. The following day we will divert to the Javaro, which will take us into different country."

"Okay, then," Mel said, "*no problemo*. Let's do it."

"Shouldn't we clear it with Dr. Scofield first?" Tim asked.

Mel shrugged. "So we'll clear it with him." He laughed. "You think he's going to object to putting the whole Amazon River between us and the Chayacuro?"

"Well, but . . ." Tim was frowning. "Cisco said he was guessing. What if there *are* Chayacuro on both sides? How do we know that the ones on the south side won't warn the other ones that we're coming?" Tim, it appeared, was not as ready as some of the others to consign the Chayacuro revenge idea to the trash basket.

Cisco responded with a derisive snicker. "How the hell would they know what we're going to do? And what would they warn them with? Cell phones? E-mail?"

Tim took offense. "Hey, you're the one who said they

had all these"—He put his hands up beside his ears and waggled his long fingers—"all these *woo-hoo* powers that us poor *norteamericanos* can't understand. What, they can't use them to communicate with each other?"

Cisco looked pityingly at him. "Not across seven miles of open water," he mumbled to his bread pudding and went back to eating it.

ELEVEN

WHEN dinner was finished and most of the passengers had gone back to their cabins to rest, or shower, or read, Gideon remained on the lower deck. The smashed side window of the bar had been boarded up with a trelliswork of one-by-three lumber, and he was peering through it at the substantial gouge that the lance had left at the junction of floor and baseboard.

"Hmm," he said. He backed slowly away from the bar until he reached the starboard railing—three and a half paces—walked back to stand in front of the bar, turned to look behind him toward the distant, darkening shore, turned again to look down the deck toward the front of the boat, looked laterally across the breadth of the *Adelita*, and folded his arms.

"Huh," he said.

Mel, who had gone into the dining room with an empty plastic water bottle a few moments earlier, came out with a filled one and a handful of miniature bananas.

He stopped near Gideon. "Trying to figure out if you can get a bottle out between the boards?"

Gideon smiled. "I figured it was worth a shot."

"Well, forget it. I already tried. Can't be done." He continued on his way to the forward stairs.

Gideon went through his pacing and gazing and arm-folding a little longer, then climbed the stairs himself, hoping to find Vargas in the wheelhouse, which was located at the front of the upper deck, forward of the cabins. He spotted the captain through the open window, looking very nautical, smoking a thin cigar and leaning over a navigational chart with a pencil while one of the crewmen steered.

Vargas looked up, smiling. "Yes, Professor Oliver? How can I help you?"

"Captain, I'd like very much to have a look at that lance again. Where'd you put it?"

"But it's at the bottom of the Amazon. I threw it overboard. Do you think I would have a thing like that on my boat?" He caught himself as he began to cross himself and turned it into a scratch of his throat instead. "Some of my crew, you know," he said in a confidential, man-to-man tone, "they're very backward, very superstitious." With a meaningful roll of his eyes, he cocked his head toward the steersman. "They think such a thing would bring us bad luck." He laughed at the silliness of it.

"Ah, I understand," said Gideon. "Well, too bad." He smiled. "Save the next one for me, will you?"

"Ha-ha-ha," laughed Vargas. "Yes, the next one, ha-ha." He waited, peering around the wheelhouse corner post until Gideon was out of sight, then crossed himself.

THE Amazon is the greatest river in the world, possibly only the second-longest after the Nile (geographers are still arguing about it), but certainly the widest, and by far the first in volume. From its mouth pours almost a quarter of the world's river water; four times that of the Congo, the second greatest river, and ten times that of the Mississippi. In one day it delivers as much water as the Thames does in a year.

Yet its pace is measured, even sluggish. From its beginnings at the base of the Andes to its mouth on the Atlantic Ocean on the other side of the continent, nearly four thousand miles away, it drops an average of a quarter inch a mile, barely enough to keep it moving, so being on it is more like drifting on an enormous, quiet lake than like being on a river. This sense of drifting, of passive floating, is enhanced in the dark, when not even a suggestion of the black, lightless jungle is visible.

It was in the dark, a couple of hours after dinner, that Phil, John, and Gideon were sitting out on deck, their legs stretched out, enjoying the tranquil, exotic ambience of the vast river. They were not in the salon on the lower deck, but on the flat, open roof of the vessel. Phil had discovered a stairwell leading up to it from the cabin deck, and they had carried up chairs from the salon to enjoy the solitude and the fresh breeze. There was no awning to protect against the sun, so the area would have been hell during the day, but at night it was different. Earlier there had been a brief, hard rain—Phil said it was very nearly a daily late-afternoon occurrence—so the heat had moderated and the gentle, moist wind from the boat's slow progress was like lotion on the skin. And more than two stories above the river as they were, there was an exhilarating feeling of being on the very roof of the world. Gideon had showered and changed clothes before dinner, and his fresh shirt was only barely damp with perspiration. Above, the carpet of stars was so stupendous and crowded that he had at first thought that the Milky Way was a huge cloud of smoke from the fires of another unseen logging operation.

The *Adelita* traveled at night with the aid of a single, powerful spotlight bolted to the front of the wheelhouse. This was flicked on for fifteen or twenty seconds every couple of minutes to sweep the milky surface of the water for a few hundred yards ahead in a slow, back-and-forth arc that brought home how very isolated they were, and in what an alien place they traveled. The stars themselves were exotic, the unfamiliar configurations of the southern hemisphere not even recognizable as constellations to a stranger's eye.

Phil had picked up a liter bottle of *aguardiente* in Iquitos and had poured generous portions into the tumblers they'd brought from their rooms.

John took a first sip, rolled it critically around his mouth, and swallowed. "Whoa boy, now this is what I call, mmm . . ." He had another judicious taste, swallowed again, and blew out his cheeks. " . . . real rotgut. How much did you pay for it, Phil?"

"Four *soles*, a buck thirty."

"That's what I thought. Jesus."

Gideon, sipping more gingerly, winced. "This is what the real people drink, am I right, Phil?"

"Absolutely. Good, plain firewater. That's what it means, you know? *Agua*, water, *ardiente*, fire."

"Gee, I wonder why that is," John said, but his views on the potent liquor had apparently changed. He held out his glass. "I guess I could stand another."

Phil picked up the bottle beside his chair, poured some for John and himself, and offered some to Gideon.

"No, thanks, I'm fine." Actually, Gideon liked the sharp, rough taste, the overtones of anise, the scraping, sandpapery sensation in his gullet (maybe that's what had done in Cisco's voice), but Phil had poured them with a heavy hand and one was more than enough. He added a little water from the plastic bottle he had brought from his cabin and had earlier refilled in the dining room.

Cisco's gargling voice, at this moment, was irritatingly audible to them in the nighttime quiet. Unfortunately, he and Tim had also discovered the roof a little while ago and had brought up a couple of chairs from below for themselves. They had apparently gotten over their earlier prickly exchange and were having an amiable, frequently uproarious conversation on the other side of the boat.

Every now and then, the cloying smell of marijuana smoke would drift over from them.

Cisco was telling a joke. "So these two guys are sitting on the beach at night, you know, smoking weed, totally psychedelicized," Cisco was saying, "and the first guy shines his flashlight up at the sky, okay? And the second guy says, 'Whoa, man, that's beautiful. I bet you could walk all the way up that beam, right up to them stars, wouldn't that be something?' And the other guy says—"

Tim interrupted, giggling. "The other guy says, 'Screw you, you must think I'm really stoned. I know you, you'd switch off the goddamn flashlight when I was halfway up.'"

Gales of choking, coughing, knee-slapping laughter followed.

John shook his head. "Is there anything worse than listening to a couple of wasted potheads thinking they're being funny when you're stone-cold sober?"

"And how would you know?" Phil asked. "You're not stone-cold sober."

Phil, far more of a free spirit than John, had gotten into more than one argument with him over the pros and cons of marijuana usage, and whether or not it was really more of a health and social menace than alcohol, and so on, and for a moment Gideon thought that this was going to be another one of them. But John was feeling too mellow to bite. Instead he sipped again and nodded gravely.

"This is true," he allowed.

The wind changed slightly so that both the smoke and the noise drifted off in another direction, and the three men sat peaceably and companionably drinking their *aguardiente*. A few minutes passed before Phil spoke again.

"I know we've been through this a gazillion times, but when it comes down to it, I just can't make any sense of what happened today."

"I think we're all in pretty good agreement about that," John said.

"Yeah, but *nothing* makes sense. I can't come up with a

single scenario that works. How could anybody out there know ahead of time we'd be close enough to shore for a spear to reach? He couldn't. So what are we left with, some guy who just happens to be carrying around a shotgun lance, which just happens to have a fake shrunken head attached to it, and who just happens to be standing around right next to the river, wondering what to do with it, when, what do you know, along comes—"

"I'd like to put forward an alternative supposition," Gideon said.

"Oh boy," John said, "watch out. When he starts talking like that, it means things are gonna get complicated."

"No, they'll get simplified. Look, why are we so sure the lance was thrown from shore? Couldn't somebody on the boat have done it?"

Like fans at a tennis match, their heads swiveled in his direction. "Somebody on the boat . . . ?" Phil repeated.

"Sure. Come on down, let me show you."

John was inclined to stay where he was and let Gideon's alternative supposition wait till morning, but the others prevailed upon him and got him, complaining affably, out of his chair. On the lower deck, Gideon stood them in front of the bar's Dutch doors, just where Scofield had been when the lance smashed through the window.

"Now. John, you and I were sitting right over there, up against the railing on the other side, watching the dolphins, right?"

A nod from John.

"Vargas was behind us, also looking at them. And Scofield was standing right here, doing the same. All of us with our eyes focused on where the fish were jumping around—"

"Dolphins," Phil stated, "are not fish."

"Even I know that," commented John.

"Pardon me," Gideon said, "where the *cetaceans* were jumping around. Okay, everybody's eyes were on them, and the lance comes crashing into the window from *behind* us."

"Where the shore happens to be," John said, "only sixty or seventy feet away at the time."

"True, but the starboard deck was right here, three feet away. My question is, why couldn't someone have come up along the deck from the front of the ship—maybe coming out the side door of the dining room—flung the lance through the side window, and then run back into the dining room and out of sight, then left later? If the door was open, he'd have been back through it in two seconds."

"Because Scofield would have seen him," Phil said. "All he had to do was turn his head."

"Is that so? Go ahead, turn your head."

Phil turned to his right. "Oh. I see what you mean. The corner of the dining room blocks the view forward."

"Yeah," John said, "I see how that could be, but how could he miss Scofield with that thing from two feet away? He'd have to be blind."

"Ah," said Gideon. "Maybe he didn't miss, maybe he accomplished what he was trying to do."

"Well, if what he was trying to do was scare the shit out of him, he accomplished it, all right."

"But that's exactly what I'm getting at. I think maybe somebody's playing games with Scofield."

Phil looked from Gideon to John and scratched at his scraggly chin. "I have to admit, that sounds a lot more plausible than some ticked-off Chayacuro warrior who's been standing there with his spear for thirty years, waiting for him to come back."

"And what about the spider?" Gideon said. "That fits too. Someone having a little fun at the big man's expense, cutting him down to size."

"It was Tim that went to get the bag with the spider in it," Phil observed thoughtfully. "So does that make him the someone, in your opinion?"

"No, the bag was in one of the luggage rooms. No lock. Anyone could have put it there."

"But how would he know Arden would open it up?"

"He'd know he'd open it *sometime*."

"Yeah," John said, "but how long could a spider stay alive in there?"

"Long enough to last the trip, that's for sure."

"Well, okay, then, it's possible. But it wasn't poisonous, so what's the point?"

"That *is* the point. Pay attention, John. If what I'm saying is right, they're not trying to kill him; they just want to frighten him, or maybe make him look ridiculous."

"But why?" Phil asked. "And who? Whom. Who."

Gideon shrugged. "No idea."

"In that case, let's go look at the stars some more," Phil said. "Maybe it'll come to us. And be careful, you guys, we're more buzzed than you think, and there's no railing up there."

John was shaking his head. "I don't know about all this, Doc," he said as they started back. "It sounds kind of crazy to me. That's taking a lot of risks just to make Scofield look silly."

"They don't like the guy, you pointed that out yourself."

John acknowledged this with a tip of his chin. "Yeah, well, that's so. Okay, it's *possible,* but that's all. At this point it's just a theory."

"Correct, only it's not even a theory. It's not even a hypothesis. It's what I said, a supposition, an inferential conclusion not based on anything close to adequate substantiation, empirical or otherwise. But it's certainly worth considering."

John sighed, as he often did when Gideon got professorial with him. "Well, whatever the hell it is, are you gonna mention it to Scofield?"

"That's a good question and, you know, I'm not sure. Probably not, I'd say. First off, it *is* just a supposition. Besides, it's pretty clear he and his people—Tim, Maggie, Mel . . . even Duayne—have some not-so-great vibes going on between them, so why should I want to stir things up any more? He's obviously paranoid when it comes to the Indians. Do I want to make him paranoid about the people he works with? I think maybe I'll just let it go—unless something else happens, and then I think I owe it to him to tell him."

Phil nodded. "I agree with that. And anyway, assuming you're right about what's going on, I'm betting that's it; it's over and done with. Whoever it is made his point. If he's trying to scare Scofield, or bring him down a few notches, how could he do any better than he did today?"

"Well, I think you *should* tell him, Doc," John said as they mounted the steps. "I think you owe it to him."

"Maybe I will, John. I haven't really decided. Let's see what he's like when he comes out of his room tomorrow."

"*If* he comes out of his room," Phil said. "I wouldn't be surprised if he doesn't, or at least doesn't show himself out on deck in the open anymore. Or if he does, I'm betting at least he finds some excuse for not getting out and going on any of the treks, even on the other side of the river."

"Nope," said John. "This is a guy who cares too much about how he comes off to other people to do that. No, I think Maggie and the rest of them are wrong. I think he'll come up with some excuse—nothing to do with what happened, of course—for calling the whole thing off and turning the ship around. No, on second thought, he'll probably get Vargas to come up with an excuse, engine trouble or something."

Gideon disagreed with both of them. "Uh-uh. If he did that, everybody would see right through it, and he couldn't live with that. My guess is, upset as he is, he'll just laugh it off and go right on with the cruise. Too much pride to do anything else."

As they approached their chairs, they were greeted first by trailing smoke that smelled a lot worse than marijuana, and then by a welcome of sorts.

"*Hola*, the three musketeers return," called Cisco, laughing away.

"The three *mouse*keteers," chortled Tim. They were both pretty much pie-eyed.

"The three *mosquitoes*," amended Cisco, engendering even greater hilarity.

"These guys are a laugh riot," John growled as he sank into his chair and put his feet up on the railing again. John had a hard time disguising his aversion to drugs and drug-takers, not that he generally made any attempt to do so; no surprise, considering that hard-drug trafficking was one of his areas of expertise and he was familiar with both ends of the long, wretched chain and all the sorry creatures in be-tween. "For Christ's sake, that stuff really stinks," he called. "It smells like a rainy day at the lion house. Go back to your Mary Jane, will you? For our sake, anyway."

"No, come on, man," Tim said amicably, "don't be like that. This is really good stuff here."

"High-quality *chacruna*," said Cisco. "Gift of the gods."

"*Psychotria viridis*," Tim explained, a professor in the making. "Mixed with tobacco and wrapped in a banana leaf. It's not illegal, not even in the States, if that's what's bothering you, not that you can get any up there. Hey, pull your chairs over, why don't you try some? It'll mellow you out. Cisco's got a ton of it."

"Sure, come on over," Cisco said, not quite as welcom-ingly.

"No thanks, fellas," Gideon said for the three of them. He wasn't quite as straight-arrow as John, but not very far behind. From the expression on Phil's face, however, he could see that Phil was more than ready to try it just to see what it was like—there were few new experiences that Phil wasn't open to—but decided to go along with his friends, at least for the moment.

"Suit yourself," Tim said.

John, Phil, and Gideon retrieved their glasses from where they'd left them on the deck, and settled back, but John was unable to let things lie.

"Hey, Tim, you really ought to know better," he said, not unkindly. "That stuff's terrible for your health. Believe me, I know about these things. It'll rot your brain." His unspoken subtext was crystal-clear: *Take a good look at your buddy there. Is that the way you want to wind up?*

"Yeah, like that crap you guys are drinking is *good* for your health?"

"It may not be good for your health," John called back, "but it doesn't turn you into a zombie."

Getting no reply, the three of them returned to their stargazing. Gideon decided on another *aguardiente* after all and poured himself a dollop. After being away from it for twenty minutes, he found that it stung his throat more than before, and he unscrewed the top of his water bottle to dilute it a bit.

Tim saw or heard him do it. "Hey, you want to talk about something that's bad for your health, what about *that* stuff? Don't you know that water'll kill you? Every glass is like a nail in your coffin."

"That's true," Cisco chimed in, "did you know that, like, every single person that ever drank it has died? Every single one! That's why I never touch it."

"That's right," agreed Tim. "And the bad part is, it's one of the most addictive substances in the world, worse than crack. What happens is that once you try it even *once*— even a tiny sip—you're hooked, and you have to have more. And then more. And more. You steal for it or kill for it; you can't help yourself. And if you can't get any more you go into withdrawal and you actually die."

They were both cackling so uproariously they could barely get the words out, but that didn't stop them. "And even if you do get more," Cisco managed, "it don't make any difference. You die in the end anyway."

They were both collapsed with laughter now, unable to carry on, but Phil picked up the baton. "Never mind the biological aspects," he said to John. "You know what water's composed of, don't you? Hydrogen and oxygen. And what do they make rocket fuel out of? Hydrogen and oxygen. I'm telling you, the stuff is too volatile to go anywhere near it, let alone *drink* it."

Gideon smiled but John, pained, bared his teeth. "Phil, I wish, I *wish* you wouldn't do that. What do you want to say things like that for?"

"Hard to say, exactly," Phil said. "It might be because I love to see the veins stand out in your neck like that."

TWELVE

AS it turned out, none of them were right about how Scofield would behave the next day, although Gideon came closest. Scofield didn't merely laugh off the incident of the lance, he acted as if nothing at all had happened. Appearing in the morning looking ruddy, bright, and well rested, he greeted everyone cordially and went enthusiastically at the buffet of cheese omelets, fried bananas, rice, salsa, and toast. When Maggie mentioned that they thought that it was a good idea to move their excursions that day to the north side of the river, he merely said, quite mildly, as if it were no concern of his, that that was just fine. It was obvious that he didn't want to talk about the previous day, and his wishes were observed.

After breakfast, the *Adelita* moored at a narrow beach topped by a thirty-foot bluff. Cisco scrambled up it and went to see about arranging a meeting with the shaman of an Ocaona settlement about two miles to the northwest, on the banks of the Punte, another of the Amazon's hundreds of tributaries. He returned two hours later with the news that the celebrated *curandero* Yaminahua would be pleased to grant them an audience. He—Cisco—suggested that they each bring along at least a liter of water. For people who weren't used to it, a four-mile round-trip jungle hike in the midday heat was going to make for a long, exhausting day.

And don't forget insect repellent, he added.

SAY *Amazon jungle* to the average person, and a picture pops into the mind of intrepid nineteenth-century explorers in pith helmets, of giant leaves, thick, tangled vines, and hostile underbrush that has to be hacked through with a machete at every step. But except for the giant leaves, most of the virgin rain forest is far different. There are thick liana vines that hang from the tree limbs, yes—some sturdy enough to swing on, Tarzan-like—but they aren't very tangled or really very prolific, and while a machete is sometimes useful, it's hardly a necessity, because the canopy high overhead shuts out so much sun that there isn't much undergrowth to contend with.

This is also the reason that what little is there is so huge-leaved; it's their way of sucking in every possible mote of sunlight that does manage to filter through. Even the water lilies are as big as wagon wheels, five feet in diameter and able to support a small child, or more likely, a capybara or a python. The canopy effectively shuts out wind too, and the birds and insects are quiet during the day, so that there is a prickly sense of hushed expectancy, of something terribly important about to happen, although of course nothing does, aside from when a howler monkey occasionally lets loose one of its deafening hoots and every previously invisible bird within range flutters and screams in response before settling down again. Ninety-five percent of the time, though, walking in such a forest is like traveling through some surreal, silent, dimly remembered dreamscape.

"These big leaves and stuff," Phil said, as the group

made its way toward the Ocaona village, "and how *still* it is—it reminds me of this painter, what's his name . . ."

"Henri Rousseau," said Gideon, to whom the same thought had occurred. Still figures, giant, meticulously detailed jungle foliage, unseen mystery.

"Right, that's the guy," Phil said. "Fantastic, isn't it?"

Gideon nodded. Fantastic it was. Beautiful. Cathedral-like, to use a well-worn metaphor that he truly appreciated for the first time. And the creatures! Jewel-like poison-dart frogs, no bigger than a thumbnail, that secrete a curare-like neurotoxin used by the Indians for their blowgun darts; three-inch-long millipedes; giant snails (giant even by the generous standards of western Washington State)—an amazing place, from every angle. But, God, was it *hot* in there! And humid—unbelievably, mind-deadeningly humid. After a few hours of it, Gideon's shirt and shorts were as wet as if he'd been in a downpour. Even his bones felt soggy. The liter of water he'd brought was long gone, and all he could think of was getting back to his cabin, downing another quart or so, then climbing into the shower and standing for half an hour in the cool—relatively cool—green-brown stream of Amazon water.

The humidity in particular had been like nothing he'd ever encountered. Mel, trying to take notes for his article, had had to give it up. First, the ink from his gel pen wouldn't dry on the page, but ran down it in streaks instead. Then, when he'd borrowed a pencil from Scofield, the point tore through the limp sheets. And as the last straw, by the end of the first hour, the glue in the binding of his notepad had liquefied and the pages had come apart in his hand. Mel, in a laid-back mood—like John, he had no trouble with hot weather—just laughed, gave Scofield back his pencil, and squeezed the notebook into a soggy wad the size of a Ping-Pong ball, which he then stuffed into a pocket.

Unpleasant climate notwithstanding, it had been a fascinating and enjoyable afternoon. Cisco, although no less spacey than usual, had proven botanically knowledgeable and articulate on the walks to and from the village, speaking confidently of epiphytes and chamaephytes and phanerophytes, so that one could see the ethnobotanists in the group rethinking their impressions of him.

The Ocaona village was a grouping of ten thatch-and-pole houses that were set up on two-foot stilts beside a marshy pond in which four exhausted-looking water buffalo lounged in water up to their nostrils while egrets strolled around on their backs. There they'd been surrounded by curious, enchanted brown children. Mostly naked, but some in T-shirts (and nothing else), they laughingly reached out to touch the newcomers and dash away, like Indians counting coup, as if to make sure they were real. They seemed to know but one Spanish word—*caramelo*—but they accepted with eye-popping delight whatever treats the visitors could find to give them: sticks of spearmint gum, Tic Tacs, and especially the cellophane-wrapped hard fruit candies that Mel had happened to have in his pocket. The only offerings that failed to be a hit were the minty breath-strips that Duayne peeled from a little dispenser and placed on their tongues. These elicited gasps, hacking, pretend-vomiting, and other evidences of extreme disgust, but even so, each child had to have a second one, as if to see if it was really as horrible as they remembered.

The *curandero* Yaminahua, a wrinkled, waspish old man in a sleeveless undershirt, clean, white Jockey shorts, and calf-length rubber wading boots, was waiting for them, smoking a cigar and sitting on the plank steps of his open-sided house, which was about twenty feet on a side, clean and spare, strung with four net hammocks across the center, and with a few open shelves along one side, on which were some old iron pots and utensils, and a few bowls. The entire structure was set on two-foot stilts. Two middle-aged women and a girl in her teens, all wearing only simple bark aprons, lay in the hammocks watching, but with no real signs of interest. The girl had a naked little boy sleeping on her abdomen. On one of the shelves, also watching, was a grumpy-looking squirrel monkey tied to a pole by a string around its waist.

On the step next to Yaminahua, who looked as if he had other things on his mind that were a lot more urgent than these pesky newcomers, were three lidless plastic containers of the sort used for fishing gear, filled with leaves and twigs. Using their contents as props, with no preliminaries whatever, aside from removing the cigar from his mouth and placing it on the step beside him, he launched into a monotone presentation that he appeared to be reciting from memory, to no one in particular, while his mind was off somewhere else, doing more important things. Cisco translated as he went along.

"This is *charcosacha*. You mash it with cow fat to cure inflammations of the throat. This is *pono* palm. You use it to cure foot fungus. Also, it makes good roofs. This is *mashunaste*, for broken bones. You mix it with juice from a rubber tree, put it on a cloth, and wrap it around the broken arm or leg. The bone will heal in eight days. This is *chuchuwasi*. You use it for headaches. . . ."

This went on for a solid hour, during which Yaminahua's gaze remained fixed on the middle distance somewhere above their heads and the listeners, one by one, took seats on the ground in front of him. Questions were entirely ignored, so much so that Gideon wondered if the man might be deaf. Note-taking was impossible because of the dampness, but Mel had a small tape recorder that he turned on, promising to have the tapes transcribed for the others who wanted them. The tape, swollen with moisture, stopped turning after a few seconds.

The conclusion of the lecture was as abrupt as the beginning. Yaminahua just stopped talking, shoved the now-dead cigar back in his mouth, and sat there looking at them, or rather through them. The women in the hammocks had never moved a muscle, except for the few that were necessary to keep the hammocks gently swaying. The monkey had disgustedly turned its back on them and gone to sleep on its perch.

Cisco took another moment to finish translating. ". . . for toothache, but it might give you convulsions for a few days. Thank you. And now somebody should give him a gift."

"But he hasn't said a single word about insects," Duayne protested. "Aren't insects a part of their pharmacopoeia?"

But Cisco shook his head. "Nah, show's over. Th-th-th-that's all, folks. Gift time."

"What do we give him, money?" Tim asked.

"No, certainly not money," Scofield said, scolding him. "It would shame him. I brought something more appropriate." He pulled from his pocket a Ziploc bag with some shiny metal objects in it and offered it to the shaman with a bright smile. "A dozen fishhooks," he said confidently. "That'll take care of it."

Yaminahua looked at them with disdain. He shook his head and said something to Cisco.

Cisco translated. "He already has fishhooks. He says he'd rather have a hat with a picture on it. Anybody got one to spare?"

"A hat with a picture on it . . . ?" an incredulous, seemingly offended Scofield echoed.

Gideon had one in his day pack, a white baseball cap with two smiling green alligators on it and the words *Woodland Park Zoo*. He pulled it out and offered it to Yaminahua, who grabbed for it eagerly. He examined it with care, turning it round and round in his hands, obviously coveting it, and yet somehow not entirely satisfied. He surprised Gideon by seizing him by the shoulder and turning him around so that, by standing on the first wooden step Yaminahua was tall enough to pull up the flap of Gideon's backpack and root around inside, right up to his skinny elbow, in hopes of finding something else, all the while querulously chattering at Cisco.

"Is there a problem?" Gideon asked Cisco.

"He says the hat's okay, but don't you have any other colors?"

* * *

THE rooftop stargazing that Gideon, Phil, and John had found so enjoyable the previous night wasn't quite as relaxing tonight. The problem was that everyone else had discovered the cool, pleasant locale as well and carried up chairs to enjoy it, so that it had gotten crowded up there. Mel, and then Duayne, had come wandering up and had decided to join Gideon, Phil, and John, so that Gideon, who was really interested in getting himself as close to horizontal as his chair would allow, turning his face up to the stars, and letting the refreshingly cool night air wash over him, was forced to participate in a coherent conversation, or at least pretend to listen to the one going on around him.

Maggie was the last to come upstairs. For the first few hours after dinner, she had been in the lower deck salon, working with a portable plant dryer that she'd set up there, processing the considerable haul of medicinal, toxic, and hallucinogenic plants that she'd collected during the hike. But at about nine, she had come up and, somewhat to Gideon's surprise, had set down her chair next to Tim's and Cisco's. He could hear the three of them comparing observations on the various exotic botanicals they had encountered. Beyond them, Scofield, who, much to Gideon's envy, had discovered an ancient, full-length, folding beach chair somewhere, lay quietly, with a pot of tea on the deck beside him. His choice of a spot at the very rear, between the guy wires that supported the smokestack and well away from the others, had made it clear that he preferred to be left alone, and he was left alone. For a while the smell of his too-sweet tobacco hung in the air but now he was sound asleep, his pipe having fallen from his hand some time before. An occasional soft, snuffling snore could be heard.

"You know what that stuff is he's drinking?" Mel was saying, looking rather unkindly in Scofield's direction. Mel had ordered a bottle of Merlot for dinner, and although he had offered it freely around, nobody had had much appetite for red wine in that kind of weather. He had consumed almost all of it himself and he was showing the effects.

"It's not tea?" asked Duayne.

"Oh, yeah, I guess you could call it tea, but your mother's orange pekoe it's not. It's made from coca leaves."

"You mean *mate*?" said Phil.

"That's what he *says*, but regular *mate* has the watcha-macallit removed—"

"The cocaine alkaloids," contributed Gideon, margin-ally awake.

"Right, whatever. Well, this stuff has *something* in it, I can tell you that. I had some after-dinner sessions with him at his house a couple of times while we were working on the book. And both times, come eight o'clock or so, he gets all wiggly and jumpy and then makes himself this tea—it's supposed to be for some stomach problem or something, yada yada yada—"

"Actually," Gideon said, "they do drink *mate* down here for stomach problems."

"Well, all I know is, both times the guy's completely out of it inside an hour. I had to let myself out. Once I came back the next morning at nine, and he shows up on the doorstep in the same clothes, all sleepy and dopey, with his hair all mussed and all. I mean, obviously, he'd been spaced out the whole time, probably never got out of his damn chair."

This was the most wordy they'd heard Mel, and the most irate, and for a few moments there was silence. "You don't get along very well with him, do you?" John asked.

Mel was indeed in a confiding mood, and there followed a list of grievances, foremost among which was that Scofield had assured him—had *promised* him—that his name would be on the title page of *Potions, Poisons, and Piranhas*, right up there with his own.

"So he gives us all the book, right? Big fanfare and everything. 'Hot off the press, fine bookstores everywhere.'

So naturally, I'm excited, I look for my name and I don't see it, and that sonofabitch tells me with a smile on his face, oh yes, sure my name's there, see? Right on page Roman numeral three, down there with his faithful typist and the nice lady at the library. And he looks at me like I'm supposed to be grateful. I swear—" He folded his hands and sank back with a sigh. "Ah, what the hell. I don't know why I'm getting so worked up. Don't pay any attention to me. I shouldn't have had that wine. I'm gonna hit the sack. Night, all."

Duayne also heaved himself to his feet. "I'm off too," he said. "I'm hoping for a better day tomorrow."

"You didn't have a good day today?" Phil asked. "I thought it was pretty cool, especially the shaman."

"Oh, that was fine as far as it went, I suppose," Duayne allowed. "Very interesting. But this is not the Amazon I'd expected. We've been here two whole days now, and I haven't seen a single cockroach, not a one!" He shook his head. "Who would have thought?"

"Yeah, that is tough," John said.

"I'm not talking about giant cockroaches, John, I'm talking about *any* cockroaches!"

"Well, cheer up, Duayne," said Gideon, "tomorrow may bring another giant spider."

Duayne's expression lightened. "It *is* a beaut, isn't it?"

"It sure is," Gideon said warmly.

And Duayne went off to bed with a smile on his face.

The three men lay back enjoying the relative quiet for a while, and then Phil said, "So what do you think? Did Mel just give us a pretty good reason for playing nasty tricks on Scofield? He's pretty upset."

"You mean just because he didn't get his name on the title page?" John asked doubtfully. "I mean, the spear and all? Isn't it a little much? He got his money, didn't he? And he got mentioned—acknowledged. What's the big deal?"

"Don't ask me," Phil said, "I wouldn't know about such things. Let's ask the academic over there. Among the weird and wonderful types you associate with, Dr. Oliver, would a person go to such lengths to humiliate someone over a failure to provide proper attribution?"

Gideon smiled. "Humiliate, kill, maim, draw, and quarter."

NOT long afterward, Maggie came up and slipped into Duayne's vacated chair. "Do you mind if I join you? The fellows"—with a tilt of her head she indicated Tim and Cisco, who were now vigorously snuffling something out of coffee cups, the visible effect of which was a lot of sneezing and hacking—"are getting a bit too empirical for my taste."

"What are they snorting now?" John asked, disapproval etched in every line of his face.

"It's cooked from something Cisco brought along. He gave me a sprig." She held up a twig with three narrow green leaves attached. "He says the locals call it *mampekerishi*, not a familiar name to me. I'm guessing it's one of the *Gesneriaceae*, but I don't know the genus. I'll check it later tonight. Possibly, it's something new. Now wouldn't that be nice?"

"What do they use it for?" Phil wanted to know.

"According to Cisco, the Nahua use it for headaches. And of course ceremonially, for visions. He says it gives you visions of eyeballs."

"Eyeballs?" Phil echoed. "Why the hell would anyone want visions of eyeballs?"

"You've got me there," Maggie said, laughing.

"What is it like?" John asked. "Did you try it? Did you really see eyeballs?"

She shook her head forcefully. "Absolutely not. I'm not one of these ethnobotanists that goes around sampling all these things. Not anymore. I found out very early that they're mostly quite unpleasant. Aside from the unsettling visions—and eyeballs would be among the least of them— there's an awful lot of vomiting involved, you know. And defecating. And half the time, the drugs induce amnesia, so that you have no memory of the experience anyway, so what's the point? No, I just want to classify them. And analyze them, of course, to see if there's some valid medicinal use. Which there often is, I might add."

After that they sprawled in their chairs, enjoying the cool, quiet night for a while until John suddenly coughed, said "Jesus!" and batted at the air in front of his face. "Now they're *smoking* something again!"

"That's just pot," Phil said, sniffing. "That's what you told them to smoke yesterday. They're just taking your advice."

"I know it's pot," John groused. "You think I don't know what pot smells like? I'll tell you what it is that gets me, though. Not Cisco, he's a lost cause; he can't help himself any more. But Tim—a nice kid, and he seems bright enough, good future in front of him—"

"He's extremely bright," Maggie said. "One of my favorite students."

"And yet there he is, snorting or smoking or drinking every damn thing that comes his way. He shouldn't be taking lessons from a guy like Cisco. He's screwing up his life."

"Oh, I wouldn't go that far, John," Maggie said. "A lot of ethnobotanists have their fling with the hallucinogens they study. I did. It's appealing to many young people. And then, you have to give Tim a bit of leeway. He's under a lot of stress right now. Arden has been giving him a hard time."

Arden was Tim's major professor, she explained, and his signature on Tim's dissertation was all that stood between Tim and a Ph.D.—and the postdoctoral fellowship at Harvard that he longed for. She herself thought the dissertation was more than good enough; she and the third member of Tim's dissertation committee, a professor named Slivovitz, had already signed off on it, but Arden was driving Tim crazy with it, sending him back to the drawing board again and again. And again.

Gideon thoroughly sympathized. His own graduate years

were not far enough behind him to make him forget what the ordeal of the dissertation had been like. "That's tough, all right. Will Arden ever go along, or is it hopeless?"

Maggie shrugged. "Oh, I suppose he'll go along eventually. It's not that his criticisms are necessarily invalid, it's just that they're . . . well, quibbles: style, punctuation, chapter organization, that kind of thing. But between us, Tim's material is certainly no worse than what you find in the published journals. Personally, I think it's a damn shame, and I've said so to Arden. But Arden's his own man, and where I come from, what Arden says goes."

"Arden's the department chair?" Gideon asked.

"The director. Formally, we're an institute, not a department, although we come under Biological Sciences. That is to say, we *were* an institute. As of September, we won't exist anymore. The ethnobotanical faculty will be whittled down from three to one—that'll be Arden, it goes without saying. The other prof, Slivovitz, saw the handwriting on the wall and lined up a job for himself down south."

"And what will happen to you, Maggie?" John asked. "Where will you be?"

"Well, technically I'm still a contender for that one slot, but that's never going to happen, and nobody's pretending that it will. So, in answer to your first question, I'm out. In answer to the second, it looks like I'll be moving down here."

"To the *Amazon*?" Phil asked.

"To the Huallaga Valley, a few hundred miles south of here. Much the same jungle ecosystem, but a few hundred feet higher, so maybe not *quite* as hot and humid . . . but close. Arden's gotten me a faculty appointment at his school down there. In the idyllic garden spot known as Tingo Maria." It was too dark to read her expression, but Gideon heard her sigh. She wasn't happy about the prospect. He wouldn't have been either.

"That sounds like a terrific opportunity for someone in your field," he said with as much enthusiasm as he could muster. "For an ethnobotanist, it must be paradise."

He heard her chuckle, a single arid note, as she got to her feet. "All things considered," she said with a side-of-the-mouth twang, "I'd rather be in Iowa City. Good night, all."

"Well, Doc," said John, watching her leave, "as far as your theory of aggravating Scofield goes, at least there's one problem it doesn't have."

"Namely?"

John laughed. "Shortage of motives."

THIRTEEN

OF the entire trip, this was the moment that *Capitán* Alfredo Vargas had most dreaded. He had managed, by and large, to keep it from his waking thoughts, but not his sleeping ones. For the past two nights he had dreamed the same dream, something out of some movie about Devil's Island: with his hands tied behind him and wearing a blood-drenched, open-throated white shirt, he was being marched to the guillotine while six drummers, three on either side of him, kept up a dismal drumbeat that grew louder and louder and faster and faster until it shook him violently awake. Both times the drumbeat had turned out to be the hammering of the blood in his ears, and the wetness had come from the sopping T-shirt in which he slept.

Well, he was wide awake right now, but it seemed to him that the thumping in his chest was loud enough to be heard ten feet away—even the leaping of his shirt front with each beat must surely be visible—and his uniform, the best, cleanest whites he had, was already dark under the arms

and at the small of his back, and spotty streaks were starting to show on the front.

Scofield had laughingly assured him that there was
nothing to worry about, that nothing could possibly go
wrong, but Vargas had heard those words before from others, spoken in the same carefree manner, and he had observed that disaster had a way of almost invariably
following them. Scofield, after all, had never dealt with the
volatile, hard-drinking, unpredictable Colonel Malagga, a
hard case if there ever was one, and a greedy, vulgar grafter
besides. And Scofield wasn't the owner and captain of the
Adelita, the man on whom all responsibility must ultimately
fall. Scofield, he was sure, already had figured out some way
to wiggle out of trouble if it came, leaving Vargas holding the
ball, or the bag, or whatever the hell it was.

He stared ruefully at the haggard face in the mirror—
why had he let himself get talked into this; was he crazy?
His heart couldn't stand it; he wasn't a young man any
more. Making a final adjustment to his cap, the good one
with the gold braid that was hardly corroded at all, he murmured a final prayer to the effect that Malagga would not
be on duty at the border checkpoint today, and stepped out
on deck.

An hour earlier, at a little after four in the afternoon, after cruising most of the day, he had swung the *Adelita*
north, leaving the broad, safe, familiar expanse of the
Amazon for the narrower, endlessly winding, more oppressive Javaro River. He had quickly pulled into a narrow inlet
to let off Cisco and one of the kitchen crew, the Yagua Indian Porge, neither of whom had papers that would pass inspection at the border. They would run up ahead through
the jungle, and once the *Adelita* was safely past the checkpoint (by the grace of God) and out of sight, the boat's
dinghy would pick them up.

A few minutes later the ship had passed the rusting *Re-
publica de Colombia* sign high on the right bank (which
was what had started the perspiration streaming), and now

they were pulling up and securing to the dilapidated pier, at the end of which was the falling-apart wooden shack that housed the Colombian military border police. At Vargas's order, the *Adelita*'s gangplank, a two-by-twelve board studded with crosspieces every couple of feet, was let down. The door to the shack opened.

El momento de la verdad. The moment of truth.

From the shack swaggered an overweight officer in mirrored sunglasses, fatigues, and combat boots, with a black baseball cap on his head and his hand resting on the heavy, black butt of the supersized handgun holstered on his belt.

Vargas's heart sank. Malagga.

"¡Buenas tardes, mi coronel!" Vargas effused, grinning away like crazy. *"¿Cómo está usted?"*

He extended his arm to assist Malagga in making the one-foot jump onto the deck, but Malagga ignored him, as he had ignored the greeting. Instead he let himself down, and without even looking at Vargas, held out his hand and rubbed his thumb and forefinger impatiently, abstractedly together.

"Pasaportes."

Vargas had them ready, having collected them earlier. Malagga riffled through them without evident interest, although he occasionally looked up, apparently to match a photograph with one of the faces of the passengers, all of whom were assembled in the deck salon at Vargas's instruction.

While Malagga shuffled the passports, two soldiers that Vargas had not seen before came aboard, one well into his fifties, wiry and sly, the other a pot-bellied, dim-looking, snaggle-toothed youth of twenty. That these were low-grade officers was evident from their ragged, stained uniforms. Both wore fatigue pants, but only the older one had a matching shirt. The other had on a dirty T-shirt with a picture of an Absolut vodka bottle on it. The older one was wearing filthy tennis shoes; the other had on flip-flops. Neither had shaved for a few days. Both had the same sinister, mirrored sunglasses and the big semiautomatic pistols that Malagga had.

But it wasn't the guns that had sent an icy, new spicule of fear deep into Vargas's gut, it was the small, friendly looking brown-and-white dog they dragged with them on a leash. A drug-sniffer, God help him. He had worried that such a thing might happen and had expressed his concern to Scofield, but Scofield had laughed it off—he was a big laugher, Scofield was, always chuckling—telling him that the balls of coca paste were hidden in the sixty-kilo coffee bags for a very good reason: the coffee beans would mask their scent so that the dogs couldn't smell them. But did Scofield *know* that this was so? Or was it only something he had heard? Vargas, in the clutch of his shameful greed, which he now so sorely repented, had not asked, but only eagerly accepted it as fact.

He stole a glance at Scofield, who was pointedly studying some kind of book, leaning his forehead on his hand to avoid any possible eye contact with Malagga. Vargas surreptitiously flicked perspiration from his own forehead. This kind of grief wasn't worth five thousand dollars, it wasn't worth *fifty* thousand dollars. Only let him get through this and, on his mother's grave, he would never—*never*—again violate even the smallest law, the tiniest, most trivial legal technicality. Well, unless, of course, there was absolutely no danger whatever of—

Malagga gave the passports to one of the soldiers for stamping, then made the quick thumb-and-forefinger gesture again. *"Sus papeles." Your papers.*

Vargas handed over the manifest and the various permits he had gotten, everything having been scrupulously completed. Malagga glanced at them indifferently, then took another look at the people around him, a long one this time, stopping at every face for two or three seconds as if to register it. At least that was the way it appeared, but with those sunglasses, who could tell for sure where he was looking? Still, his intention to intimidate them couldn't be missed. Most of the passengers did what any sensible person would do under the circumstances: they tried their best to look as unremarkable as possible. All except for the FBI man, Lau, who was glaring right back at the colonel and visibly bristling.

Don't . . . make . . . trouble, Vargas tried to convey to him with an assortment of grimaces and facial expressions. *Can't you see the kind of person you're dealing with here? Don't you know the kind of trouble this man can make? Don't you understand where we* are? But the FBI man was continuing to stare boldly back, patently uncowed. Malagga's thick lips pursed thoughtfully. For a second it appeared as if he was going to walk over and confront the Hawaiian (or Chinese, or whatever he was), but apparently he decided it wasn't worth the effort. Instead, he muttered a few curt words to Vargas.

"Sí, mi coronel," Vargas said. *"Seguro que sí."* He turned to the passengers. "In addition to inspecting our cargo, Colonel Malagga respectfully requests your kind permission to examine your cabins. He also asks that you remain here while this is being accomplished, if there is no objection."

"I have an objection," Lau said, despite the eye-rolling facial contortions Vargas was now sending his way. "I'd like to know what his grounds are for examining our cabins."

"Oh, it's routine, merely routine," Vargas said, smiling through his perspiration. "Very standard. It's done on every ship." *Now shut up, will you?*

"Yeah, but is he looking for drugs, or what?" Lau persisted. "He should have a reason."

Malagga's heavy eyebrows rose. *"¿Pues qué pensa este?"* he said ominously, his hand back on the butt of his gun. *What's with this guy?*

Before Vargas could reply, he heard Lau's friend, the anthropologist, come to his aid. "John, will you shut up, for Christ's sake? Let the guy do his job, don't bug him."

"I just don't like to see a cop act like that," Lau answered, still glaring at Malagga. "I hate that crap."

"So do I, but look around, we're not in Seattle at the moment, if you haven't noticed. This is Colombia. This is the Amazon jungle. Different rules."

Lau, thank God, appeared to see the sense in this, even if reluctantly. "Okay, forget it," he said to Vargas.

Now Malagga's eyebrows lowered behind his sunglasses. He didn't like Lau's tone. *"¿Qué es lo que dice?"* *What's he saying?*

"El Señor Lau se equivocó, y le pide su perdón," the conciliatory Vargas explained, embellishing a little. *He misunderstood. He asks your pardon.*

The crazy Lau looked anything but apologetic, but Malagga, with a shrug, chose to let the matter pass.

Tim Loeffler, the gangly student, held up his hand. "Is it okay if I go to my room for a minute first?" he asked in reasonably good Spanish. "I want to get some—"

"No, it is not all right," snapped Malagga in Spanish. "You will wait here with the others." He slapped the manifest and permits back into Vargas's hand. "These appear to be in order." In fact, he had hardly looked at them.

Malagga's head swung toward the bar and Vargas thought he was going to demand an explanation for the broken, boarded-up glass pane, but instead he remarked amicably on how fortunate Vargas was to have all those bottles of Scotch, and how difficult it was to get decent whiskey in this miserable jungle outpost, where all that was available was the miserable, homemade *aguardiente* you could buy in that so-called town of Potrero de Mineros, and—

Vargas, lamentably slow on the uptake, finally leaped willingly for the bait. "I hope, Colonel," he said, "that you will accept from me as a friendly gift a bottle of our finest—"

Malagga's brow lowered. His mouth pursed again.

"—I meant to say, four bottles—*six* bottles—"

The colonel's brow relaxed.

"—of this fine Scotch whiskey for the pleasure of you and your men, when you are not on duty, of course." *Not that your men are likely to see a single drop of it, you thieving bastard.*

"That is most kind of you, Captain, and I accept with pleasure on behalf of my officers. You can have someone bring it to the office." He extended his hand in a limp, three-fingered handshake. "I wish you a safe continuation of your journey," he said, and jumped up on the gangplank.

Vargas's world, so dark for the last hour, lit up. Was that it then? They could go? There would be no inspection after all?

No such luck. The other two men and the dog stayed. "Do your work, Sergeant," he said to the older one, who wore no insignia of rank. "Captain Vargas, accompany them, if you please."

The next twenty minutes, spent in the hold of the ship, were the worst of Vargas's life. With the two soldiers dourly tagging along, the little dog merrily explored every crevice, every item, sniffing away at the lumber, the boots, the guitar . . . and finally the coffee sacks, stowed neatly in stacks of three. Stopping at the very first stack, he put his nose right up against the bags and went over them like a vacuum cleaner gone crazy. Then, God in heaven, he *barked*, sat down, and looked proudly up at the sergeant, eyes bright, tongue lolling, tail wagging against the floor, as if to say, "Here it is, I've found it. It's coca paste, all right. Quick, arrest that man right there!"

The younger soldier leaned curiously over the stacks, poking at them with a finger, as if that would tell him something. Vargas, about ready to faint by now, crossed himself with a trembling hand. Hidden deep in thirty of the forty-eight sacks of beans were sealed, white, plastic bags, each containing five kilos of coca paste. Scofield, damn him, had said it would be impossible for a dog to—

"Open this one," the sergeant said to him, slapping the central sack.

"Open the sack? Are you serious?" Vargas babbled. There was a tiny sign, a black triangle made with a marker pen, under the folded down tops of the sacks that contained the paste, but Vargas, in his panic, couldn't remember whether that particular sack was one of them or not. "I can't open any sacks. Can't you see they're sewn shut? They're not my property, I can't—"

At a tilt of the head from the sergeant, the soldier shoved the top sack off, produced a stubby folding knife, and sliced into the burlap of the center sack, slashing it from top to bottom. The contents spilled like beige lava onto the floor, filling the hold with the sharp aroma of dried, unroasted coffee beans. Vargas, grasping at the corner of a crate to keep from collapsing, closed his eyes. He was hyperventilating. He could feel his soul flying away, leaving him. This was what it was like to die. He heard the soldiers burrowing through the pile of beans. And to make it even worse, he had wasted—thrown away—six 1.14-liter bottles of Cutty Sark, his best—

"Nada," mumbled one to the other.

Nada? Nothing? Was it possible? He opened one eye. They were still sifting through the beans with their feet, but it was clear that there was nothing to find. Beans, only beans. The dog was happily sniffing at them. A dog that liked coffee, that was all it was. Vargas's soul returned to his body. His heart soared. He opened his other eye.

"Look what you've done," he told them severely. "How am I going to explain this? This is going to cost me a lot of money. I'm warning you, you'd better not damage anything else. I'll file a complaint with Colonel Malagga, I'll—"

"These boots," the one holding the knife said. "Are they extra?"

"Extra?" He was so thickheaded with fear and relief that it took him a few moments to understand. "Yes, as a matter of fact," he said more agreeably, "two of the pairs happen to be extra. I wonder, would you gentlemen like them? It would save me the trouble of transporting them."

They grinned their acceptance, the knife was folded up and put away, and the worst, the longest, twenty minutes of Alfredo Vargas's life came to an end.

AFTER leaving the hold, the two soldiers and the dog started going through the cabins, as instructed by Malagga. Vargas went joyfully up to join the passengers, where he opened the bar early and offered a free round of drinks to make up for the inconvenience of the check. In a few minutes, the young soldier returned to the salon.

"Cabin six, whose is that?"

"Mine," said Tim in a voice from the tomb.

The soldier motioned to him. "Come with me, please."

Tim, with panic in his eyes, looked to Vargas for help, but all Vargas could do was shrug. "Go with them, don't worry."

He was back in two or three minutes, in even deeper distress. He took Vargas aside. "They found my stash. They want to arrest me." He looked every bit as frightened and desperate as Vargas had been a little while ago. "They told me to ask you for advice. They told me you understood the law, you'd know what to do."

"Your 'stash,' what is it?"

"It's just pot."

"Nothing else? No coca? No cocaine? Are you sure?"

"Yes, marijuana, that's all, I swear. Captain Vargas, I can't go to jail here. I couldn't—"

Vargas gave him a friendly pat on the shoulder. "Relax, *amigo*, they don't care about marijuana." He smiled and rubbed his thumb and forefinger together, much as Malagga had earlier.

Tim frowned. "I don't understand. They want money? A bribe?"

"A gift, let us call it. Not necessarily money. Did they admire anything in your cabin?"

"No, they just . . . wait, I've got a big bag of Jelly Bellies—jelly beans—on the shelf. They were asking about them. I gave them a couple to try and they really liked them, but—no, that's stupid—"

"There you are, then."

The young man stared at him. "They want *jelly beans*? That's the bribe?"

"Offer them and see what happens."

"You mean, just . . . go back and . . . offer them? Just say, 'Would you like these jelly beans?' "

"That's as good a way as any," Vargas said, laughing. He was feeling marvelously relaxed, and even somewhat paternal toward Tim. "You'll see, don't worry. They're not interested in putting you in jail, my friend, trust me. It's too much work."

As Tim began to understand that he was not really going to rot for the rest of his life in some jungle hellhole of a prison, other matters came to the front of his mind.

"Will they let me keep my stash?"

"That I cannot tell you. Be polite and hope for the best. Now go back and do as I say. These people are not known for their patience." He waved him affably on. "Go go go."

AN hour later, the *Adelita*, having stopped to pick up Cisco and Porge, was on its way once more, lighter by six bottles of Scotch, two pairs of rubber boots, and a twelve-ounce bag of jelly beans. There were, as well, a number of lightened moods: Vargas's because he'd actually come through this horrible experience in one piece and his additional $5,000 was now as good as certain; Scofield's, because the coca paste was safe in the hold and, having been sealed and certified by customs, was immune from further official prying and his $120,000 was as good as certain; and Tim's because he had his freedom, his stash, and a deeper understanding of the Colombian system of criminal justice.

FOURTEEN

THE main dish that night was something a little different: freshly caught piranha. While the *Adelita* had been tied up at the checkpoint, the crew had passed the time fishing from the deck. Using bloody gobbets of lizard as bait (according to Vargas, the bait, if untaken, had to be changed every couple of minutes; as soon as the blood drained away, it was of no interest to the piranha), they'd hauled them in by the dozen. The piranhas were served up from the buffet table in filets of firm, white meat, much like halibut in taste and texture. In addition, a sort of centerpiece for the dining table had been made up of four whole ones arranged in a circle, with their tails together in the center, and their ferocious little sharp-toothed mouths facing out.

Gideon had seen photos of them, and some dried specimens as well. Still, he was surprised at how small the celebrated "cannibal fish of the Amazon" were: six or seven inches long, chubby and pink, and almost cute when looked at from the side. But seen head-on, there was nothing cute about that open mouth crammed full of those justly famous little teeth, as sharp and pointed and vicious-looking as a shark's.

Because Scofield was the only one at the table who had any personal knowledge of piranhas, they were naturally a subject of curiosity to the others. Scofield, feeling his oats—he was almost manic—was regaling them with scientific and not-so-scientific piranha lore. These particular specimens were *Pygocentrus natterreri*, the infamous red-bellied piranha, that could strip an unlucky live cow or human down to a bare, white skeleton in thirty minutes or less. As far as Gideon knew, this was an exaggerated account. He was fairly certain that there were no verified accounts of human beings having actually been *killed* by piranhas, although many a barefoot native fisherman had less than his full complement of toes as a result of standing in a dugout and continuing to fish while freshly caught, still-living piranhas flopped about on the floor. And there was no doubt about their ability as scavengers to peel the flesh off an already dead creature in short order (even if thirty minutes was pushing it a bit). But tonight it was not an issue. The piranhas were the eatees, not the eaters, and it was they who were being made short order of.

Cisco showed up late for dinner, as he did now for most meals—when he bothered to show up at all. As usual, he was weaving a little, as if the boat were on the high seas and not on a slow, brown, jungle river. Also as usual, he ignored the main dishes and went straight for the dessert, which was local finger-length bananas sliced up in honey. He loaded up a good four servings' worth in a soup bowl, the tip of his tongue sticking out with the effort at eye-hand coordination that was required. Holding the bowl carefully in both hands, he wandered unevenly back to the others, where he took his usual place as not quite part of the group, his chair pushed back from the table, so that he had to hold the bowl in his lap, where it claimed his whole attention while Scofield continued regaling the others.

"What's more . . ." Scofield continued, "this is known to be the only species—"

Cisco laughed abruptly. "Hey, piranhas," he mumbled, apparently his first notice of them. "Whoa. How you doing, little guys?" He put his emptied bowl aside and leaned forward to run his fingers over the razor-sharp teeth.

"Little . . . tiny . . . teeth," he said dreamily, moving from tooth to tooth with each word. And once again, as if he were reciting something: "Little . . . tiny . . . teeth."

The helper behind the buffet table tonight was the cook, Meneo, a wizened, five-foot-tall Huitoto Indian who spoke no English and only a few words of Spanish, but who seemed to find everything the passengers said sidesplittingly funny. Cisco's crooning was no exception. Narrow shoulders jiggling, tears of glee streaming from his eyes, small, brown hands keeping time, he sang along with Cisco.

"Widdoo . . . ty'ee . . . teet'.   Widdoo . . . ty'ee . . . teet' . . ."

Meneo's hilarity was hard to resist, and pretty soon everybody was doing it, hooting with laughter and beating time on the table. "Widdoo . . . ty'ee . . . teet' . . ."

Gideon, chortling and beating away with the rest of them, shook his head in self-amazement. "Somebody send for a doctor," he said to Phil. "I think we're all getting jungle fever."

ON Wednesday afternoon, twenty minutes into their trek to meet with the famous Orejón *curandero* Tahuyao (celebrated for his plant cure for inflammation of the kidneys, reputed to be highly effective and entirely risk-free—other than its propensity to turn the skin iguana-green for four to six months), the outing was called off. Cisco was not feeling well. According to what he told Scofield, his headaches had flared up. According to what he told Phil, an old knee injury was bothering him. To Tim he explained that his back just wasn't up to a long hike that day.

Whatever the cause, he disappeared back toward the ship, sighing and groaning piteously. The passengers had to content themselves with a self-guided botanical exploration of the jungle within easy range of the *Adelita*, a disappointment to most, but not to Duayne. Before he left, Cisco had pointed to some pendulous, bulbous birds' nests hanging from low branches over the river. "Oropendela nests," he'd told Duayne. "There ought to be some cockroaches in there. They love the birdshit."

Ten minutes later, an overjoyed Duayne had come back cradling a trembling, monstrous, black, gold, and brown cockroach that completely covered the palm of his hand. "*Blaberus giganteus*," he'd proudly told anybody who would listen. "I admit, it may not be the most massive cockroach in the world—that'd be the Australian burrowing cockroach—but it's every bit as long or even longer. This particular beauty measures more than four inches in length, and that's not counting the antennae! And I'm betting the wingspread is a good twelve inches, maybe even more! And they can actually fly, you know—really fly—unlike our earthbound homegrown variety. They say they do it in great hordes. Wouldn't that be something to see? Ten thousand of these on the wing, flapping away?" His eyes turned dreamy at the thought; a small, blissful smile played about his lips.

Gideon too enjoyed the outing, but for a different reason. Not long after Duayne had returned to his cabin to carry out the regrettable but necessary execution of his *Blaberus*, Gideon noticed that the already dim rain forest was growing rapidly darker. Then came a sound he couldn't place at first, a deep, resonant thrumming from above, like thousands—millions—of wingbeats, that made him look up apprehensively, with thoughts of giant flying cockroaches. But after a moment he realized it was the sound of heavy rain hitting the canopy. Despite the volume, it seemed a mere sprinkling at first, barely getting him wet, but that was only because it was working its way down through the foliage. When it finally hit with all its force, it pelted him in huge, warm drops, and then in streams, as if a thousand faucets had been turned on, and then in choking sheets. Most of the others ran for the boat, but Gideon just stood there, arms and face held up to the sky, coughing as the clean, fresh water filled his mouth and nose, but letting it soak him through. It was like a baptism, a wonderful break from the unrelenting closeness and humidity of the jungle.

AFTER dinner, Gideon found his mood depressed. Unlike John and Phil, he still hadn't adjusted to the temperature, and especially not to the strangling humidity. He'd been in climates with 100 percent relative humidity before, so, technically speaking, it was impossible for this to be any worse. Except that it was. The air was more like damp wool than air, lying heavy and hot on the skin and making breathing a struggle. He was listless and restless at the same time. And Lord, he missed Julie. Not feeling very social, he lasted only a few minutes at the by-now de rigueur night session on the roof, before saying good night. Back in his cabin, although he'd been told his cell phone wouldn't work, he tried calling her. Nothing, not even static.

At nine o'clock he slid open his window to let in the river's night breeze—after dark, it made things cooler than the air-conditioner did—and went to bed, hoping that a long night's sleep would pep him up. It had been a mistake not to bring any work with him. The idea had been that this was to be a genuine vacation for a change, an opportunity to relax in an interesting locale with nothing pressing on his mind to interfere with the enjoyment of the experience. It had worked for a little while, but now he had gotten fidgety. How many days were left? Two? It seemed like a long time still to go.

He needed something to *do*.

HIS opportunity wasn't long in coming.

It was the stifled, piercing cry—*"Ai!"*—that broke through to his webbed, sleeping mind, but even as he swam unwillingly to the surface, he thought he remembered that it had been preceded by some kind of distant thumping or scraping. (He'd incorporated it into a nonsensical dream, something to do with a dying horse trying to stomp its way into its locked stall.) With his head still on the pillow, he looked at the softly glowing dial of his watch: 1:45. It was perfectly quiet now, with no sound but the hissing of the water along the side of the ship below his cabin window. *Had there really been a cry, or had he been—* The hollow, ponderous *pa-loosh* of something substantial plunging into the river dissolved the last shreds of sleep.

"Somebody's overboard! Stop the ship!" he yelled instinctively, jumping out of bed and springing for the cabin door. Before he reached it there was another cry, this one shrill with panic: "Help me, somebody! I can't swim! *I can't swim!*"

Maggie?

Then, with his hand on the door handle, there was yet *another* resounding *pa-loosh. Two* people overboard? Good God—

In another second he had yanked the door open and was on the deck, leaning over the railing and peering into the darkness. After a moment he was able to make out Maggie, thrashing and gasping in the black water about twenty yards behind the slowing *Adelita.*

"Hang on!" he called. "I'm coming!" He jerked an orange *M/V Adelita* life preserver from its clasp, hooked it over his arm, and vaulted feet-first over the railing, trying not to think about the fact that the last lifesaving instruction he'd had had been in junior high school. Or about little tiny teeth and the fact that his toes were bare.

He panicked slightly himself as the warm, rank-smelling water closed over his head—Gideon had never been altogether at home in the water and especially not under it—pulled himself to the surface, grabbed the life preserver, which had been plucked from his grasp by the impact, and sidestroked toward the struggling Maggie, who was beating her arms against the surface to keep from going down. When he reached her and touched her shoulder she fought him blindly, catching him painfully in the mouth with her fist, but then she saw who it was and calmed down enough for him to get the ring over her head and under one of her arms.

"Thank you!" she gasped. "I thought it was— Thank you!" He hardly recognized this wild-eyed woman as the formidable person of the last few days. Her face was bunchy with distress, and her hair, ordinarily so neatly arranged, was plastered over her face in limp, black strands that looked like seaweed. And she was weeping frenziedly, a sloppy, snuffly, child's sobbing that convulsed her body, or at least the little of it that Gideon could see.

"You're okay, Maggie," he said, his hand comfortingly on her shoulder. "I've got you, you're safe. Are you hurt?"

"No, I'm—I don't think so, no."

"What happened?" he asked. "Is there someone else in the water? I heard two splashes."

"Yes—*uck*—" Choking on swallowed water, unable to speak, she turned her head away from him, coughing and spluttering.

The *Adelita* had swung around now and was turning to get back to them. Some of the others were out on deck in their underwear or pajamas, gesticulating and calling encouragement. Maggie, held by Gideon and supported by the life preserver, had sighed shakily a couple of times and begun to relax, when suddenly she went rigid. Her hand clamped on his forearm. "You have to get him!" she shouted, her face only inches from his. "He's going to get away!"

"Who's going to get away? Maggie, what *happened*?"

"No, you have to get him! He grabbed me! He threw me over!" She was crying again, and shoving against him.

"Catch hold now." John's reassuring voice came from above. "We'll pull you up."

The ship had come up alongside them, and the gate in the railing had been opened. John, dressed in T-shirt and boxers, as was Gideon, was kneeling in the opening, holding out a boat hook with a ten-foot-long shaft.

"You have to get him!" she said to Gideon again, even more urgently. "Don't you understand what I'm telling you? He tried to kill me! He . . . he . . ."

"We'll talk about it when we're aboard," Gideon told her firmly. "Let's get ourselves up there first."

"No, but . . . !" She stopped herself and nodded. "All right, yes."

She caught hold of the proffered pole, and with Gideon steadying her from below and John pulling from above, she more or less climbed up the side of the boat to the deck, a distance of perhaps five feet. Gideon quickly followed. They both stood dripping on the deck while questions came at Maggie from all sides: "Are you all right? Are you hurt?"

Still wracked with coughing, she shook her head at them. "Not hurt."

"What happened? *Who* tried to kill you?"

In frustration, she shook her head again. "That's what I'm trying to tell you—" She held her hand up while she went through another bout of deep, painful coughing. When it had run its course, she took in a slow, steadying breath, and let it out, cheeks inflated. Then she raised her head, feeble but very much more in control of herself.

"Cisco," she said.

FIFTEEN

"*CISCO* tried to kill you?"

It seemed to Gideon that everyone there—John, Tim, Mel, and Vargas—said it at the same time, in exactly the same astonished tone. He wasn't sure if he'd said it himself, or only thought it.

She seemed taken aback by the chorus of incredulity. "Well, I . . . I *think* it was Cisco. I mean I couldn't see. It was dark, it was—"

She shuddered, then suddenly glanced down at herself, at the flimsy, wet summer bathrobe that was clinging to her and the men's pajamas underneath, and then at the circle of males surrounding her. She lifted her chin and drew the robe around her with her arms. "I have to change," she said stiffly. "Give me twenty minutes, if you please. Captain, I don't suppose there'd be such a thing as hot chocolate on this ship?"

"Of course there is, professor. I'll have it for you at once."

"Thank you." She turned to leave.

"But wait, where is he?" John asked. "Where is Cisco?"

"He jumped," she said. "He's gone. After he threw me in, that's what I was trying to tell you!" An angry glare at Gideon. "But you'll never find him now, not after all this time." Then, with a final, penetrating, accusing glance at Gideon, she turned and swept away and up the stairway, with considerable élan.

"What did you do to her?" John asked Gideon. "I thought you just saved her life."

Gideon shrugged. "I thought so too. I guess I took too long."

"Dames," Mel said, the voice of experience. "You can't please 'em."

SHE had been sound asleep, she explained. She had been roused by what she thought was scuffling that seemed to be coming from next door—not from Gideon's cabin, of course, but from Scofield's, on the other side. Then, still three-quarters asleep—she wasn't sure if it was minutes later, or only seconds—she heard what seemed to her to be someone being violently sick outside her cabin. She put on her robe and went out on deck to see if she could help. Cisco—if it was Cisco—was standing there with his back to her in what looked like a nightshirt, or maybe it was just a long shirt down almost to his knees, gripping the railing with both hands, mumbling to himself, and staring fixedly down into the moving water.

She paused to sip the hot chocolate that Vargas had given her, hunched over the cup and holding it with both hands as if to warm them, although the temperature was still in the eighties. It was two-thirty in the morning, still pitch-black. Everybody but Scofield, who had been observed to have had a couple of pots of his "digestive" tea up on the roof earlier that night, was there now, gathered around her at their table in the dining room. They were all in walking shorts and polo shirts or tank tops, the established daily uniform of choice. Vargas had made "fresh" coffee by opening a new jar of Nescafé.

She continued. Something about his rigid posture, about how tightly he was clutching the rail, told her that something terrible had happened. She was frightened. She began to back quietly away, back to the safety of her room, but the movement must have caught his eye. He had her before she'd taken two steps, both of his arms around her, squeezing the breath out of her. In what seemed like a fraction of a second he'd wrestled her to the railing and heaved her over. Cisco was incredibly strong, far, far stronger than he looked. If it *was* Cisco.

"Maggie," Duayne said, "Cisco's a pretty strange-looking man. So skinny . . . and the way he holds his head . . . I'd think he'd be recognizable, even from the back."

"Well, he wasn't," Maggie snapped. "It was dark, he had on this long thing, he was turned the other way. Maybe I should have asked him for an ID?"

"No offense, Maggie," Duayne said, taken aback. "I only meant—"

"Captain, where does Cisco sleep?" John asked.

"In the next to the last cabin on the port side, next to the storage rooms."

"Tim, would you go check that room, please? Knock, and if you don't get an answer, open the door and peek in, see if he's there." Gideon could see that John had assumed his cop persona. A crime had been committed, there was no responsible official there to look into it, and so John, being John, had readily jumped in as the man in charge, a state of affairs that no one seemed about to challenge.

"Why didn't you yell for help?" he asked Maggie.

She blinked, as if it was something that hadn't occurred to her before. "I don't know," she said, frowning. "You think that's what you'd do, you know that's what you *should* do, but when it happens to you, your mind doesn't work right. And it was so quick! The whole thing couldn't have taken two seconds. I was flying through the air before I knew what was happening. It was as if I was paralyzed," she mused. "I couldn't struggle, couldn't scream, couldn't—" She ran out of words and shook her head.

"Maggie, that's a pretty bad gash you've got on your leg," Gideon said. He'd only noticed it a moment before. "You'd better get some antiseptic on that and cover it up. In this kind of climate you don't want to take any chances."

"What?" She stared down at her leg—the wrong leg first, then the right one, then reached down to touch, very gingerly, a still-bleeding wound on the inside of her left ankle. Blood had seeped down into and spotted her white sneakers, worn without socks. "I didn't even know I had this," she said with wonder. "I didn't feel a thing." She produced a Kleenex and dabbed it against the wound.

"That's because your system's still in shock. Don't worry, you'll feel it when the vasoconstriction reverses. Any minute now."

"I remember, I hit my leg on the railing as I was going over. That's when it must have happened. I think I even gave a yelp, but—"

"You did," Gideon said. "That's what woke me up."

"And thank heavens it did!" she said fervently, and then her face softened. "Gideon, I haven't really said thank you to you."

"As a matter of fact, you did. The very first thing. After you finished slugging me."

She laughed. "I'm sorry about that. I thought you were Cisco. Oh dear, I split your lip, didn't I?"

"It's nothing," said Gideon, who had been dabbing a tissue at his mouth. By now the bleeding, hardly copious to begin with, had almost entirely stopped.

"Well, when we get to Leticia, I owe you the biggest, best dinner money can buy."

"Oh, I think a beer'll cover it," he said, smiling.

She returned the smile. "You've got it. Anyway, as soon as I landed in the water my brain started working again and I screamed for help. Then when somebody yelled 'Man overboard'—"

"Me again," Gideon said.

"—he just climbed over and heaved himself into the river too."

Ah, and that was the second splash, thought Gideon. Until then he'd been uncertain whether he'd really heard two splashes, or if he'd imagined—dreamed—one of them.

"I saw him hit the water," Maggie continued, "but it was too dark to really see anything. Then you showed up and I thought it was him coming after me. I don't know what happened to him. I hope he drowned."

"He probably just swam for the shore," said John. "Probably made it without any problem too. The Javaro's not much more than a hundred yards wide here. Maggie, do you have any idea of why he would have attacked you?"

She shook her head slowly back and forth, still cradling the mug of hot chocolate. "I don't have a clue. I guess he was . . . well, you know how he was."

"Yeah, the cheese slid off his cracker a *long* time ago," Mel said.

"I want to apologize," a visibly disturbed Vargas said. He had run off to get some antibiotic cream and a super-sized Band-Aid for Maggie, and having applied them, he was hovering over her with the pot of hot chocolate, punctiliously topping off her cup every time she had a sip. "I had no way of knowing the man was . . . was crazy, insane. I assure you, if I had any idea—"

"Nobody's blaming you, Captain," John said. "All right, let's—"

"He's not there." Tim had returned. He was standing at the entrance to the dining room, looking sick and shaky, making no move to approach.

"Hey, buddy, what's the matter?" Phil asked.

"I—" He had to steady himself on the doorjamb. It seemed to take all his courage to continue. "I checked Dr. Scofield's room too. He's not there either. He's . . . he's dead, I'm sure of it."

"Oh, hell, he's probably still up on the roof," Mel said,

"sleeping it off. He lapped up a hell of a lot of 'tea' last night."

Duayne nodded. "Yes, that's probably so. Yesterday morning, I was up there early to see the sunrise, and he was still in his deck chair, sound asleep."

Tim was shaking his head, back and forth, back and forth. "No . . . no . . ."

"Well, why would you think he's dead?" Maggie said irritably, perhaps vexed at being yet again shoved from center stage by Scofield.

"Because—"

"No, hold it," John said. "Before we go there, let's just see if he *is* upstairs."

"I'll go and check," Phil said, getting up.

But Tim continued to shake his head, looking sicker by the second. "I'm telling you. You won't find him."

PHIL soon returned, shaking his head. "Not there."

A search of the nonpassenger section of the ship by one of Vargas's crew produced the same result.

Arden Scofield was no longer aboard the *Adelita*.

"Okay, Tim," John said. "Let's hear it. What's going on here?"

Tim had joined them at the table by now, and Vargas had had the galley scare up some hot, predawn *picarones* and honey for them, which all but Tim were attacking as if they'd had nothing to eat for a week.

"I should have told you before," Tim said miserably. "I almost did, really—but I never thought—I mean the idea that he would—Jesus Christ, I still can't believe it! I mean—" And his face was in his hands.

"Goddamn it, Tim—!" John began, but Gideon stopped him with a hand on his arm. He made up a cup of heavily sugared coffee for Tim and put it in front of him. "Tim," he said gently, "take a couple of sips. That's right, good. Okay? Now. Take your time. Who are you talking about? Who is 'he'?"

Tim lifted a haggard face. "Cisco. Cisco killed him."

In the general burst of exclamations that followed this, a thought flitted briefly across Gideon's mind: it seemed as if an awful lot was being blamed on someone who wasn't there to speak for himself.

"He threw him overboard," Tim continued.

"You *know* that?" Gideon asked.

"No, I don't *know* it; how could I know it? But it's obvious. That was the scuffling that Maggie—Dr. Gray—heard, don't you see?"

"Well, why would Cisco—" Mel began.

With a wave of his hand John quieted him and retook command. "Captain, don't you think you'd better run up to the wheelhouse and turn the boat around and go back and see if you can spot Professor Scofield? You might have a look for Cisco as well."

Vargas, at his usual station overseeing the buffet table, jumped to comply. "Meneo, you come too," he said in Spanish. "I want you and Chato up front searching for them. Take the other lamp."

"Okay, Tim," John said, "go ahead. Why would Cisco want to kill Dr. Scofield?"

"He hated him, that's why. That stupid spider in his bag? That was Cisco. That thing with the spear and the shrunken head? That was Cisco too. He just wanted to, to scare him, to humiliate him."

Gideon permitted himself a small, internal *a-ha* of satisfaction, and from across the table Phil doffed an imaginary hat in his direction.

"You knew about that—about the spider and the shrunken head—and you didn't tell anyone?" John asked, seeming to swell as he grew more stern.

"I . . ." Tim's expression had become more shamefaced than anything else. "I didn't know about it at the *time*, no. He told me later, up on the roof that night."

"But you kept it to yourself. You didn't tell anyone."

"I . . . no. I'll tell you the truth, I thought it was funny—

well, I did." He paused to drink more coffee. "I thought he had it coming."

"And did he tell you he was going to kill him too?"

A sudden twitch of his fingers jammed the cup onto its saucer, slopping coffee over the side. "*No!* It's just that it makes sense now, after what happened to Maggie and everything. He threw Dr. Scofield overboard too. How hard would it have been to dump him over the side if he was all doped up from that tea?"

"That's a pretty big leap, Tim," Gideon said.

"No, it isn't. Last night—I don't mean tonight, I mean the one before—he told me, all mysterious and weird-like, that he wouldn't be around the next day, that he had something to take care of, and that he'd be back the day after, or maybe not. Maybe we wouldn't be seeing him anymore at all. He had other things on his plate. It all adds up now, but at the time, I never thought he meant to *kill* anybody, I just thought he was— Dr. Gray, you were there, remember?"

"I was?" Maggie said, startled. She had been vacantly pushing the remnants of her *picarones* around her plate with her fork. She put the fork down. "Yes, that's right, I was. I do remember that, Tim. But I thought it was just more of his wild talk, I didn't take it seriously."

"Well, of course not," Tim said eagerly, "I didn't either, that's my point. I mean, who knew what he was talking about half the time?"

"But Tim, I never heard him say anything about the lance, or the spider—"

"No, no, he wouldn't say that in front of you. That was after you left, when we started on that *mampekerishi* shit he brought." He winced. "Oh, hell, excuse me, I—"

"Tim," Gideon interrupted, "why would Cisco hate Scofield? How did he even know him?"

Tim gathered himself together, visibly trying to collect his thoughts. When he sucked twice at an empty coffee cup, Gideon got up and got him some more, which he sipped equally absently. "I think everybody knows that old story about Dr. Scofield," he said, addressing the whole of his rapt audience. "About how the Chayacuro attacked him and his friends, the two brothers?"

Nods all around.

"And how they had to leave the first brother after he got hit by a poison dart, and they heard the Indians chop his head off, and then the second brother got hit by a dart and died in Dr. Scofield's arms?"

They nodded again, expectantly now.

"Well, it's not true. He didn't die in Dr. Scofield's arms. Dr. Scofield just ran away and left him there to die. But he didn't die. When the Chayacuro found him they knew him, see, because he'd done some fieldwork with them when he was working on his dissertation. They've got an antidote for the poison—they make it from sugarcane—and they gave it to him. He lived with them for three months, became what they call a shaman's apprentice, got really deep into their drugs, and never went back to the States after that. He's lived in South America ever since, in Bolivia and Colombia, I think, but mostly right around Iquitos."

"This can't be going where I think it's going," John said.

"Anybody remember his name—the second brother?" Tim asked.

"Frank," Mel said. "Frank Molina."

"That's right. And *Frank* in Spanish is *Francisco*. And short for *Francisco* is—"

" 'Cisco,' " breathed Gideon.

"Jesus, Mary, and Joseph," said Duayne after a moment's stunned silence.

SIXTEEN

THE fact that Cisco and Scofield had wound up on the same ship after thirty years, Tim continued, was just an unlucky fluke, not anything that Cisco had worked out ahead of time.

"Hold it right there," John said. "It's not that I don't believe in coincidences, but that's a little too much to swallow."

"I'm just telling you what he told me," Tim said, chewing vigorously. His appetite had caught up with him, and although the *picarones* were now cold and getting soggy, he was stuffing them in.

"It's true, what he says," Vargas said, having just returned from the river search for Scofield and Cisco, which had been fruitless. There was no sign of them. "I could think of no one else who could be a guide for such a group as this. I went to him and offered him the job, and he took it."

"You're saying he didn't even know Scofield would be aboard?" John asked. "So we're supposed to think he just carries around a giant spider and a shrunken head in case they come in handy? And a spear?"

Vargas offered a supplicatory shrug. "No, no, of course not. I'm sure I mentioned to him the name, so yes, he knew Professor Scofield would be here. Still, it was I who went to Cisco, not Cisco who came to me."

"No, it's too much of a coincidence," John repeated, shaking his head.

"I don't know, John," Gideon said. "Coincidence, yes. Too much of a coincidence? Maybe not. Look at it this way. Cisco's been hanging around Iquitos on and off for thirty years. He knows more about ethnobotany—he practically has a Harvard doctorate in it—than anybody else in the area, and he's familiar with the local shamans and what they do—plenty of experience in that regard. Well, those things are just what Scofield was interested in, right? And, if I understand it correctly, this was Scofield's first Amazon expedition—"

"Yes, that's so," Maggie said. "Until now, he'd held them down in the Huallaga Valley."

"So he needed someone knowledgeable to guide them. He asked Captain Vargas to find someone—"

"Exactly right, exactly right," Vargas said, nodding along.

"And Captain Vargas quite naturally came up with Cisco."

"Exactly! Naturally!"

"Okay," John said, "I'm not convinced, but okay." He turned to Maggie. "Maggie, you said you heard scuffling—"

"I *think* I heard scuffling."

"—coming from Scofield's cabin."

"I think it was from Arden's cabin."

"All right, fine," John said, showing some impatience. "But I don't remember you saying you heard a splash. Do you *think* you heard a splash?"

She looked blank. "A splash?"

"If he threw Arden in, there would have been a splash, wouldn't there? Right outside his cabin. Pretty much right outside your cabin."

Maggie frowned. "I'm not certain. Now that you've

asked the question, it seems to me, maybe I did. But I can't really say . . . no, I'm sorry, John, I can't say for sure that I did."

Duayne lifted his head, sensing something in the air. "What's happening? Are we turning around again? Why are we going back?"

"No, we're not going back," Vargas said. "The river here, it's making a big loop, a big bend. That's what the Javaro is like."

"Tim, you got anything else to tell us?" John asked.

Tim mutely shook his head.

"Captain Vargas," John said, "I think we need to turn this over to the police."

"The *Colombian* police?"

"Well, it happened in Colombia, so obviously, yes."

"You want to go back to the checkpoint? You want to report a murder on my ship to Colonel *Malagga*?" Vargas was horrified.

"Not a murder, we don't know that yet," John said. "A missing person for sure, a homicide, maybe—"

"And an attempted homicide—on me," Maggie said. "Let's not forget that delightful little incident."

"Absolutely," John said. "But yeah, I see your point about Malagga, Captain. What do you suggest?"

"That we continue to Leticia. It's not much farther ahead than the border is back. We'll be there tomorrow night or Friday morning. There you will find a much more professional, more competent headquarters of police. Real policemen, not scoundrels like Malagga."

John nodded his approval. "Sounds good."

CAPTAIN Vargas was once again in a dither, and once again the cause was Arden Scofield, who was as much a source of trepidation and self-recrimination dead as he'd been alive. For the hundredth time, Vargas cursed himself for ever getting involved with the vile man. The problem was, what the hell was he supposed to do now? He knew next to nothing about the arrangements for the contraband coffee at the San José de Chiquitos warehouse. The plan had been for Vargas to unload the shipment of coffee as if it was no different than usual. Scofield would take it from there. But with Scofield no longer in the picture, how would it work? Were the sacks with the coca paste in them supposed to be treated differently in some way? He supposed so, but how? Would there be people there to receive them? If so, would they be in on what was in them? Acceding to Vargas's own wishes, Scofield had kept him out of the loop on almost everything.

Beyond that, he was unsure of whether to unload the coffee at all. Was there supposed to be some signal sent to the drug boss in Cali to the effect that it had been deposited? Undoubtedly, yes, but the identity of the boss was another thing he had foolishly not wanted to know and therefore didn't know. Should he simply leave the coffee and let whoever else was involved worry about it? Should he *not* unload it, but rather take it back to Iquitos with him? And then do what with it? Did the Colombian boss know who *he* was? If so, what would be his reaction when he learned the paste was not at the warehouse but still in Vargas's possession? He wouldn't be pleased, that was certain. Had he already paid money to Scofield? Vargas didn't know that either, but he imagined so, since he himself had already received money from Scofield.

These were serious questions, life-and-death questions. The people in the cocaine trade were brutal in the extreme. When they were crossed, their vengeance was a terrible thing: death, certainly, but death in the most horrible ways imaginable. He himself had a cousin whose wife's brother had been fed to ravening pigs—alive—because he had skimmed some trifling amount from the boss's profits.

He came to a decision. *Not* unloading the coffee was out of the question. *Somebody* would come after him; there was too much money involved, and he had no wish to be fed to the pigs. He would simply unload everything, let events take care of themselves, and hope for the best.

He closed his eyes and crossed himself. God would protect him. He was not a gangster, a criminal; he was weak, that was all—the most human of failings. He had been led down the garden path by a clever, deceptive man. Only let him get out of this with his skin intact, and on his mother's grave, he would never—*never*—again . . .

"SO what do we think happened, exactly?" Phil asked. "I'm a little confused. Somebody go over the sequence for me."

Phil, John, and Gideon were sitting in a nook at the rear of the upper deck, aft of the cabins. It was four-thirty and the first pale pink smears of the day were just beginning to show up ahead on the eastern horizon, although high in the sky, a single, torn shred of cloud was lit a flaming orange. The meeting in the dining room had broken up half an hour earlier, and the three had come up here to talk things over on their own.

"All right," John said. "Apparently Cisco came after Scofield and—"

"When?"

"Well, it would have to have been right before Maggie came out of her cabin."

"Where?"

"Where?"

"*Where* did he come after Scofield?"

"In his cabin," said Gideon. "Maggie heard them scuffling, remember? And Scofield's room is right next to hers."

Phil nodded. "Okay, so he walks in on Scofield, who is not only asleep, but pretty much gaga from that crap he drinks, and drags him out of bed, and flops him over the side, is that it?"

"Probably something like that," John said. "Could be, he slugged him or . . . You know, I should take a look at the room, see if there's any blood or anything."

"Okay, and then what happens?" Phil asked.

"Then Maggie wakes up, goes outside, sees Cisco

standing at the rail admiring his handiwork, and he turns around and sees her, and over the side she goes too, letting out a yell that Doc here hears."

Gideon nodded.

"And then?" Phil persisted.

"And then," said Gideon, "after I yell 'Man overboard'— and probably make a racket falling all over myself trying to get to the door in the dark—Cisco bids us good-bye too."

"Uh-huh." Phil was plainly doubtful. "And that's it?"

"As far as we know," John said. "What's the problem?"

"Well, first, why would the guy just toss Maggie overboard? I mean, couldn't he figure out she'd scream? Wouldn't he, you know, knock her out or choke her or something?"

"Yeah, a rational person would," John said, "but we're talking about Cisco here. Who knows what he had in his system by that time of night?"

"Not only that," said Gideon, "but if the guy had really just killed Scofield, Maggie's showing up would have thrown him into a panic. And when you're talking about panic, there's no such thing as a rational person."

"Okay, I can see that," Phil allowed, "but what about the splashes?"

"What *about* the splashes?"

"There should have been three of them, but we only heard Maggie and Cisco hit the water. Why didn't we hear Scofield?"

"What do you mean, 'we'? As far as I remember, I'm the only one who heard any of the splashes. You two were snoring away, right up to the 'man overboard.' "

"Well, hell, we were farther away," John said. "You were right next to Maggie's room."

"And just one more down from Scofield's," Phil added. "So why didn't you hear him go in too?"

"Phil, I was lucky to hear Maggie go in. It wasn't the splashes that woke me up. It was that yelp when she cut her ankle. If not for that—"

John's head came up. He sniffed once, twice. "Do I smell smoke?"

"Must be some more logging up ahead," Phil said, as they got up to peer around the corner of the cabin block.

BUT there weren't any logging projects along this stretch of the Javaro. The acrid smoke was coming from a charred, one-story wooden building built on the right bank above a rickety old pier that was under repair, with some jarringly clean new planks among the dark, rotten ones.

"Looks like a house," Phil said. "What's left of it, anyway."

"No, I don't think so," Gideon said, looking at the blackened structure. "It's pretty big for that, and that's a fairly good-sized unloading pier down below. I think it's some kind of commercial building. A warehouse or something."

The fire had occurred not long before, sometime during the previous day, in all likelihood; there were no longer any flames to be seen, but curling gray wisps still rose occasionally from the burnt wood, and a few embers could be seen glowing here and there in the shadows. The flooring had buckled in places, but the walls still stood, and the corrugated metal roof had held. Fifty feet from the building was a simple, open-walled, thatch-roofed house on waist-high stilts, much like the ones they'd seen at the Ocaona village, untouched by the fire and deserted.

As the *Adelita* pulled up to the pier, a stricken Vargas stood gazing up from the deck like a man who's just been told he has five minutes to live. "What am I supposed to do now?" he was saying to himself over and over in Spanish, sometimes with a desperate little hiccup of a laugh. "What in the name of God am I to do now?"

Gideon, standing not far from him, asked, in English, what was the matter.

"Is our warehouse. San José de Chiquitos. I be to unload the . . . the coffee beans here. Now how I do it? I don't can!" In his extremity, his command of English had fled him again. He jerked his head to stare at Gideon. His eyes, protuberant to begin with, bulged a little more. "What I do with the coffee?"

He asked it—wailed it—as if he were really counting on Gideon to give him the answer, and Gideon didn't know what to say. "Well, it isn't as if it's your fault," he began soothingly. "Obviously, you can't unload it here—"

"How this can happen?" Vargas muttered, barely hearing him. "Are guards, guards what live right here! How they can don't see? And where they are now, why they don't be here, can you tell me this?"

"Captain Vargas, however it happened, I guess you'll just have to take it back to Iquitos. No one would expect you to—"

But Vargas, not listening at all now, was wandering dazedly away. "You don't can understand . . . you don't know . . ."

A few minutes later, the narrow gangplank was let down, and Vargas, some of the passengers, and most of the crew came down it and climbed the dozen or so rough steps dug out of the bank to get up to the building and look around. Although the still-smoldering structure was too hot to enter, it could be seen through gaps in the walls that the place was empty; nothing was stored there. John, who had some experience investigating arson, guessed that the fire was twelve or fifteen hours old.

While most of the others poked gingerly along the outside of the building, some with sticks they'd picked up, Gideon and John went meandering, with no real purpose, around the clearing. There were stacks of fresh lumber, corrugated metal roofing, and other building materials nearby, and lumber scraps and power tools on the ground. Under a crude little waist-high lean-to of its own stood the tools' power source, a new-looking, gasoline-powered 5.5-horsepower Hitachi air compressor. (Gideon, not much of a hand around power tools, knew this only because John, who did know about such things, had just told him what it was.)

"Looks like there was some construction going on," said John.

"Yup. Enlarging the place, repairing it, something."

On top of the small lean-to were a few more power tools. "These are pretty good tools, you know?" John picked one up. "Hutchins rotary sander," he said enviously. "Top of the line. I wish I could afford one. And this . . ." He hefted another. "Whoa, a Makita nail gun, also top of the line. This little baby doesn't come cheap." He put it down, seemingly with regret. "Doc, does it strike you as a little strange that in a place like this"—he waved vaguely about them—"way, *way* out in the boondocks, middle of the jungle—that they'd have expensive stuff like this? It all looks new too."

"Not really, no," Gideon said. "This is a warehouse, a pick-up point for other places, isn't it? Not just some local storehouse. We don't know how much money is behind it." He leveled a finger at his friend. "Let me guess. You're thinking there are drugs involved, right?"

"Yeah, I guess I got a one-track mind. But you know what the DEA people call this stretch of the Amazon Basin? The White Triangle. Sixty percent of the North American cocaine trade comes through here, either on the ground, down the river, or in the air. And here we have this falling-down little shack of a warehouse, way, way in the tules, and there's about ten thousand dollars worth of new tools laying around." He shrugged. "So, yeah, I'm thinking there might be more than coffee beans that come through here. You don't agree with me?"

"I agree you've got a one-track mind. It's hard to picture Vargas as a drug trafficker. The guy's a bundle of nerves. He'd never be able to stand it."

"Yeah, I guess."

They walked on a little. "And here's something else," John said. "You know that old prof of yours, Abe Goldstein, and that theory he was always talking about, when too many things happen—"

"The Law of Interconnected Monkey Business. When

too many suspicious things—too much monkey business—start happening to the same set of people in the same context, you're going to find a connection between them."

"Yeah, that's the one. Well, don't you think it maybe applies here? Yesterday Cisco goes bonkers and throws Scofield overboard, then throws Maggie overboard, then throws himself overboard . . . and then when we arrive at the warehouse to drop off the coffee, the warehouse has just been burnt down—"

"I see what you're saying, John, but in this case I don't think it applies. We know why Cisco hated Scofield, and it had nothing to do with the warehouse, or coffee, or drugs for that matter. That was between them, something personal. This is something completely different, a different context."

"Is it? Tell me, what's Vargas so shook up about? He looks like a balloon that somebody let all the air out of."

"Well, he was supposed to make a delivery here. That coffee—"

"Big deal, so he can't deliver his coffee. So what? He brings it back with him, that's all. Dried coffee beans'll hold for months." John's relatives were in the coffee business and he knew a lot about the subject. "But Vargas goes around acting like a, like a . . ." But his search for another metaphor to match his deflated balloon failed and he just shook his head. "I think, I just think . . ."

"You think there's more going on here than meets the eye."

"Right, and I think there's more than coffee in that hold."

"I gather we're still talking about drugs?"

"Yeah, drugs. Sometimes they put cocaine or heroin inside sacks of coffee. You ever hear that? It makes it harder for the sniffer dogs to smell it. I tell you, I'd really like to have about twenty minutes alone in that hold."

"John," Gideon warned, "you're not on duty here. You're not in America here. You have no jurisdiction—"

John held up his hand. "I know, I know, I know. Just dreaming, that's all."

They wandered over to look at the nearby platform house. Through the open sides they could see that there were two hammocks strung crosswise to each other in the center, and that the shelves along one side held canned food, cups and plates, and cooking utensils. A half-full sack of rice leaned against one of the poles that held up the roof. It was impossible to tell how old the house was—it could have been five years, it could have been five days— but it looked very much as if it were currently being lived in. It must have been where the construction workers, or maybe the watchmen (who were perhaps the same) were housed, they concluded, as they sat heavily down on the front step.

"Doc, there's something else that I can't figure out," John said, his elbows on the step behind them. "I did take a look at Scofield's room this morning, just before I got off the ship."

"And?"

"It was strange. His bed hadn't been slept in. It hadn't even been sat on; it was tight as a drum."

"And this is strange why?"

"Well, the thing with Cisco happened at two in the morning, right? What was he doing, if he wasn't sleeping?"

"Who knows? He'd had all that 'tea' of his. Maybe it put him to sleep up on the roof, all right, but interfered with his sleep when he came down later on. The way alcohol does. Maybe he was reading, or—"

"Where?"

"Where?"

"Yeah, where?" John said. "Where was he reading? His cabin is the same size as ours. There's nothing in the damn thing but a bed. There's no chair. There's no *room* for a chair. There's only the bed, and he wasn't on that. What's more, the whole damn place was neat as a pin. Maggie heard scuffling, right? How could two guys scuffle in there without messing things up? There's barely room for two guys to *stand* there."

"Ah," Gideon said, nodding. "I see what you mean. Maggie thought it came from his room, but it couldn't have, could it?"

"That's what I'm saying, right."

"Well, it probably came from the cabin on her other side. We should—"

John was looking curiously at him.

Gideon looked back. "What?"

"*You're* in the cabin on her other side. Were you doing a lot of scuffling?"

"Oh. Yeah, that's right. Okay, maybe—"

They were interrupted by a shout from Phil, who was part of a knot of people—crew and passengers—standing in front of the warehouse's scorched double doors.

"Hey, Gideon, come look. I think we have something in your line of work here."

When Gideon, with John, got closer he saw that they were all peering at a round, silver-dollar sized object that appeared to be stuck or pinned to the outside of one of the doors. The crowd parted respectfully for him, then eagerly closed in again.

"It *is* bone, isn't it?" Tim asked.

"Well, let's see . . ."

It was a glistening, perfect disk of—yes, bone—a little less than an inch in diameter, with a quarter-inch hole at its center; essentially, a ring of bone. It had been nailed to the wall through the hole in the middle. There was a very slight convexity to it, with the concave side pressed up against the wall. He ran a finger gently over it.

"Hmm," said John, smiling.

"Hmm," said Gideon.

"It could be an ornament of some kind," Maggie declared when she grew tired of waiting for something from him beyond "hmm." "A pendant, perhaps; part of a necklace."

"Meneo says he thinks it must be another sign," Tim offered excitedly. "From the Chayacuro again."

Meneo, the tiny cook, nodded energetically. "*Sí, Chayacuros. Muy malo.*" Very bad.

"He thinks they burned down the warehouse and left this as a warning."

"A warning to whom?" a wide-eyed Duayne asked. "About what?"

"About everything, about every damned thing you can name," Vargas mumbled.

"Is it human?" Mel asked Gideon. "Can you tell?"

"I don't know," Gideon said slowly. "Let's get it off." He tried to slide the ring off the nail, but the hole in the center wasn't quite large enough to slip over the nail's head. The nail itself, about two inches long, wasn't deeply embedded in the wood, however, and with a twist of his hand he was able to jerk it out. The bone fell gently into the cupped palm of his other hand.

He turned it over, studied it, fingered it, turned it over again. And again.

The ring, he saw now, wasn't as perfect as he'd thought. For one thing its rim beveled slightly outward from the convex surface to the concave one. And while superficially circular enough, it showed rough edges and some excrescences, as if it had been drilled from the surrounding bone, but never finished, never sanded or polished. But the quarter-inch opening in the center, about a quarter of an inch across, was indeed perfectly circular, as smooth as the hole in a Life Saver, although its rim also beveled outward from the convex surface to the concave one.

"Well?" Maggie demanded when her patience ran out again.

Phil laughed. "Forget it, Maggie; it's hopeless. When the Skeleton Detective is engaged in examining a skeleton or any part thereof, he is not to be distracted. He is no longer really with us."

Gideon, as if to prove the point, continued his examination, hearing neither of them. More fingering, more up-close scrutiny, even a little sniffing.

"Okay," he said at last. "First of all, it's from a skull; a piece of cranium. These brownish streaks are dried blood. From its thinness and its convexity, I'd say it's from the frontal bone—the squamous portion, the left or right frontal eminence." He tapped his own forehead. "Could be parietal, however. Not temporal, though, and certainly not occipital, which is thicker and not as—"

"But is it *human*?" Maggie ground out through clenched teeth. "For God's sake, Gideon!"

"Ah, well, that I can't be sure of. There's nothing to suggest it *isn't* human, and if you want my guess, I'd say that it is. I can't think of any animals that you'd find around here that would have a skull both as globular and as large as the one that this must have come from. Oh, and I can also tell you something else. It's fresh. See, you can feel how slippery, how greasy, it is." He proffered it for them to see for themselves.

"We'll take your word on it," Phil said.

"Also," Gideon continued, turning it over so that the concave side was up, "see this sort of skin, this membrane on the inside? That's meningeal tissue—brain tissue—that's still adhering to the bone. And it's hardly dried out at all. So . . . definitely fresh, yes."

" 'Fresh,' meaning like yesterday?" John asked.

"Yesterday would be a good bet," Gideon said.

"So it could be connected with the fire?"

"Could well be," said Gideon, who was beginning to think that John might have a point after all; there had been an awful lot of strange things going on in the last day or so.

"Wait a minute," Mel said. "You're losing me. A hole like that in your head—you'd be dead, wouldn't you?"

"Interestingly enough, not necessarily. Many people have survived a trephining operation that removed this large a chunk of skull. But in this case, I think so, yes. He would have been dead. This would have done him in."

"So what you're telling us is that Meneo probably got it right? The Chayacuro—"

"*Sí, sí, los Chayacuros!*" Meneo loudly agreed.

"—burned the place down and killed somebody—"

"The watchman, probably," Duayne supplied eagerly. "There must have been a watchman."

"—and . . . and cut a piece out of his head and nailed it up on the wall to . . . to . . . what?"

"Take it easy, Mel," John said. "Don't get carried away. That's not what he's telling us. He's telling us . . . well, what the hell are you telling us, Doc?"

"Only that somebody was killed in the last day or so, and this piece of his skull wound up nailed to the wall. The rest—the Chayacuro—"

"Los Chayacuros, sí!"

"—the burning down of the place on purpose—is strictly conjecture. No evidence one way or the other, at least that I can see."

"But who else would do something like this?" Duayne asked, his lips curled in disgust. "Maybe not that particular tribe, but some band of primitive . . . savages. I mean, cut a piece out of a skull and nail it—" He shuddered. "Ugh."

"I wonder how they did it," Phil mused. "Look at how clean that hole in the middle is. You couldn't do that with a knife, let alone a machete. It's as if someone did it on a drill press in a factory. How could they bore a hole like that?"

"Oh, I know exactly how it was done," Gideon said. "I've seen this before. Only once, but it's not the kind of thing you forget."

They fell silent, waiting. Even the non-English-speaking Meneo, staring expectantly at Gideon's lips, seemed to be waiting for an explanation to emerge.

"Well, first of all, nobody cut this thing out of his skull," Gideon said. "Secondly, nobody nailed it to the wall."

"Nobody nailed it to the wall!" Mel exclaimed, almost angrily. "Nobody— What the hell are you talking about?"

"Nobody nailed it to the wall in the sense you're thinking," Gideon amended. "I'd guess it wound up there accidentally."

After a few moments of blank stares all around, John spoke up. "Oh, well, now that we've had that explained . . ."

Gideon couldn't help laughing. In spite of himself, in spite of the grisly situation, he enjoyed these public moments of seeming wizardry. They were as close to *fun* as anything in the forensic business came. "Wait a second," he said and walked back to the lean-to that had the tools on it. He came back with the Makita nail gun. "Now," he said, scanning the ground, "anybody see the nail I pulled out of the door?"

"Here it is." Vargas bent, picked it up, and handed it to Gideon.

"See these spiral grooves in it?" Gideon said.

"It's a roofing nail," John said. "The grooves help anchor it."

"Fine, a roofing nail," Gideon said. "Now look at the nails that are still left in the cartridge of the nail gun."

"They're the same!" Tim exclaimed.

"Yes."

"So that means . . ." Maggie began, then frowned and shook her head incredulously. "*What* does it mean?"

"It means," said Gideon, "that someone almost certainly killed him with this nail gun. Or let's just say he was killed with the nail gun. Possibly he did it to himself by accident— or not by accident. People have tried committing suicide with them, sometimes successfully, sometimes not."

"Yuck," said Tim.

"You've lost me, Doc," John said. "Okay, this piece of bone, this ring of bone, was maybe nailed up with a nail gun—this nail gun right here, it looks like—but how does that translate to the guy was *killed* with it? How do you know what killed him?"

"And I still want to know how they made this," said Phil, who had finally taken the bone from Gideon and was peering at the smooth, circular border of the hole in the center. "It's like it was made with a, with a . . ."

"It was made with the nail gun," Gideon said, "which also nailed it to the wall—and on its way from doing the first to accomplishing the second, it made a hash of his brain."

His open-mouthed audience waited for more.

"Well, first of all, you have to remember that a good nail gun can generate a fantastic velocity; around fourteen hundred feet per second, if I remember correctly."

"You're kidding me. That's faster than the muzzle velocity on my old Detective Special," John said. "And that could sure do a lot of damage."

"And so can a two-inch steel nail, especially with a flat, round head, although more often than not, it just makes a hole in the skull and merely gets embedded in the brain."

Duayne winced. " 'Merely,' the man says."

"But once in a while, especially with a powerful gun driving it, it doesn't happen that way. It happens the way it happened here."

The sequence would have been like this: The point of the nail would have easily perforated the skull, making a small, circular hole—smaller than the one now visible in the bone—but a millisecond later the round, flat head of the nail would have struck the skull as well, creating a larger opening. It would have driven partway through, then gotten wedged in the hole it had made, which would have transferred its energy to the immediately surrounding bony tissue, breaking away the ring of bone he now held in his hand. The nail would then have continued plowing through the brain, dragging the ring along with it and doing dreadful destruction, then exploded out the back of the head, bony ring and all, and then kept going a few feet—it couldn't have been far, because so much of its energy would have dissipated, which would have been why it wasn't embedded very deeply in the door.

"And that's how it happened," he finished. "I think."

They had listened to this virtuoso analysis, part enthralled, part horrified, and for a moment it almost seemed as if they were going to break into applause, but they only shook their heads, or clucked, or softly whistled.

Except for Duayne, who murmured, "Amazing, just amazing."

"Question," Mel said. "Where's the rest of him?"

"Very good question," said Gideon. "Obviously, the body's not here."

"Burned up inside, perhaps?" suggested Maggie. "In fact, maybe they set the fire to cover it."

"Oh no, I don't think so. You can see this wasn't an especially hot fire—apparently no accelerants involved, no gasoline or anything like that. A fire like this, or an ordinary house fire—it's not nearly hot enough to consume a body. If he was inside, we'd be able to spot him."

"Well, if it worked the way you said, Doc," John said, "then he would have been standing a few feet in front of the door, just about where we are right now, when he got shot. We're only ten or fifteen feet from the edge, and there's no beach right below. It would have been easy enough to roll him over the edge and into the river."

"That's true, but whatever happened, there's probably some of him—blood, brain tissue, hair, pieces of his head—left around where he was shot. Which, as John says, was probably right where we're standing."

"And which we'd better get off of," John added. "The police aren't going to appreciate our stomping around a crime scene."

"What police?" Vargas said with a guttural laugh. "Malagga? You think he'll care enough to get his fat rear end all the way over here? Why should he?"

All the same, Vargas moved off six or seven steps, as did everybody else except Gideon, who had dropped to his hands and knees to have a better look at the ground.

"You mean Malagga would be responsible for investigating this?" John asked Vargas, as most of the others somewhat uncomfortably checked the soles of their shoes for any human residue that might be sticking to them. From the relief on their faces, it was obvious that none was found.

Vargas shrugged. "We're still closer to the checkpoint than we are to Leticia, and there can't be any police stations between them . . . there's *nothing* between them except a few Indian villages . . . so, yes, I think it would fall to Malagga—if it fell to anybody."

"Well, all the same, the cops have to be told. We'll add that to what we tell them when we get to Leticia and let them decide what to do."

"I've found something," Gideon called. In the variegated red, yellow, and brown forest litter it would have taken more than the naked eye to spot blood spatter or brain tissue, but bone was different. He held up a roughly triangular chunk of bone an inch across at its widest point.

"This is a piece of the occipital—the rear of the skull, way down low. I can see some of the superior nuchal line and just the start of the occipital protuberance, and here on the inside, what I think is the transverse sinus . . . the left transverse sinus." He hefted the piece. "This would have happened when the nail blasted out the back of his head. There are probably some more pieces around."

For the next twenty minutes he continued crawling around the general area, coming up with another chunk of occipital, and five more pieces—no more than crumbs, really—that he recognized as bone but were too small to identify. By that time, everybody but Phil, John, and Vargas had grown bored and gone back to the ship. Vargas had gone to sit on the steps of the nearby shack and shake his head and mumble to himself, and John and Phil were idly watching Gideon.

"So what are you going to do with the pieces?" Phil asked.

"Turn them over to the police in Leticia, I guess. As John said, tell them about all this, and leave it up to them. Although I'm hoping I'm able to keep that ring of bone from the frontal. It'd make a hell of an addition to my study collection."

Phil grimaced. "Jesus, you're as bad as Duayne with his bugs. How come Julie hasn't divorced *you*?"

"I'm referring to the collection in the forensic lab at the U," said Gideon. "I don't keep the damn things in my living room."

"So what do we have here?" John was musing. "Can't be a suicide."

"Why can't it be a suicide?" Phil asked him.

"Because where's the body? Suicides don't get up and walk away. And from what Doc said, this would have been pretty much an instant death, am I right? He would have dropped right here."

"You're right," Gideon said, still on his knees. "Something as big as that bone ring, with the nail attached, tearing through the brain? He was dead before he hit the ground."

"Well, maybe he committed suicide and somebody else moved him," Phil suggested. "Buried him, or threw him in the river."

"Yeah, it could be," John said agreeably. "There isn't exactly a lot to go on."

"One thing we *can* assume," said Gideon, getting slowly to his feet, "is that this wasn't a premeditated homicide."

"You mean because of the weapon," John said. "Nobody with murder in his mind plans on doing it with a nail gun."

"Right, a weapon of impulse, of opportunity." Gideon brushed leaves and soil from his knees and got up. "One thing, though, John. I have to say I'm starting to agree with you."

"About the Law of Interconnected Monkey Business?"

"Uh-huh. There's just too much going on. All that craziness last night on the boat, and now the warehouse burning down and somebody getting killed . . . What do you think, Phil?"

The question caught Phil in the middle of a vast yawn. "What do I think?" he said before it had quite finished. "I think I need a nap. I'm going back to the ship. See you guys later."

"Why don't you have a talk with Vargas, Doc?" John suggested. "Maybe you can get something out of him about what's going on."

"Me?" cried Gideon, who had no taste, and not much talent, for the guileful subtleties of interrogation. "Why me—why not you? You're the cop."

"That's why; I'm a cop. I'll scare him. And this isn't my jurisdiction, you're right about that. But you, you're just a private citizen being friendly. Besides, he likes you."

"He likes you too," Gideon said lamely.

"No, he doesn't. I make him nervous. Come on, look at the poor guy." He tilted his chin toward the house, where

Vargas was sitting forlornly on the steps, his elbows on his knees. "Aside from everything else, he looks like he can use a friendly ear to talk into. I mean, I'm not saying he's guilty of anything, but something's going on, and he knows more about it than he's been telling us."

"Okay," Gideon said with a sigh, "I'll give it a try. Um, how do I start?"

John shrugged. "Any way you want. Ask him when he expects us to leave. After that, just play it by ear."

"Oh, thanks, that's a huge help. They must teach you that stuff at the academy."

"See you back on the boat, Doc."

"Captain Vargas," Gideon said, approaching the house, "I was wondering when you think we might be getting the *Adelita* going again."

Vargas raised his head and made an attempt to smile. "Very soon, professor. I was hoping that the workmen who live here would come back. Surely they will, soon? Perhaps I give them one more half hour, no more." He brightened at a rustling at the edge of the jungle a few yards away. "Ah, you see? Here they . . ." He leaped to his feet, eyes practically popping from his head as the newcomers emerged from the bush. *"Madre de Dios!"*

SEVENTEEN

THERE were three of them, the kind of beings for whom there is no longer a polite term: savages, primitives. Wild men. You could sense that, instinctively and at once, from their veiled eyes, from the way those dark, impassive eyes looked at you but didn't look at you, focusing on nothing, as if the consciousness that lay behind them was in some other place and time. The men seemed to hold their bodies apart as well, standing tall (or as tall as they could; the biggest was perhaps five-foot-four) and poised and aloof. Their foreheads and cheeks were tattooed with complex designs of undulating lines and dots in orange, blue, and black. Their lips were dyed blue and their eyebrows plucked and replaced with thin, painted, blue crescents. Their thick black hair hung loose in back and was chopped into bangs in front. Quills or small, thin bones ran horizontally through their nasal septa. Although they wore no earrings, the holes in their ears showed they often did. Their earlobes had been dragged and stretched by heavy ornaments into two-inch long flaps. Their smooth chests were daubed with more dots and waving lines, this time in white. Their clothing consisted of short bark kilts—aprons, really. All were barefoot, all had yellow-gray teeth in terrible condition.

Vargas couldn't stop staring at them. "Chayacuro?" Gideon whispered, about equally scared and enchanted.

"No, Arimaguas!" Vargas whispered agitatedly. "God help us, real tree climbers! Be careful." He grinned at them, bobbing his head. *"¡Hola, amigos!"* Slipping off his watch, he held it out invitingly. *"¿Le gusta? ¡Un regalo!* OK?" *Do you like it? It's a gift!*

The nearest one took it from him, a casual flick of the hand without any change in his stone-faced expression, more or less without looking either at Vargas or the watch, then gestured at Gideon's wrist.

"Give him your watch," Vargas said.

"Wait a minute, why—"

"Give it to him!" Vargas urged. "They're as bad as the Chayacuro. Worse! Give them what they want, don't upset them. Trust me, give them the watches and they'll go away."

Gideon unclasped the watch and handed it to the Indian. *"Un regalo,"* he said, with markedly less enthusiasm than Vargas had shown. And a gift it had been, from an appreciative fellow professor for whom he'd filled in for a couple of weeks. Well, at least it would make a good story when he told her about it. *Oh, the watch? Sorry, Marilyn, it was taken from me in the Amazon by a bunch of Indians with bones in their noses.*

The second watch was handed to another man, and both objects disappeared under their aprons. That they had some contact with modern life was shown by the shotguns that all three carried on their shoulders with the grace and ease of long custom. Also by the fact that at least one of them, the one who'd taken the watches, spoke a primitive Spanish.

"You come," he said, not particularly threateningly. Not particularly friendly, either. Not anything. Just an announcement. *You come.* He was the oldest of the three, a man probably in his late thirties or early forties, with a nose that had long ago been diagonally split across the bridge with a knife or, more likely, a machete. (In addition to the shotguns, each had a machete slung over his back in a sheath of woven palm fronds.) Gideon could see that the vicious, ropy, white furrow of a scar extended upward from his nose, over his right brow all the way up to and under his clipped bangs. Below, it ran down his left cheek to the corner of his jaw. It was deep enough to have done some serious bone damage, and indeed, his left malar—the cheekbone—was conspicuously caved in, making one eye appear weirdly lower and bigger than the other, like a head in a Picasso painting. Clearly, someone had once tried to cleave his head in two and very nearly succeeded, but here he was, spectacularly disfigured but otherwise apparently hale. *I'd hate to see what the other guy looks like*, Gideon thought.

"Come? Come where?" Vargas demanded, gathering up a few shreds of his dignity. "I am the captain of a ship, I have a ship to—"

"You come," he repeated in exactly the same toneless tone, and at his nod the other two unshouldered their shotguns. Gideon noted that a firearms safety course had not come with the weapons. Each carried his gun with the action closed, and with his finger curled on the trigger, not alongside it or on the trigger guard. He had no doubt at all that there were live shells in the chambers. A jag of one of the double muzzles in Gideon's direction made it clear that he was included in the invitation as well. He thought briefly of yelling for help, but everybody else was back on the *Adelita*, and the *Adelita* was at the base of a forty-foot bank that was sixty or seventy feet away. It was unlikely that they'd hear him, and even if they did, what would ensue in the thirty or forty seconds it took anyone to reach them? Besides, what could they do against three men, whatever their size, who were armed with shotguns and machetes?

"We'd better go with them, Captain," he said.

"You come, yes?" He was grinning now, and his voice had taken on a wheedling, nasty tinge, like a Japanese soldier's in a World War II movie. "Now."

With one of the Arimaguas in front leading the way, and the other two behind them, Vargas and Gideon were marched into the bush.

"Captain Vargas, what's this about? I think you know more—"

"No talk," said Split-nose. An unexpected and painful jab of the gun into Gideon's lower back emphasized his point. Both of the following Indians chuckled merrily at Gideon's "Hey!"

The jungle closed in at once. In thirty seconds, the warehouse clearing was completely obscured from sight. In a minute, they were unable to see more than ten feet in any direction. The path, if there was a path, was invisible to the two white men, although the Indians clearly knew where they were going. Their naked, callused feet moved with speed and certainty over the uneven ground.

Gideon absently watched their rhythmic, confident motion for a few moments, and then did a double take that nearly brought him to a standstill (and no doubt another jab with the shotgun). These were feet such as he'd never seen in life before, and they filled him with a sense of wonder that almost made him forget the uncomfortable circumstances he was in. He'd read descriptions of tribes with feet like these in the accounts of nineteenth-century jungle adventurers, and had even seen group photographs of them, but he'd thought of them as historical curiosities at best; things of the past, long disappeared from the earth. Certainly, he'd never expected to see them for himself, except in a rare individual case, and here were three pairs of them!

In most respects they were like anybody else's feet; a bit broader across the sole perhaps, and more callused, but not all that different, generally speaking. But the big toes were another thing entirely, twice the size of normal big toes—three inches long, at least, and proportionately thick. Moreover, they were splayed outward at an incredible angle, very nearly a right angle, from the rest of the toes. This was a deformity not unknown in the modern world. *Hallux varus* it was called, and you saw it once in a while, usually as the result of a botched operation for bunions, although it could also show up as a congenital deformity. Three-million-year-old footprints in Africa showed that it was nothing new in the human condition. But to see *three* sets of them at once . . . !

Clearly, the huge, muscular, near-prehensile appendages would permit their owners to easily clasp two-or-three-inch-thick branches between their toes and give them a far more secure grip on branches that were larger. "Real tree climbers," in Vargas's words, these people were what the old explorers called "arboreal dwellers," thinking that they pretty much lived in the trees. Whether the condition was genetic in these cases, or rather the result of behavioral adaptation, was unknown then and unknown now. There had been argument, in fact, among the learned professors of the nineteenth century, as to whether they were humans at all, or some kind of tree apes. Well, they were indisputably human, all right, and here they were, alive and well, in the middle of the Amazon, in the twenty-first century!

For a very little while, his extreme gratification at seeing them for himself and his similarly extreme regret at not having a camera with him were his uppermost thoughts, but others soon enough intruded. Where were they going, and why? How would they possibly get back? Would they be *permitted* to come back? But within an hour—it seemed like five, but the sun had barely moved and wasn't yet directly overhead—even those concerns about the future had been driven from his mind by the present, by the nightmarish immediacy of the trek itself. The jungle they were slogging through—the Indians so effortlessly, so *sweatlessly*, the two white men stumbling and cursing at the thorns and bugs—was nothing like what they'd been in during the last two days. This was not Scofield's "awe-inspiring" virgin rain forest, but second- or third-growth, scrabbly and wretched in the extreme, not mature enough yet to have created its own high, protective canopy. It was all thorns, mud, brambles, ankle-grabbing ground vines, mosquitoes, and terribly persistent clouds of vicious, biting, black flies. And except for the occasional blessed patch of shade from a quick-growing ceiba tree or banana bush, all of it in the roasting, shriveling heat of the sun.

Once they had to cross a small, fast-running green river on a "bridge" consisting of a section of an old, rotting tree trunk, twenty feet long and slimy with algae. The first Arimagua trotted easily across—those toes *were* prehensile, a marveling Gideon observed; he could see how they clutched the curving, slippery surface and pushed off from it—and turned, beckoning with his shotgun. A motion from Split-nose's gun encouraged Vargas onto the log, on which he managed two wavering steps before losing his balance and tipping over, arms swinging, to plunge backside first into the river, which was fortunately only about four feet deep.

The rest of his crossing was accomplished in the water alongside the log, with a muttering Vargas holding on to it for balance, to the indescribable mirth of the three Indians, who were clutching their sides with laughter. There was nothing particularly mean about it, it seemed to Gideon; nothing contemptuous or cruel. They just plain found it absolutely hilarious. Vargas, still grumbling, climbed onto the opposite shore and shook himself like a dog.

Gideon's turn. The Indians looked at him with the obvious anticipation of more good fun. *Well, I'm going to disappoint you*, he vowed. *I am* not *going to fall in.* But in his heart he knew he would. And did, although he managed four whole steps before it happened. Only whereas Vargas had keeled over in a slow, relatively stately manner, like a toppling tree, Gideon's feet went out from under him on the slick log, setting them into a frantic pedaling while he fought to keep his balance. It was like something out of a Charlie Chaplin movie, and the Arimaguas were convulsed even before he hit the water, flat on his back and hard. Like Vargas, he had to go the rest of the way up to his armpits in the river, with the remaining two Indians jogging easily across the log to beat him to the other side, still chuckling.

"If I had toes like yours, I could do it too," he griped up at them in English, bringing more gales of merriment, so artless and happy that they even forced a smile from Gideon. *Well, anyway, it's cooled me off*, he thought.

But a few minutes later, all five of them were wriggling and slapping at themselves like a whole crowd of Charlie Chaplins that had blundered into a hornet's nest, and nobody was laughing. They had apparently disturbed a colony of fire ants, and with astonishing speed thousands of the ferocious, minuscule insects had charged out of their mound a few yards away. These were tiny creatures, half the size of the fire ants of the American South, and their sting, Gideon quickly learned, was more itch than pain, but itch of a truly excruciating intensity. Back to the river they ran to plunge in and get rid of the things.

"Don't worry," a grimacing, panting Vargas told him as they vigorously scrubbed themselves. "The itch, it doesn't last long if you don't have too many bites."

"No talk," growled Split-nose, who had never let go of his gun, and whose cool good humor had been severely strained by the ants. *"Vamonos."* Let's go.

In what Gideon estimated was another hour's tough trekking they reached a second, larger river and turned left along it. They were back in virgin jungle here, with a welcome green canopy overhead to shield them from the sun. There was even a recognizable path, with no brambles to tear at their bloodied legs (the Indians' legs showed plenty of old scars, but not a single fresh wound), and the Arimaguas speeded up the pace. With the increase in humidity, Vargas's glasses immediately steamed up so much that he had to take them off.

After a while they came to a squalid riverside settlement of tar-paper, tin-roofed shacks, ugly, concrete-block houses, and mud streets "paved" with planks here and there over the worst of the potholes. An occasional swaybacked, dejected horse stood tethered to a wooden post, its head hanging. The few surly, furtive, unshaven men they passed didn't bother to look twice at them. Apparently, there was nothing unusual about the sight of two filthy, bloody white men being practically frog-marched down the street by a gang of gun-toting Arimaguas.

At the riverfront there was a small, primitive pier, and at the head of it was a wooden shanty, a jungle cantina, into which Vargas and Gideon were marched. Inside there was a plank counter, behind which were a few crooked shelves holding bottles, cans, and glasses, an ancient refrigerator with a clanking old generator, and an even more ancient woman, milky-eyed and toothless, chewing on her gums, who watched them come with no sign of interest. The Arimaguas immediately went to her, asked for and got Inca Kolas, and retreated with them to a wall, at the base of which they squatted, their shotguns propped upright between their knees. Gideon and Vargas were left standing in the middle of the room.

There were three rectangular, battered, extremely dirty tables—stains, crumbs, empty, toppled beer bottles, used glasses—with five or six old cane chairs around each. The nearer tables were unoccupied. At the farthest one sat four decidedly rough-looking men, the sole occupants of the bar other than the old lady. All of them were smoking cigarettes. Two of the three had rifles leaning up against the table at their sides. Another had a revolver in a shoulder holster, and the fourth appeared to be unarmed. The table held three brown bottles of beer, a clear, half-empty bottle of what looked like *aguardiente*—there was no label—a crumpled blue pack of cigarettes, and four stubby, thick-bottomed tumblers. All the place needed to look like the *bandido's* hideaway to end all *bandido's* hideaways were some cartridge belts slung over the chair backs.

Three of the men raised their heads to look speculatively—amusedly?—at the newcomers. The fourth didn't turn, remaining as he sat partially facing away from them—purposely facing away, it seemed—very relaxed in his tipped-back chair, one hand loosely hanging, a cigarette between his fingers, and the other hand apparently tapping his knee under the table, slowly, appraisingly, as if he were considering the pros and cons of some difficult issue.

The boss, Gideon knew instantly.

This was confirmed when, with a tip of his head, he sent the other three to another table, taking their guns and their beers with them. They sat down, also watching. The boss man simply continued his contemplative smoking and knee tapping. He had yet to look at the newcomers, let alone acknowledge their presence.

Thirty seconds of this—of standing there filthy and parched and edgy and uncertain, waiting for who knew what—was enough to snap Vargas's fragile self-restraint.

He stepped forward. *"Señor—"*

"Shut up," the man said offhandedly in Spanish, and now he turned fully toward them, ground out his cigarette on the tabletop, dropped the butt on the floor, and brought his hand up from under the table. In it was a lovingly polished stainless steel knife that he laid in front of him with care, aligning it so that it was at a right angle to the table's edge. But this was no ordinary knife, this was a Rambo knife, a Crocodile Dundee knife, a foot long, with an olive-drab handle and a broad, heavy, faintly scimitar-shaped blade, saw-toothed on top, that curved upward to a vicious hooked point. Gideon had seen a knife like this before. He even knew what it was called: a Krug Assegai combat knife. It had been used in the most horrific homicide that it had ever been his misfortune on which to consult.

We're going to be killed, he knew with sudden, cold certainty. *We've been brought here to be murdered. Murdered and carved up, not even necessarily in that order.*

The man was watching from under lowered lids to see their reaction to the weapon, and he must have loved Vargas's. The captain's eyes bugged out, his mouth popped open and then closed with a click as his teeth snapped together, and he took a stuttering step back.

Gideon was determined to provide no similar satisfaction. Swallowing down the seeming ball of cotton that had suddenly clogged his throat and crossing his arms to make sure his hands didn't tremble, he said in Spanish: "We could use some water."

"Oh, they could use some water," the man said, grinning, and there was some low chuckling from the other table. "Sure. Why not?" He called out a command to the old woman. As with so many other people in this part of the world, his teeth were in wretched condition, some of them nothing more than yellow nubbins barely protruding from his gums.

"*Señor*, I don't know what this is about . . ." Vargas said pitiably, practically wringing his hands. If he'd had a forelock, he would have been tugging on it. "But I assure you, there has been a misunderstanding of some—"

"I told you once to shut up," he was told. "I'll deal with you later. Right now, I want to talk to the professor."

That came as a shock to Gideon. *How did he know I was a professor?* That meant he had been brought there not by pure accident, not because he'd happened to be with Vargas at the wrong time in the wrong place, but on purpose, because he was who he was. *But how does he know me? What the hell was going on here?*

"I am called Guapo," the man said, speaking directly to Gideon.

Guapo. It meant *handsome*, but if this Guapo had ever been handsome, it had been a long time back. A fleshy, beetle-browed man, he was cut from the same cloth as Colonel Malagga: gross-featured, brutal, thuggish, with the high, thick shoulders of a bull buffalo, no neck to speak of, and small, mean, piggish eyes. A lush, silky, jet-black mustache (the only conceivable basis of the "guapo" nickname) drooped over the sides of his mouth, Pancho Villa style. Like the other men Gideon had seen in this settlement, he hadn't shaved for three or four days. He wore jeans, sandals, and a dirty, white soccer jersey with *Alianza Lima* on the chest. The belly-ballooned front of the jersey was smeared with finger marks where he'd wiped his hands on it.

"So, you heard of me?" Guapo prompted. He had a serious drinker's voice, husked and whispery, from deep in his throat.

"No, I never heard of you." Gideon's own voice, he was glad to hear, remained steady, although his breath was a little short. He was looking about him as inconspicuously as he could, with his mind working at top speed. What were the ways out? Forget the way they'd come in. There were three white men and three Indians with guns between him and the door. But in the wooden wall right behind Guapo were two large, windowless openings. Could he get by the man and his knife and through one of them before someone with a rifle could get a bead on him? No, not if he made a run for it around the table. But what if he acted with enough suddenness, at a moment of inattentiveness, launching himself right onto the tabletop, kicking or swatting Guapo over in his chair and vaulting over him through the opening . . . maybe even grabbing the knife on the way, if he could? But what about poor Vargas? What about—

The corners of Guapo's mouth turned down. "No, he never heard of me," he said sarcastically, and unpleasant laughter came from the three men at the other table.

"Sit down, Professor." With his foot, Guapo kicked out one of the chairs. Gideon took it, angling it slightly and moving it back a little to give himself room for a better shot at the opening.

"I'll go and sit over there," Vargas offered, indicating the one unoccupied table. "I don't want to intrude."

"No, you'll sit here. I want you to see what happens to him. I want you to have a real good view, so you'll remember."

It didn't seem possible for Gideon's stomach to sink any lower than it already had, but it did. Guapo didn't intend to kill *them*, he intended to kill *him*. He noticed that Guapo's fingers lay loosely on the knife, but he wasn't actually holding it. If he were to move his hand or turn to look away, even for an instant . . .

The woman shuffled over with a bottle of mineral water

and two cloudy glasses. She was blind, Gideon realized from the way she touched the table before setting them down. Guapo himself poured for them with the expansive, benevolent air of a host providing for his guests—first moving the knife out of their immediate reach and keeping his hand on it—and Gideon and Vargas each gulped down a glass of the closest thing to nectar Gideon had ever tasted.

"More?" Guapo asked hospitably and was answered by two vigorous nods. The second glasses were emptied as fast as the first and once again eagerly held out. Strange. Minutes from probable death—an unimaginably unpleasant death—and yet one could take so much grateful pleasure from a glass of cold water.

When Gideon had put down his glass again without signaling for another, Guapo said something to him that he didn't understand. Something about the river and the *Adelita*. Gideon asked him to repeat it.

He said it again and Gideon still couldn't make it out. "I'm sorry, I don't—"

Guapo was suddenly furious. He slammed the table with a heavy hand (Vargas actually jumped out of his chair; Gideon managed—just—to stay in his), grabbed the monstrous knife, and waved its point at Gideon's eyes. "Don't play dumb with me, you bastard! I know you speak Spanish."

"I speak *some* Spanish, yes."

"You speak *perfect* Spanish."

No, I don't, Gideon thought, his stomach moving up just a little toward its normal location. *Vargas was right. It was some kind of misunderstanding. They had him confused with someone else. Talking their way out of this might still be a possibility.*

"Look," he said evenly, reasonably, "I don't know who you think I am, but—"

Guapo got up, leaned on his hands—on the knuckles of the one holding the knife—and loomed aggressively over him. Gideon smelled whiskey, cheese, cigarettes, sweat. "You're telling me you're not the professor?"

"I'm *a* professor, but I'm obviously not the one you think I am." And now a sudden burst of reckless but welcome righteous anger surged in him. He jumped up too, so he was nose to nose with Guapo. (Vargas, sitting between them, skidded back, out of the likely range of the knife.) "Why don't you tell me who the hell you think I am? This is . . ." He sought the word for *outrageous*, but had to settle for *terrible*, the same in Spanish as it was in English. "You send your Indians to . . . to . . . you . . ." But his Spanish wasn't good enough and he was reduced to waving his arms and sputtering: "Mud . . . thorns . . . mosquitoes . . . threats . . ."

His language difficulties had more effect than his protestations. For the first time, Guapo's heavy, cruel face showed some doubt. He sat slowly down again, peering hard at Gideon.

"So who are you then?"

"Look . . ." Gideon zipped open the fanny pack he wore near his belt buckle, in which he kept his passport, airplane tickets, and money (and for the moment, a miscellaneous collection of fresh cranial fragments), then fumbled through a wad of damp *nuevos soles* and ten- and twenty-dollar bills to pull out the passport, its familiar blue cover somehow reassuring, as if he were at an airport and simply showing it could get him out of whatever this mess was. He opened it to the identification pages and pushed it across the table to Guapo. "See? Gideon Oliver, that's me." He tapped his photograph.

Guapo peered sulkily at it. "And how do I know it's not fake? Why should I think you're not trying to fool me?"

"Fool you? How could I know I was going to see you? How could I possibly know your Indians would come and get us?"

"My Indians, my damn Indians!" Guapo exploded, jumping out of his chair. He flung the passport at Gideon's face. "Luis!" he called, and the man with the revolver came to sit at the table in his place. A snake-necked, fox-faced, crazy-eyed man with an inch of burning cigarette dangling

from his lower lip, he was missing the thumb and first finger of his right hand. But with his other thumb, he steadily
clicked the revolver's hammer back, eased it forward,
clicked it back, eased it forward . . . all the while keeping it
pointed at the center of Gideon's chest. Gideon did his best
not to think about it, but his eyes kept returning to the moving thumb.

"Would you mind not doing that?" he said. "Or at least
pointing it someplace else?" *A mistake*, he thought immediately.

Oozing malignance—whether it was general or directed
specifically at Gideon was impossible to tell—the man
smiled meanly, revealing yet another mouthful of discolored, rotting teeth, and kept on doing what he was doing.
Click . . . click . . .

Gideon shrugged one shoulder in what he hoped was a
show of unconcern, and turned to watch Guapo, who had
stomped to the three Arimaguas, where they still hunkered
down at the base of the wall with their rifles and their Inca
Kolas. He began shouting at them, waving the big knife for
emphasis. None of them looked at him, but only stared
straight ahead. Split-nose was the only one who replied, his
answers surly and curt. Like the others, he stared straight
in front of him, into the middle distance, his eyes on a level
with Guapo's hips, as still, and as impassive, as a stone
idol, and just about as grim.

A long silence after his last answer, and then Guapo
suddenly lashed out, kicking the bottle out of the Indian's
hand and sending it skittering over the worn plank floor,
spewing yellow-green liquid. Split-nose didn't move a
muscle: no start, no blink, no change of expression or fo-
cus. Guapo yelled even louder, a mix of Spanish and something else. Gideon couldn't pick up most of what he was
shouting, but he managed to make out *imbécile* and *es-
túpido*. Split-nose's answers were more of the same:
monotonic and obstinate. He seemed unreachable, immov-
able, but Gideon suspected there would come a time when
Guapo would pay for this.

Now would be a good time, he did his best to convey to Split-nose. *Now would be a* perfect *time*. But the Indian sat immobile and oblivious.

"What are they talking about?" he asked Vargas in English. The man guarding them frowned and watched them intently, as if trying to understand the words, but he didn't tell them to be quiet.

"Guapo, he thought you were Scofield."

"Scofield? Why would he think I was Scofield?"

"He sent the Indians to get him . . . and me. He told them Scofield was called 'professor,' and the fellow with the chopped-up nose, he heard me call you 'professor,' so he thought . . ." He shrugged away the rest of the sentence. "At least, I think that's what they're saying."

"This Guapo, have you heard of him?"

Vargas nodded. "He's a very big man, the boss in North Loreto," he whispered, then stopped himself. With a wary glance at the man with the revolver to assure himself that he didn't understand English (the obtuse, openmouthed expression satisfied him), he went on: "A tough customer, a killer. He'd as soon take your eye out with that knife as—"

Guapo's heavy returning footsteps silenced him. "Stupid bastards," he grumbled in Spanish as he fell into the remaining chair and poured himself three fingers of *aguardiente*. "Trained monkeys would do better." With a grunt and a sudden jerk he jammed the point of the knife into the tabletop, which Gideon now noticed was covered with splintery pockmarks from a hundred previous such spearings. There the knife remained, upright and quivering, about three inches from Guapo's hand and five long, impossible feet from Gideon's. And both Vargas and the guy with the gun and the itchy thumb now sat between them. Plan A—going up and over the table and through that opening in the wall—wasn't going to work any more, that was clear. Guapo drained half the tumbler and smoothed his mustache with thumb and forefinger, a surprisingly dainty motion. "So where is Scofield?" he asked in a low voice, staring at the table.

A promising sign? Gideon wondered. *He believes me?*

"Professor Scofield has . . . has died, I regret to say," Vargas stammered, clearly realizing how extremely unlikely it sounded. "Only last night."

Guapo eyed him suspiciously.

"I swear it on the grave of my mother," said Vargas. "A crazy person, a drug-crazed lunatic, threw him from the ship. He also threw another passenger, a—"

"And what do you say?" Guapo asked Gideon.

"It's true. Scofield's dead." Well, that had hardly been established beyond doubt, but it was highly probable, and this was not the time for complicated answers.

"They're lying," said the fox-faced one. "Why are we wasting all this time?"

Thoughtfully, Guapo drained the tumbler and poured a little more, finishing the bottle. Another sip, another delicate smoothing of the silky mustache, and he turned to Vargas to address him directly for the first time, other than having told him to shut up. "And you, I suppose you're going to tell me you're not Vargas."

"No, *señor*, I'm Vargas, all right, that's completely correct. Alfredo Vargas, Captain Alfredo Vargas, at your service." His hand reached up to his braided captain's hat, but it was no longer there, having been lost when he fell into the river.

"That's good. I'm very glad you didn't lie, my friend. *You* should be even more glad you didn't lie. Now I want you to tell me exactly what happened to Scofield."

"Of course, with pleasure—"

"And I want you to tell me exactly—*exactly*—what your boat is doing on the Javaro River."

"Certainly, I have nothing to hide from you—"

Guapo held up his hand. "*You* know who I am, don't you? You've heard of El Guapo?" With a jerk, the knife was pulled from the table.

Vargas's eyes followed it as if magnetized. "Of course, *señor*. Everyone has heard of El Guapo."

"And have you heard of what happens to people who

tell falsehoods to El Guapo?" With the point of the huge knife he gently, almost tenderly, touched Vargas's left earlobe, then ran it around the entire ear. Gideon saw a single spot of blood where it nicked the top rim. Vargas sat through it as rigidly and motionlessly as was possible for a human to sit, although his Adam's apple, beyond his control, glugged up and down a couple of times.

"Yes, *señor*," he croaked through barely moving lips.

Guapo withdrew the knife, but his fingers remained around the handle. "Then go ahead. And don't be nervous."

Fox-face laughed nastily. "No, no, don't be nervous, what is there to be nervous about?"

And so the story came out. The first part, about how Scofield and Maggie had been thrown overboard, and Maggie, but not Scofield, had been rescued, was told pretty much as it had happened. Gideon was asked to verify the details once or twice and complied. Guapo didn't ask *why* Cisco would have wanted to kill Scofield. He seemed to accept Vargas's description of a "drug-crazed lunatic" on the loose (which was accurate enough), and neither Vargas nor Gideon volunteered anything more about it. The simpler, the better. "You are very lucky you are not Scofield," Fox-face said to Gideon with undisguised regret.

Gideon nodded his agreement. Any way you looked at it, it was the truth.

The rest of Vargas's story, which he told with an occasional shamefaced glance at Gideon, and with many self-serving asides ("He talked me into it against my better judgment," "Never have I done this before," "It was my intention to do it only this one time, for enough money to upgrade my poor ship," "I didn't realize, I never thought, that we would be in a region of interest to El Guapo; had I known, I would never have agreed, never!") was pretty much what Gideon was expecting by now. He had realized from the moment he had walked into the cantina and set eyes on Guapo and his men that John had been right: he, John, and Phil had gotten themselves into the middle of a drug-trafficking imbroglio. And Guapo's original certainty that the Indians had brought him Arden Scofield, and his incensed disappointment that they had not, had made it clear that Scofield was the major figure in it.

The substance involved was coca paste, Vargas said. He understood that there were sacks of it hidden within the coffee bags (he himself, of course, had never seen any of it, but had only taken Scofield's word for it; he himself had no part in the arrangements, but only provided the space and transportation) that were to be deposited at the warehouse—

"Was it you who had the warehouse burnt down?" Gideon asked Guapo.

"Hey—who told you to speak?" Fox-face said, but Guapo waved him down.

"Yes, sure, that was my man," Guapo said. "Do you think I didn't know what was happening? Do you think I would permit such a thing? Do you think anything happens in North Loreto Province about which I don't know?"

"I guess not," Gideon said, which seemed to please Guapo.

"How many coffee bags?" he asked Vargas.

"Forty or fifty, I believe."

"Forty-eight," said Guapo. "And how much paste?"

"About . . . about a hundred kilos, I think."

"A hundred and fifty," Guapo said, his voice hardening. "Be careful, my friend." He sat back, slowly rotating the knife in his left hand, its point gently rotating against his right forefinger. "And for whom was it destined?"

"Destined? I—"

"Think before you answer. Tell the truth when I ask you a question, and you may yet get out of this with your life, and maybe even with all your appendages."

Vargas fished in his pocket for his glasses and put them on, as if they might help him think more clearly. "Guapo . . . *señor* . . . I honestly don't know the answer to that question, I didn't *want* to know, I had no wish to be—"

"It was destined for Eduardo Veloso of the Cali cartel, whose carriers were to pick it up tomorrow night," Guapo said, and Gideon began to think that there really wasn't much going on, at least in this particular aspect of the regional commerce, that got by El Guapo. "And how is it hidden? Is there some in all the coffee sacks?"

"It's in plastic bags—so I was told by the professor—not *him*"— a gesture at Gideon—"the other professor—in several of the sacks, fifteen or twenty of them, I think—"

"Thirty," said Guapo warningly.

"Yes, thirty, that was it, that was it!" Vargas gibbered, the perspiration actually dripping off him onto the floor so that there was a little puddle on each side of his chair. Was he lying because he yet hoped to siphon off some of the paste for his own profit? Or was lying simply his instinctive reaction to stress? "Yes, thirty, that's right, now I remember, of course. It's thirty, all right. Now, *señor*, the honest truth is I do not know which bags it's in, I was never told—"

"That's all right, Vargas. It doesn't matter."

Vargas licked his lips. "*Señor*, you are only too welcome to come and take it, to take it all. I regret extremely that I allowed myself to be used in this way, that I caused offense to you. I only want to go home and forget I was ever so stupid. It would be an act of kindness to me to take it away. Please—"

"What, and have the Cali people find out I have their paste? No thank you. I have no interest in taking any of it from you at all."

If wheels turning in one's mind made a sound, the room would have been filled with grindings and squeakings from Vargas's quick brain. His eyes darted right, then left, then right, as he assessed the rapidly changing situation. Guapo had practically said he would be allowed to live. Was he going to get to keep the paste—*all* of the paste—as well? Surely it was worth many thousands—hundreds of thousands—of *soles*. It would change his life, he could go away from Iquitos, leave all this behind him, start fresh in the south with a fishing franchise, down by Pucusana—

Guapo could read Vargas's thoughts as readily as

Gideon could, and he laughed; a voiceless rumble that changed his expression not at all. "You are not going to keep any of it either, Vargas."

Vargas blinked. "Ah . . . no?"

"No. You are going to throw it overboard. Into the river."

"Into the—? But, sir, as I told you, I do not know which bags it's in."

"That doesn't matter because you are going to throw *all* the coffee bags into the river. My Indian friends will take you back and will watch you do it. And my sincere advice is not to try and trick them. And never, never let me hear of you in this province again. Do you understand?"

"I understand, Guapo, but *all* the coffee? I have no insurance, I will have to pay for it myself—"

"Are you arguing with me? Negotiating with me, goddamn you? You should be thanking me for not burning your lousy boat and you with it," Guapo said, looking as if it was still a distinct possibility.

"No, no, Guapo, of course not, Guapo," Vargas mumbled. "Whatever you say. Thank you for your understanding. I can promise you—"

"And in case you're wondering whether the Arimaguas have a number for 'forty-eight' (which was exactly what Gideon was wondering), I should tell you that they will have a bag with forty-eight pebbles in it. Each time a coffee sack goes in the river, a pebble is removed from the bag. When you have finished, you'd better hope that there are no pebbles left in the bag."

"Of course, Guapo," Vargas said glumly.

"And you," Guapo said, turning to Gideon. "Now what are we to do with you?"

"I have some good ideas," said a grinning Fox-face. The burning cigarette stuck to his lower lip couldn't have been more than a half inch long.

"No, no, an American professor," Guapo said, "I don't think we want that kind of trouble. I'll tell you what, Professor. You give me those pretty American dollars you have in that wallet of yours—you can keep the lousy *soles*—and I will send you back to the ship with your good friend the captain to go on with your life. You'll have a good story to tell. What do you say?"

Gideon looked at Guapo, at the big knife, at the leering Fox-face, at the other armed men, and sighed.

"Sounds fair to me," he said.

EIGHTEEN

SHOWERED, changed, his cuts and bug bites attended to, Gideon felt like a human being again. The hike back to the ship hadn't been as bad as the one from it (the fire-ant mound was given plenty of room this time), and a glorious pint of *carambola* juice—looking like orange juice but tasting like cool, thinned-down papaya juice—that he had poured down his throat had brought him back to life. They had been gone a mere three hours, he was shocked to learn. It had seemed like ten.

He had told his story to a fascinated, half-incredulous John and Phil and answered their hundred questions. Now they were lounging at the grassy edge of the thirty-foot bank overlooking the *Adelita*, having just watched a gray-faced Vargas, who looked like death on two legs, supervise the dumping of four-dozen sixty-kilo sacks of coffee—and presumably a fortune in coca-paste balls—into the Javaro River. The other passengers had watched from the deck, subdued, shocked—and no doubt thrilled—with the knowledge that Arden Scofield had been up to his eyeballs in drug-trafficking. The Arimaguas had disappeared back into the jungle, leaving their forty-eight pebbles behind in six neat rows, and the three-man crew that had dumped the sacks—Chato, Porge, and the cook, Meneo—were sitting on some logs along the muddy riverside a few yards downstream, taking a cigarillo break.

"I knew that Scofield was a blowhard," John was saying, "but a drug-trafficker?" He shook his head. "What a piece of crap. What did I tell you, Doc? Did I say it was all about drugs, or didn't I?"

"That you did," Gideon said. "You were right, and I was wrong."

John's hands flew up. "Phil, did he just say what I think he said? Write it down, nobody's gonna believe it!"

They sat companionably for a little longer and then Phil said: "Oh, there were some developments while you and Vargas were on your little junket."

"Oh?"

"The guy that was shot with the nail gun? We found out who he was."

Gideon sat up. "You did? Who?"

"Well, not exactly who," said John. "We know what he was doing here, and why he got shot. And who shot him." A ghost of a smile. " 'Nailed him,' I guess we should say."

Phil took up the narrative from there. Two Indians, who said they were members of a peaceable, fairly well-assimilated Yagua settlement a day's canoe journey upstream, had appeared at the warehouse site not long before to collect what they said were their belongings—hammocks, cups and utensils, a few articles of clothing—from the platform house near the warehouse. Phil had gone to chat with them. They were frightened and shy and in a hurry to leave again, but Phil had wormed a surprising amount of information out of them with the aid of a couple of bottles of Inca Kola, a little rum, and two cigars. They had been the property's caretakers and had been engaged for the past week in the construction work necessary to strengthen and enlarge the warehouse.

"Who were they working for?" Gideon asked. "Who was paying them?"

"I didn't think to ask," Phil said, and then after a moment, with some irritation: "Why would I ask that? Jeez. Anyway, they told me they'd been fishing for dorado from the bank about five o'clock yesterday afternoon when they smelled smoke. And when they climbed back up to the warehouse, they found this guy in the doorway, right in the act of setting a match to a pile of newspapers and scrap wood. A couple of other piles were already burning inside, on the wooden floor."

"Ah, that would have been Guapo's man," Gideon said. "One of the Arimaguas, I bet. He was an Indian, right?"

"I have no idea."

"You didn't ask what he looked like?"

"No."

"You're kidding me. You don't know if he had a bone in his nose, or was wearing a loincloth, or had shoes, or, or—"

Phil sighed and looked at John. "What do you think, does he really want to hear the rest of this or not?"

"Sorry," Gideon said. "I'll be quiet."

They had yelled at the man, who had turned, screamed something unintelligible back at them, and begun to fling burning pieces of wood at them. One of them—they wouldn't say which—had threatened him with the nail gun, meaning to scare him off, but when a flaming chunk of plywood hit him in the shoulder the gun had gone off, and the man had been shot through the head and very, very obviously killed. Terrified, they had fled into the jungle. Today, they had come back for their things, unaware that the *Adelita* was moored below.

"I scared them half to death by showing up, apparently out of nowhere," Phil said, "but I got them to open up with my celebrated friendly, open, and unthreatening manner."

"And Inca Kolas spiked with rum," Gideon said. "Am I permitted to ask a question yet?"

Phil responded with a gracious wave. "Speak."

"Did you happen to inquire as to what happened to the body?"

"As a matter of fact, I did," Phil said. "They said he staggered away, fell over the edge into the river, and disappeared."

"No, that part never happened. When your brain is blown apart, you don't do any staggering. You drop where you are."

"Yeah, you already told us that. So my guess is they just picked him up and dumped him in the river themselves. Either way—"

"—he's in the river," said John.

Any further thoughts were interrupted by an excited clamor from the crew members on their break down below at the riverfront. They were jabbering in pidgin Spanish, pointing down into the water, and calling, apparently, to Gideon. He was able to understand a few words: *"¡Oiga, esqueletero! ¡Aquí le tengo unos huesos!"* Hey, skeleton man, I have some bones for you!

He jumped up. "They've found some bones."

"More bones?" John said, getting up too. "What is it about you, Doc? Do you bring this on yourself?"

"That's what Julie thinks," Gideon said, laughing, as they made their way down the bank. "And remember your weird friend Hedwig, in Hawaii? She thinks it's because of my aura."

The three Indians were on a narrow, muddy, log-littered beach, and one of them, in the act of tossing a cigarillo into the water, had spotted what he was sure was a human skull, caught by an eddy and lodged in a pool formed by a tangle of downed tree branches.

"It's *him*!" Phil exclaimed the moment he saw it, gazing placidly back up at him from empty eye sockets, through twelve inches of brownish water. "The nail-gun guy."

"Looks like it," Gideon said. It was a human skull, all right. There was the expected round hole in the forehead, just right of center—no radiating or spiral cracks, just a clean hole—and a jagged-edged empty space where the back of the head should have been. No mandible was visible. "Should be easy enough to confirm, though."

He leaned down, and grasping a branch for support, dipped into the water with his other hand and brought up the broken skull. The Indians, whom he half expected to quietly back away and leave, sat down and watched avidly. The perforated disk of bone from the warehouse door was still in his fanny pack. He took it out, wrinkling his nose a little—the fanny pack would have to go; it was getting nasty in there, what with the heat and humidity making the still-fresh bone fragment reek—and fitted it to the circular hole in the skull, which had to be done from the inside because the beveling of both the hole and the disk made it impossible to do from the front. This was no problem, however, what with the fist-sized hole in the back of the skull. He adjusted the disk until he had its irregularities matched to those of the hole and gently pressed it in. It slipped in with a solid little click, and held. A perfect fit.

"Consider it confirmed," he said. For a while he held the skull up to his face, turning it this way and that. "Amazing," he murmured.

"What is?" John asked, after it became clear that further elucidation wasn't on its way.

"Well, look at it," Gideon said. "This guy was killed yesterday afternoon, not even twenty-four hours ago, and *look* at this thing! It's perfectly clean . . . okay, a little crud clinging to the inside of the brain case and the nasal aperture, and in the orbits, and so on—back of the palate, auditory meatuses, hard-to-reach places—but no muscles, no ligaments, and just a few shreds of tendon. In the lab, it'd take a colony of Dermestid beetles weeks to get it this clean."

"Piranhas?" said John.

"*Sí, piranhas,*" the three crewmen agreed in sober unison.

Gideon nodded. "I really didn't believe they were as fast as this, though. And all these tiny scratches over every square millimeter of it . . . as if it's been . . . well, scoured with a pad of heavy-duty steel wool." He shook his head.

"Amazing," he said again. "If you look closely, you can see that most of the scratches are really nicks, kind of triangular in cross section."

"Little . . . tiny . . . teeth," John said.

"Little tiny *pointy* teeth," Gideon amended.

"Gideon, did I just hear you say you used beetles to clean your skeletons?" Phil asked.

"Uh-huh," he said abstractedly. "Dermestids. You get them from biological supply houses. There's nothing like them for corpses. They love to eat dead flesh."

"Big deal, so do I," John said.

"Mmm," said Gideon. He had sat down on a log with the skull and was slowly turning it in his hands again, studying it from various angles, running his fingers over eminences and concavities, gently inserting them into the nasal aperture, stroking the teeth.

"I always thought you boiled the bodies or used some kind of caustic or something. You just put them in a tank with a bunch of *beetles*?" Phil persisted. He was fascinated with the idea. "Gideon? Are you there? I think we've lost him again," he said to John.

"He'll be back," John said. "You just have to be patient." They seated themselves on a log to await his return.

It took him another minute to surface again. "Well," he murmured, "it's a male, all right; not much doubt about that. The rugged muscle-attachment sites, and these rounded orbital margins, and the bilobate mental eminences—"

"That means he's got a square chin," John said for Phil's benefit. Over the years of his association with Gideon, he had picked up the occasional bit of forensic jargon. "That's just the way these people talk, you see. It's to make sure no one else can understand them."

"I know, I'm very familiar with the language myself."

"—all those things yell 'male.'" Gideon continued, more or less talking to himself. "And he's a grown man, in his thirties at least, and probably not more than, oh, fifty or so. All we have to go on there are the cranial and palatine sutures. None of them are still anywhere near open, but none of them have been obliterated yet either, inside or out. Now, as to race . . ."

Another period of intense, silent examination and palpation before he looked up again.

"Well, I'm pretty sure he's not an Indian, at any rate. The nasal aperture is too narrow, the nasal sill is too sharp, there's no prognathism to speak of, the malars aren't very prominent at all; if anything, they're reduced. And you can see that the interorbital projection is pretty high . . ."

"True, true," said John, as if he still knew what Gideon was talking about.

". . . and the palatine suture . . . well, see? It's really jagged, not at all straight, and the mastoid processes"—he fingered the rough, cone-shaped eminences to which the large muscles of the neck attached—"see how narrow they are? Almost pointed, not stubby. And no sign of shovel-shaping on the incisors. No, there's nothing about this guy that makes me think 'Native American.' And definitely not one of the local Indians. He's way too big."

"What then?" Phil asked.

"White, I'd say. Everything points to Caucasian."

He had the skull upside down on his lap, so that the palate and the teeth were uppermost. John and Phil leaned forward to see. So did the crewmen, from a distance.

"Guy could use a dentist," John said. "It hurts just to look at those teeth."

"Most of them, yes. They're crumbly and discolored and full of caries, and two of them are missing and, ugh, here's an abscess well underway. He's let his teeth go for years, maybe decades. The poor guy must have been in some pain, and if he'd lived, it was going to get a lot worse. But it's these two that are really interesting." With his ballpoint pen, he tapped the two right bicuspids.

"Oh, yeah, look at that," said Phil. "Fillings. He's had a little dental work done."

"But not just any dental work," Gideon said, "excellent, *expensive* dental work. This is gold, gold foil, and beautifully applied. You don't see this type of work anymore. It sure as hell isn't the kind of work you *ever* would have seen down here."

"So the guy's not from around here, that's what you're saying?" Phil said.

"Well, yes, but it suggests a little more than that. When you find this kind of dentistry on a down-and-outer, a guy whose teeth haven't seen a dentist in twenty years, it usually tells you one of two things. Either he's somebody who once had money, but who's seen a change in fortune, or else, more likely—"

"Or else," John said, "he spent some time in prison, where they took better care of his teeth than he could get for himself on the outside."

Gideon nodded. "Correct."

"Not too surprising, considering what he was doing when he got himself killed," said John.

"Hey, am I wrong?" Phil asked. He was staring at the shallow, eddying pool from which the skull had come. "Or are there some more bones down there? There, see? Caught in the branches, right on the bottom, a couple of yards—"

"You're right!" Gideon said. "Vertebrae. Human too. And that's the mandible under there!" He slapped the side of his head. "How could I not have looked! There might be more. Let's fan out a little along the shore. Phil, could you ask these guys to do the same? I bet there is more. Something like the pelvis tends to get caught because it's so big and irregular . . . I'd really like to see the pelvis. . . ."

But there wasn't anything else. Only the mandible—the lower jaw—and a collection of vertebrae. Seven of them to be exact: all seven cervical vertebrae, the ones closest to the skull, the vertebrae of the neck. Somehow or other, the poor guy's head and neck had gotten lodged there in that niche. The piranha had stripped them, and the bones had remained behind, almost as clean as the specimens you'd get from a supply house. Where the rest of what was left of him was at this point was anybody's guess.

When they had fished them all from the water and laid them on a piece of plywood that one of the crew had brought from the construction area to keep them out of the mud, Gideon started with the mandible as the most likely one to provide more information, but there wasn't much. The first thing was to fit it to the skull to make sure that they were really from the same person, and this was quickly verified. The few healthy teeth abutted perfectly and the two mandibular condyles fitted neatly into the gle-noid fossae of the temporal bone, or as neatly as was al-lowed by the absence of the cushioning cartilage that would have been there in the living person. Beyond that, it pretty much confirmed his assessment of race and sex, and that was it. No interesting anomalies, no visible injuries, new or old. No additional clues to the living man.

On his knees in the muddy soil, he began to arrange the vertebrae in their top-to-bottom anatomical order, from C-1 to C-7, on the plywood sheet. The first two and the last one were easy, of course. C-1, the atlas, was like no other vertebra in the spinal column, essentially a simple ring— no spinous process, no vertebral body—a sort of collar on which the skull rested. C-2, the axis, had the smooth up-ward column of the odontoid process, essentially a pivot on which the atlas, carrying the skull, rotated, which was how one is able to freely turn one's head. And C-7 was big-ger than the others, so that was simple too. The middle four were a bit harder to differentiate, and Gideon settled down to comparing them two by two.

"Can I ask you a dumb question?" said Phil. "What are you doing all this for?"

Gideon continued working. "Well, I'm trying to learn a little more—ah, this is C-3, and this is C-4—about who this guy was—that is, what he was like."

"Yeah, but what difference does it make what he was like? I mean, who cares? There's no way to actually iden-tify him, is there?"

"Well, no, not by me—"

"He can't help himself," John explained. "He never met a skeleton he didn't want to know better. You ought to know that by now."

Gideon smiled. "You never know what you're going to find," he said as he figured out the final two and laid all seven in a row. "But there's always something interesting."

He leaned forward to study them, propping his hands on the plywood. Sweat dripped onto the board from the tip of his nose. Minutes passed. The crew members lost interest and wandered a few yards upstream to sit on a nest of fallen trunks, light more cigarillos, and chat among themselves. Phil lost interest and went to join them, but John sat down on a log and remained to watch. He had seen Gideon pull too many surprising and instructive rabbits out of the hat to go wandering off.

"Ah, there *is* something interesting," Gideon said after a while, then quickly lapsed back into silence, picking up the vertebrae one by one, peering at them, poking at them, turning them round and round. John, well accustomed to this, waited patiently, twiddling—literally twiddling—his thumbs.

What had caught Gideon's attention were the two lowest vertebrae, C-6 and C-7. Both had suffered some pretty serious injury to their vertebral bodies—the thick cylinders of bone that stacked one upon the other (separated only by the soft, pulpy, and so often troublesome intervertebral discs) to form and give strength to the vertebral column. Both bodies had a collapsed, caved-in look, especially at the front. He showed them to John, comparing them to the healthy, solid look of the others.

"Whoa," John said, getting down on his knees in the mud beside Gideon to have a closer look and to handle them. "They look . . . it's like someone just grabbed them with a pair of pliers and squeezed the hell out of them."

"That's not a bad metaphor, actually, but what did the squeezing were the vertebrae above and below them. These are compression fractures, John. They're not broken in the usual sense of a fracture—that is, they're not broken, as in 'broken into pieces'—they're squashed. The pressure on them has compressed the cancellous bone inside."

John was holding the C-7, running his fingers over the surface. "So what would do something like this?"

"Well, a lot of the time they're associated with osteoporosis, where the bone is already thin and weak, and maybe the person falls and lands square on his rear end, and that jams the vertebrae up against each other. Sometimes the person doesn't even know there's been a fracture."

"You mean it doesn't hurt?"

"Oh yeah, it hurts all right. But it's not like when you actually break a leg, or an arm, or a rib—*snap*—when that happens you *know* it the minute it happens. But something like this—he might just think he's got a chronic headache or a pain in the neck from a strain, or a sprain, or something like that. People will go months before they finally see a doctor."

John fingered the crushed part and grimaced. "Man, I think I'd know it."

"But what's interesting about these particular bones is that this guy wasn't osteoporotic. Except for these two vertebrae, everything else that's left is fine. That's one thing that's odd about it. The other thing is . . . mmm . . ."

"The other thing is . . . ?" John prompted patiently.

"That you don't see this kind of thing in the neck. It usually occurs down in the lower thoracic or lumbar vertebrae, right in that S-curve in our backs, because that's where the pressure on your spine is concentrated—one of the unfortunate outcomes of our walking around on two legs instead of a more sensible, balanced four. When you see it in the cervical segment, it's usually something like a motorcycle accident, or an automobile crash where the person's head is driven up against the frame of the windshield, say. But in something like that, you'd expect some associated trauma, whereas in this case the other bones don't show any. The skull's fine—other than that hole, of course—the mandible's okay, and none of the other five vertebrae are damaged. In fact, the only times I can remember coming across cases like this one were . . . I'll be damned. Is it possible . . . ? I bet . . ." He trailed off in mid-sentence and wandered abstractedly upstream to where Phil and the crew members were yakking away like lifelong buddies.

"Were *what*?" John yelled after him. "Is *what* possible? Damn it, I wish you wouldn't—" With a sigh and a shake of his head, he followed after him.

Gideon spoke in Spanish. "Chato, the other day, the first day of the cruise, when we were all meeting each other, you were there, standing on the side."

"Yes," Chato said warily.

"And when Cisco got introduced as the White Shaman, you laughed and called him something else."

"I mean nothing bad, *señor*, I only joke with my friends, I very—"

"No, I realize that. I just need to know what you called him."

Chato licked his lips and looked to his pals for help, but they gaped blankly back at him.

"You're not in any trouble, my friend; there's nothing to worry about. I didn't mean to frighten you."

"I called him . . . everybody calls him . . . the White Milkman."

"Ah, that's what I thought," Gideon said with satisfaction. "And why was he called the White Milkman?"

"What does this have to do with the price of tea in China?" Gideon heard Phil ask John.

Chato's explanation, a torrent of overexcited pidgin Spanish-English, was too much for Gideon, and he had to ask Phil to translate. Phil listened, nodding, then explained:

Cisco had been labeled the White Milkman by many of the locals in Iquitos in sarcastic reaction to his self-aggrandizing references to himself as the White Shaman. Cisco's knowledge of authentic shamanism, it seemed, was held in low repute by those who—

"Fine, fine, but why do they call him a *milkman*, specifically?"

"Because that's what he is. Well, not the kind who delivers milk—there's no such animal in Iquitos, because apparently nobody drinks it—but there's this little dairy farm nearby that makes cheese, the one and only Amazonian dairy farm they ever heard of, and sometimes he worked there, taking care of the cows, milking them, feeding them—"

"What do they mean, 'little'? How big is 'little'? How many cows?"

"Gideon, what the hell does this have to do with anything?"

"Just ask them, Phil."

Phil shrugged and asked. "Maybe a dozen, they say. Maybe less. Little." Another shrug. "Which proves?"

"Which suggests that it wasn't big enough to make milking machines worthwhile. The cows would have been milked by hand, the old-fashioned way."

"Which proves?" This time it was John.

"Plenty. In fact, that about settles it." He went back to where the bones lay, picked up the skull, and gazed with extreme attentiveness into the face that was no longer there.

"'Alas, poor Yorick. I knew him, Horatio,'" Phil intoned as the crewmen, increasingly uneasy, quietly went back to the ship.

With a half smile, Gideon slowly looked up. "I did know him, Phil. So did you two."

Phil and John stared mutely at him.

"It's Cisco," he said quietly.

NINETEEN

THE crushed cervical vertebrae, he explained, were part of a syndrome known to forensic anthropologists as "milker's neck."

When a cow was milked by hand, the milker sat on a low stool beside it and leaned his head at a somewhat awkward angle against the animal's flank while he reached underneath to do the milking. So far, no problem. But a cow does not stand perfectly still while being milked. It shuffles its feet. It shifts its weight. And when it shifts its considerable mass sideways against the milker, he is more or less pinned between the cow and the stool . . . with his neck sharply bent—that is, flexed. When this happens, the vertebral column can "give" at its most stressed point, the junction of neck and torso, where the flexion occurs. In other words, the already flexed neck is hyperflexed, and pressure is focused on the lowest two cervical vertebrae, C-6 and C-7. The result—by no means always, but often enough— is a crushing of their cervical bodies.

"Like these," he finished, holding the two vertebrae up

again for their inspection. "Remember Cisco's headaches? And the way he held his head, kind of on the side? Well, you're looking at the reason."

John looked at them with a puzzled frown. "Yeah, sure, well, that's all great stuff, Doc, but how could it be Cisco? It *can't* be. This guy here was killed in the middle of setting the fire. That would have been yesterday afternoon some time. Cisco was still on the *boat* yesterday afternoon. He didn't jump off till almost two this morning."

"Did he? Maggie wasn't that positive it was him. And I'd say that what we've got here pretty strongly suggests it wasn't."

"Well, if it wasn't Cisco, who was it?" Phil asked. "I mean, whoever did it jumped ship, right? So he should be missing. But who's missing? Everybody's still there." He paused, his eyebrows lifted. "Well, everybody but Scofield, of course."

This thought occupied them for a few seconds of concentrated reflection, but none of them could find a way of making sense of it.

"Maybe it was another crewman," Phil suggested. "We need to check with Vargas and find out if one of them is gone. Let's get back to the boat."

But Gideon was now in full professional throttle, more interested in dead bones than in live conundrums. "Whoever it was then, *this* is Cisco now, and the interesting question is—"

"Are we really that sure?" Phil asked. "Okay, I buy the milker's neck thing, that's interesting, but couldn't there be other milkmen?"

"Phil's right," John said. "Even if that's the only dairy anywhere around here—which we don't know for a fact—there must have been other people doing the milking too, since Cisco only worked there once in a while. You have to milk cows every day, you can't just do it when you feel like it."

"And what's the likelihood of running into two cow-milkers on this trip?" Gideon said. "But forget about the milker's neck thing for a minute." He bent to put down the vertebrae and pick up the skull. "What about this gold-foil work? How do you explain that? With Cisco, it's easy. He would have lived in the Boston area when he was at Harvard thirty years ago. Plenty of good dentists—and in the seventies gold foils would still have been popular. How many other Amazonian dairy workers would have this kind of work in their mouths?"

"Okay, that part of it makes sense," Phil said. "We're not about to argue forensics with you. But the timing doesn't. There's no way Cisco would have been able to get here in time to set the fire."

"Well, let's think about that," Gideon said. "Tell me, when was the last time anybody saw him for sure?"

"That would have been yesterday afternoon, as far as I know," John answered after a moment's thought. "Remember? He called off the trek and went back to his cabin. And he didn't show up for dinner."

"And he wasn't up on the roof later on," Phil added. "I remember, Tim looked kind of let down because his buddy didn't show up. He was wondering if anybody knew where he was. Nobody did."

"Right. So if no one saw him all that time, nobody can say for sure he *was* in his cabin—or even still on the boat. How do we know he didn't just take off into the jungle while we were still moored? That would have been well before the fire."

"And do what?" asked Phil. "Shoot right up here and get himself killed?"

"Why not?"

"Nah, Doc, you're not thinking," John said. "That hike in the jungle broiled your brains a little. Now look: when Cisco called off yesterday's trek and disappeared on us, it was maybe three in the afternoon, right?"

"Right."

"And the fire here at the warehouse happened around five o'clock, two hours later."

"Right."

"And the *Adelita* got going again yesterday at what time?"

"Just after dinner, a little after six," Gideon said. "We were still having coffee."

"Okay. And we didn't get here till around five this morning, so it took us eleven hours to make it, and we were doing six or seven knots all the way—well, except for an hour or two when we were looking for Scofield, so say the distance had to be a minimum of fifty miles, am I right?"

"Yeah . . ." *Oh, jeez*, he thought as he finally, belatedly grasped the point that Phil and John were making. Maybe his brains *had* been a little scrambled. They were absolutely right; how could it be Cisco? Whatever the bones said, it was impossible. He would have had to be in two places at the same time.

"I see—" he began, but stopped himself before the words were out of his mouth. John didn't very often get to win a Socratic argument with him, and Gideon didn't want to deprive him of the experience.

"So," declared John exultantly, "you want to tell me how Cisco could beat the boat here? How he could cover fifty miles in *two* hours? There aren't any roads out there. What'd he do, run?"

Frowning, honestly mystified, Gideon shook his head. "You're right, it doesn't compute, does it? And yet I can't make myself believe . . . I mean the odds against—" His face lit up. "Wait a minute. Maybe, just maybe, it does compute. Maybe he did beat the *Adelita* here!"

Now it was their turn to look confused. " 'Splain yourself, Lucy,' " Phil said.

"Come on back to the boat," Gideon said. "We need to check something out."

THEY carried the bones back to the *Adelita* on the plywood square, left them on the bed in Gideon's cabin, and went looking for Vargas. They found him in the wheelhouse with Chato, apparently preparing to get underway again for Leticia, but before they opened the door he slipped somewhat furtively out to meet them, closing the door behind him. The trip had begun a mere five days ago, but the captain looked as if he'd aged twenty years.

"Professor, you told them"—he indicated John and Phil—"what happened?"

"Yes, I did."

"Everything?"

"Yes."

His face fell. "Did you . . . did you told anyone else?" He was still shaky, and so was his English.

All three shook their heads no.

"I got a big favor to ask." He chewed on his lip and gazed beseechingly at them. "I never done nothing like this before. I never going to do it again, I swear! Was all Dr. Scofield. Please, don't tell no one else."

"Yeah, but didn't the others already see you throwing the coffee overboard?" Phil asked.

"Yes, sure, and I explained them everything."

Not quite everything, it turned out. He had faithfully given them the essential details of all that had happened— the "rocks" hidden in the coffee bags, the runners who were to pick it up at the warehouse, the forced meeting with Guapo, the reason the bags were being chucked in the river, and so forth. All he had omitted was the little fact that he had known anything about it before being informed by Guapo (to Vargas's horror and amazement) that the *Adelita* was carrying coca paste. It had all been Scofield's doing, accomplished without Vargas's knowledge. Vargas was merely an innocent, victimized by a cunning criminal.

"And they believed that?" asked John.

Vargas shrugged pitifully. "I hope." He awaited their response as if his life was in their hands, which wasn't that much of an exaggeration. "I don't want to go to jail!" he blurted.

"Up to you, John," Gideon said, and Phil signaled his agreement with a nod.

Gideon was willing to believe Vargas when he said that this was his first experience with drug transporting and that he'd been scared enough by Guapo never to do it again. His inclination was to go along with him, to let the poor guy put it all behind him, and he knew that Phil, being Phil, would feel the same way, only more strongly. But John was the arbiter in such matters, and Gideon honestly didn't know what he would do. He could be unbending when it came to breaking the law, especially concerning drug-trafficking, but he was also a genuinely nice guy with a lot of sympathy for people in trouble.

"I'll take everything into consideration, Captain," he said magisterially. "For the moment we'll keep it to ourselves. In the long run, we'll have to see."

Vargas's eyes closed in relief. Obviously, he took it (as did Gideon) as meaning that he was off the hook.

"But I'll tell you this: if I ever hear your name in connection with the drug trade again—even a *suspicion* of connection—and I have my contacts—I will get in touch with the Peruvian authorities instantly. You understand?"

Vargas's eyes misted. "God bless you, Juan." He looked as if he might kiss John's hand if given the chance. "God bless you all."

"There was something we wanted to ask you," Gideon said, embarrassed. "Do you have a chart of the river that we could look at?"

"A chart? You mean, a nautical chart? Of the Rio Javaro? There isn't no such thing. All there is is a map."

"That'll do fine."

"Come, is inside."

A narrow, four-foot-long strip map that followed the snakelike river, from where it left the Amazon to where it rejoined it at Leticia, had been tacked to the back wall of the wheelhouse. It had been folded and unfolded so many times that it was coming apart at the creases despite several yellowing layers of transparent tape laid along them.

"Can you show us where it was that we stopped yesterday afternoon?"

"Mmm . . ." Calculating, Vargas moved his finger in little circles and brought it down on a spot. "Here."

Gideon laid his right forefinger on it and left it there. "And the warehouse, where was that?"

A painful little wince wrinkled Vargas's forehead at the hated word, but he pointed to another spot. "Here. San José de Chiquitos."

Gideon realized he had been holding his breath. Now he exhaled with satisfaction. *There. He'd been right.* He laid his left forefinger down on the spot and smiled. "See?"

"Wow," said John.

"Whoa," said Phil.

IT was so obvious that no explanation was necessary. Gideon's forefingers were only an inch apart, approximately two miles. Because the Javaro was a giant series of undulating, incurving loops, it doubled back on itself in places, creating slender necks of land that were only two or three miles wide. The warehouse and the place they had stopped yesterday—the place where Cisco had last been seen—were on either side of one of these necks, directly opposite each other. Thus, while the *Adelita* had to negotiate a wide, fifty- or sixty-mile arc to get from one to the other, Cisco had only to cross a two-mile strip of land. Sweltering, brutal, unforgiving jungle land, to be sure, but Cisco was no stranger to that. Two hours would have given him ample time to reach the warehouse and start the fire. And get himself punctured by a nail gun in the doing.

The question was: Why? Guapo had said that "my man" had started the fire. But surely Cisco—poor crack-brained, strung-out Cisco—couldn't have been tied in with El Guapo?

"Ah, but he could, he could!" Vargas cried. "He used to run errands for some of those people—dirty little jobs they didn't want to do for themselves." Now that the worst was presumably over, his easy command of English was back. "Sure, they probably paid him a few *soles* to set it. That's the answer."

A few minutes' further discussion laid out a probable scenario: Guapo or his representative had gotten in touch with Cisco when he'd learned that Cisco would be on the *Adelita*—or possibly Cisco had gotten in touch with Guapo to see if there was any little paid service he could perform. And Guapo had taken him up on it. The plan, and it was a good one, seemed evident now. When they stopped for their trek the previous day—and, tellingly, it was Cisco who'd chosen the place to moor—Cisco would call off the hike to the shaman's village and say he was going back to the boat. Instead, he would head on foot for the warehouse and set it afire. When the *Adelita* showed up the next morning and the passengers got off to look around, he would get back on the boat when they did. No one would be likely to notice that he hadn't gotten *off* there. Why would they?

The presence of the two caretakers that had so fouled things up had probably been a surprise to both Cisco and Guapo. The warehouse, after all, had been empty at the time, and would be empty until the *Adelita* unloaded its cargo. Why guard it before then? Possibly it had been empty for weeks. Guapo, despite his self-professed knowledge of everything that went on in North Loreto Province, might well have been uninformed that the two men had arrived early to get started on the construction work.

And so Cisco—Frank Molina, brilliant Harvard graduate student, promising ethnobotanist—who had almost died from a poisoned blowgun dart thirty years before, had ended up in one of the world's most remote rivers, dead from an even more bizarre weapon, his skull pierced by a two-inch roofing nail. Food for the fishes.

Little tiny teeth.

THAT left one critical question unanswered. If Cisco had been killed at San José de Chiquitos the previous afternoon, who was it that attacked Maggie on the boat that night?

TWENTY

IT had to be Scofield, that was the consensus.

"It *has* to be Dr. Scofield," Tim said in the same incredulous tone that Duayne had just said it, and before him, Mel.

"It also explains why nobody heard any more than two
splashes," Mel added. "That's all there were. Arden never
got thrown overboard by Cisco at all. How could he? Cisco
wasn't even there. First you went in, Maggie—splash
one—and then Arden jumped in after you. Splash two. End
of splashes. It all adds up."

They were halfway through dinner, a fruit salad followed
by a gluey mix of mashed beans, chicken, and rice that a
sprightly, much-rejuvenated Vargas told them was *tacu
tacu*, Peru's national stew (everything they had seemed to
be Peru's national something), and they had spent the last
twenty minutes working their way toward this conclusion.

Except for Maggie. She had eaten only a few forkfuls of
salad and had not gone back to the buffet table for the stew,
and she just kept shaking her head, refusing to accept it. "It

LITTLE TINY TEETH   237

couldn't be. No. Not Arden. Why in God's name would he want to kill me?"

But there simply weren't any other possibilities, Duayne pointed out to her for the second or third time. Vargas had already told them that all the crew members were still aboard, which left only Cisco and Scofield unaccounted for. Cisco's few remaining bones now reposed in a black plastic garbage bag in the hold—actually, two layered garbage bags, inasmuch as a developing, unwelcome odor had by now become apparent. Which left only Scofield.

"Now, wait a minute," Maggie said. "Why couldn't it have been one of the crew? Maybe when we turned the ship around to go looking for Arden, he got back on board. Why isn't that possible?"

"Climbed back aboard a moving ship?" John asked. "In the dark?"

"He could have had help from the others, couldn't he? You pulled *me* up."

"The ship was stopped. It never stopped when we went back looking for Scofield."

Maggie shook her head impatiently. "Well, I can't explain everything that happened. All I know for sure is—"

"Maggie, how tall was the man who attacked you?" Gideon asked.

"How tall? I have no idea. I told you, it was all so quick, so shocking—"

"Was he taller than you?"

"I don't know."

"Was he *as* tall as you?"

"I—" She saw where he was leading. "You're right, Gideon, they're all Indians, aren't they? Smaller than I am. I would have noticed if he was only five-three or five-four. And he wasn't."

"Well, then—"

"Well, then, it wasn't one of the crew," she said stubbornly. "That hardly proves it was Arden." She spread her hands, a gesture of frustration. "Okay, he's a drug-runner.

That's crazy enough, but I accept it. But to say that he's a . . . a murderer, that he tried to kill me . . . and besides, I haven't heard anybody come up with a *why*—or with what he was doing out on the deck talking to himself in a . . . in a nightshirt or something, or what the scuffling I heard was, or—"

"I looked in Arden's room afterward," John said. "Nothing was disturbed. If you heard scuffling, it came from someplace else."

"No, I'm quite positive—"

"*Are* you positive? You said you were sleeping. Are you sure you didn't dream it?"

"Well . . . all right, I grant you, that could be, it might have been a dream. Let's put aside the scuffling, then. But to suggest that it was Arden that . . ." She folded her arms. "No, I'm sorry."

"Maggie," Mel said thoughtfully, "what did he smell like? The man who threw you overboard."

The question, like most of the others, seemed to annoy her. "What did he *smell* like? You mean, did he smell dirty, or—"

"Uh-uh. Arden was a steady pipe smoker, though. My brother always has a pipe in his mouth too, and the smell doesn't just soak into his clothes and his hair, it soaks into *him*. It comes out of his pores. Get close to him and you can't help smelling it. Do you remember anything like that?"

Good point, Gideon thought. Smokers *do* smell of their tobacco—pipe smokers more than anyone else, it seemed—and he himself had noticed the sweet, coconut-and-vanilla scent that hung around Arden.

But Maggie rejected it with an impatient shake of her head. "No, I don't—" She stopped abruptly, staring hard at nothing, her thoughts obviously turned inward. "Oh my God," she said slowly, looking at each of them. "I *did* smell it. I smelled it and didn't realize what it was. I thought it was something Cisco smoked, something familiar . . . marijuana . . . only it didn't quite smell like marijuana. Sweetish, yes, but different. I guess I assumed it was something else like that, I don't know, something from around here. But it wasn't. It was Arden's Sultan's Blend—he gets it from England—how could I not have realized it? It just never occurred to me to think that . . . that . . ."

She was rocking her head back and forth, hands steepled in front of her mouth. "My God . . . it's so unbelievable . . . Arden. But *why*?"

TWENTY-ONE

BUT why?

That was the question that absorbed them for the remainder of dinner, but no persuasive or even credible answers emerged, and the flow of ideas slowed and eventually stopped. Everybody was tired. Everybody had missed most of the previous night's sleep. Once the rice-pudding dessert was finished, people began leaving, talking about getting to bed early. There would be no convivial gathering under the stars that night. In the morning they would reach Leticia, and nobody knew what awaited them when the police were informed of the bizarre goings-on of the last few days. John had told them that they might all very well be detained—they would certainly be interrogated—and it wouldn't hurt to be well rested. The Colombian police did not rank among the world's most considerate forces.

Phil went off to wash clothes, John disappeared somewhere, and Gideon went to the ship's "library," a two-foot shelf of fly-specked novels in German, Spanish, and English, apparently none of them less than fifty years old. He found a dusty copy of Sinclair Lewis's *Main Street* and took it out to the salon, hoping to read for a couple of hours in the early evening breeze and calm his mind. It had been a hell of a day. But the posture he chose—sprawled back in one chair, with his feet propped on another, proved too comfortable. It wasn't long before the book fell open on his lap and dropped to the deck.

"Hey . . . Doc." John was shaking his shoulder.

He had been deeply, dreamlessly asleep. "What time is it?" he said, unwilling to open his eyes.

"What time is it? It's seven o'clock. What difference does it make what time it is?" He was brimming with impatience and enthusiasm. "Come on, you've been snoozing for an hour. Open your eyes, wake up—I got something to show you. Come on. *Hey.*" More shaking.

Gideon grumpily brushed at his hand. "Okay, okay, don't nag." He squeezed his eyes open one at a time, reluctantly pulled his feet from the chair, stretched, and stood up.

John was standing there, bouncing on his toes and holding a manila envelope. Beside him was Phil, looking scrawnier than ever in nothing but his baggy shorts and a pair of flip-flops.

"All my shirts are in the sink," he explained.

"Really? All both of them?" Gideon yawned and stretched once more. "All right, I'm awake. What's all the excitement?"

"Don't ask me," Phil said. "Ask him. He practically dragged me out of my room by the scruff of my neck." He frowned. "Do people have scruffs?"

"Well, see, the whole thing didn't make sense to me," John said, herding them toward the stairwell, "so I've been wandering around looking at things, trying to see everything, you know, from a fresh angle. I went to look at Scofield's room again, I looked at Cisco's room, I went over the ship pretty much from top to bottom, to see what I could see. And I found something up on the roof that changes everything."

"The roof?" Gideon repeated. "Where does the roof come into it?"

"That's what I'm going to show you. I want witnesses." And then, portentously: "You'll probably have to give depositions later."

Once on the roof, he took them to the rearmost part, where Scofield had isolated himself behind the smokestack in the evenings. The sun was still above the horizon, but it had dropped below the evening cloud bank and it was tolerable to be out in the open, especially in the breeze that came up every late afternoon.

"Oops." One of Phil's flip-flops had caught on one of the stanchions to which the two guy wires that secured the smokestack were attached.

"Watch out, Phil!" John exclaimed. "And for Christ's sake, keep away from the other one!" This exhortation, emphatic enough to begin with, was made still more forceful by his grabbing Phil by the elbows, lifting him bodily, and setting him down three feet to the right. "In fact, don't move. Jesus."

Phil docilely allowed himself to be transported, but looked puzzled. "What's the big deal?"

"Give me a minute and you'll see. Look around, you guys. What do you notice that's different?"

"From?" Gideon said. He brushed at a waft of gritty smoke that had drifted down from the smokestack.

John waved it away too. "From what it was last night, and the night before, and the night before that. What's changed?"

Gideon and Phil looked around them. "Where exactly are we supposed to be looking?" Phil asked.

"Right here. Right where we're standing."

"Well," said Phil, "this is where Scofield was, right?"

John nodded. "Right. Sitting right here in his beach chair."

Phil shrugged. "Give us a hint."

"I just gave you a hint."

"Here's his teapot and his cup, still on the floor,"

Gideon said, "and a plate with some crumbs in it. Well, the cup's on its side, is that what you mean?"

"That probably figures in it, but no, that's not what I mean."

Gideon spread his hands. "I don't know, John. How about letting us in on it?"

John folded his arms somewhat crossly. "For a guy who sure loves to take his time when he's telling other people about his brilliant deductions, you're a little impatient when you're on the other end of it."

Gideon saw the justice in this. "I beg your pardon. Please continue."

"Where's his chair, Doc?"

Gideon scowled. "His, uh, chair."

"Yeah, his chair."

"I don't know. I guess somebody moved it."

"Really? Look around. Nobody's moved any of the others. They're all where they were last night, roughly anyway. There's where we were, there's where—"

"Okay, so somebody took it downstairs."

"Why would anyone carry a beach chair downstairs? Except for the dining room and the salon, this is the only place there's enough room for it. And I already checked the dining room and the salon. It's not there. Besides, who's gonna have the nerve to take away Scofield's chair?"

"All right, then, maybe the crew was up here cleaning up."

"They cleaned up his chair, but they didn't clean up the teapot and cup that he left on the floor? Nope, no good. Besides, I talked to Vargas. The crew hasn't done any work at all up here. He didn't even know we were using the roof."

"Okay, already, we give up," said Phil. "Where is it?"

"In the river," John said triumphantly, "probably a good hundred or hundred and fifty miles back."

"And why is that?" asked Gideon.

"Because somebody threw it in . . . along with Scofield."

"You've lost me," Phil said.

"It wasn't Scofield that tossed Maggie overboard," John

said. "It couldn't have been. He was already in the river. Someone threw *him* in too."

"But she smelled his pipe tobacco," Phil pointed out.

"Maybe she smelled someone else's pipe tobacco," John said. "Or maybe she imagined it. She imagined she heard scuffling, didn't she? No, Arden was gone. Dead."

"And you know this, how?" asked Gideon.

"Well, I don't *know* it—" He smiled. "It's what you'd call an 'unverified supposition,' of which you've made plenty, Doc—but it all adds up, and it explains a few things too. Scofield's room hadn't been slept in last night, remember? Well, the reason's obvious: he never went to bed, probably never went back to his room at all. He was up here, probably asleep—"

"Probably zonked out of his mind," amended Phil.

"Probably, which would have made it even easier for someone to throw him off."

"But why?" Gideon asked.

"And who?" said Phil.

John shook his head. "That I can't tell you. I'm not there yet."

"And what then? Then he, whoever it was and for whatever reason, went downstairs and Maggie heard him, and he threw *her* over too? And then jumped in himself?"

"Yeah, that's what I'm assuming. Unless more than one person was involved, which is something to keep in mind."

"But how did he get back on the ship?" Gideon asked. "When we got Maggie out of the water, everybody was standing there, perfectly dry. Everybody except Scofield."

John shrugged. "Hey, look, all I can tell you is what I can tell you."

"Why get rid of the chair?" Phil asked.

"Ah, see, that's a crucial part of it. Scofield must have been cracked on the head, or knifed, or something that involved blood, and naturally it got on the chair. So it had to go too, or somebody was sure to realize what happened. Now, then— What?" he said in response to the dubious looks being directed at him. "You don't buy it?"

"It's not that I don't buy it," Phil said gingerly. "It's plausible. That is, it's not *im*plausible, but—"

"John, I think what Phil is getting at is that we could use a little verifiable supposition at this point," Gideon said. "What are we supposed to be witnesses to? What are we going to be deposed on? A chair that wasn't there?"

"If you guys would let me finish, you'd find out." He cleared his throat. "Now, gentlemen, may I direct your attention to the, what do you call it, the stanchion . . . no, not the one you got caught on, Phil. The other one."

They looked at it. Like its companion six feet away, it was a foot-long piece of angle iron attached at its bottom end to a metal plate, which was then solidly bolted to the floor—that is, to the top of the roof. Two parallel holes had been drilled in its upper end, and through them one of the two guy wires that stabilized the smokestack had been pulled, knotted, and snipped off.

"Not the stanchion itself," John said, when there was no response, "the floor near it. Over here."

"These spots, you mean?" Phil asked. "Is that what you're talking about?"

"Damn right, that's what I'm talking about. Doc, what do they look like to you?"

Gideon shrugged. "Could be anything."

"Pretend you're a famous forensic anthropologist. Pretend you're looking for clues."

"Well, I know what I'm supposed to think. I'm supposed to think that's blood, right? And it could be blood, I guess." Hands on his knees, he leaned closer. "Could also be old tomato juice or ketchup or—"

"What would ketchup be doing up here?" Phil asked. "They don't even use ketchup in Peru."

"That's not the point," John said petulantly. "The thing is, I'm betting it is blood, and I'm betting it's Scofield's. See, there's some more spatter over here, right on the very edge. It was nighttime. Whoever did this wouldn't have seen them and wouldn't have worried about them anyway, because who's going to notice a few spots on the floor?"

"But you did," said Gideon.

"Damn right I did. I already took pictures, and I wanted you to witness the spots before I collected the blood. I'd be real surprised if a DNA test doesn't show it's Scofield's."

Gideon nodded doubtfully. "Well, a DNA test would settle it, all right. That'll be a long time coming, though."

"The blood's all dry," Phil said. "How do you collect dried blood?"

"Not a problem," John said. "Watch and learn."

From the manila envelope he took some things he had gotten from Vargas: a single-edged razor blade, several sheets of white paper, and a few letter-size envelopes, the latter items bearing an impressive, thickly embossed *Amazonia Cruise Lines* logo.

With the razor he scraped the crusty brown spots near the stanchion onto one of the sheets, and the ones near the edge of the roof onto another. Both sheets were then folded and refolded to keep the material inside, and put into the smaller envelopes, which were then placed in the larger manila one.

"You'll notice that I didn't seal the envelopes yet," he explained for Phil's benefit. "I'll use some water from the sink instead of licking them. I don't want to take a chance of contaminating them with my DNA."

"I knew that," Phil said.

The manila envelope and its contents were deposited on one of the alcove shelves in John's cabin. His air-conditioner, which the heat-loving John had previously set at mid-range, was now turned up to *máximo*. "The cops better appreciate this," he said. "I'm gonna freeze tonight."

"Yeah," Gideon said, "the temperature might plummet all the way down to ninety. Maybe Vargas can get you a couple of blankets."

TWENTY-TWO

"I'M still having trouble with the pipe tobacco," Phil said. "Maggie seemed pretty sure she smelled it."

"After someone suggested it to her," Gideon pointed out.

They had gone from John's cabin, barely big enough to hold the three of them, to the deserted salon, first stopping at the dining room buffet table to bring out glasses of water and a basket of fruit to snack on—bananas, tangerines, and some objects that looked like cucumbers, but which Phil said had fluffy insides that tasted like lemon-flavored cotton candy, which they did.

"Yeah, someone," John said, and looked meaningfully up at them from the tangerine he'd been peeling. "Mel."

"But she even knew the brand," Phil said.

"Sure, that's what she thinks now. But you have to remember, she was in a state of shock at the time. She didn't remember any smell until Mel brought it up."

"So you're voting for Mel?" Gideon said.

"No, but I wouldn't rule him out either. He was pretty ticked off at him over the book, don't forget that."

"Tell me someone who wasn't ticked off at him," Phil said. "What about the screwing over he was giving Tim on his dissertation?"

"That's true," John agreed. "And Duayne had something against him too."

"He did?" said Phil.

"Oh, sure, you could see it right off," Gideon said. "When Scofield started talking about his daughter— Duayne's daughter—Duayne looked as if he wanted to kill him then and there."

"Oh yeah, you guys mentioned that before. I never noticed it."

Gideon smiled. That was the way Phil was, quick to see the good side of people, unobservant to the point of obtuseness about seeing the other. "I assume she told her father some things about Scofield's behavior that got him upset."

"Not too hard to imagine what," John said. "Okay, so if they all had it in for Scofield—"

"Yes, but who had it in for Maggie?" Gideon asked. "That's the problem I'm having with this. Why try to get rid of her too? What was that all about? When we all thought it was Cisco, it made some sense because Cisco was batty enough to do anything. But now we know it wasn't Cisco, and if your hypothesis is correct John—about Scofield's having been dumped off the boat from the roof—then that means that whoever did it then came downstairs to the cabin deck and stood around making some kind of noise until Maggie came out of her room, at which point he grabbed her and tossed her in the river. Why? What kind of sense does that make? Now if Maggie—"

"The three best-looking guys on the ship talking about me?" said Maggie, who had come downstairs with her empty liter bottle of water. "Be still, my heart."

John laughed. "How's the ankle doing, Maggie? I see you took off the bandage."

"Oh, that. It's fine, not nearly as bad as it looked. See?" She put her foot up for inspection on a chair and indeed, with the blood wiped away, it could be seen to be a nice, clean gash, as gashes went: no abraded, torn edges, no nasty, radiating pink tentacles of infection, no deepening, blue-brown bruising of the surrounding skin.

"Looks good," Gideon agreed. "But I'd still keep it covered, if I were you. It's open, and a lot of strange things grow down here."

"You're telling me," she said. "Well, I just came down to refill my water . . ." She paused awkwardly. "Uh, Gideon, I, uh, just want to thank you again." It was one of the few things he'd heard her say with no tinge whatever of sarcasm or irony. "You saved my life. You risked yours to do it. I couldn't have lasted two minutes."

"Oh, heck—"

"And"—she offered a crooked grin—"I'm really sorry I socked you. How's the lip?"

He laughed. "Forget it, Maggie, the lip's fine. However," and he leveled a finger at her, "you still owe me that beer."

When she went into the dining room, Gideon sank into a pensive silence while Phil and John continued to toss around ideas. A grotesque thought, almost too bizarre to consider seriously, had begun noodling away at him. Was it possible that they had it wrong, that everybody had it wrong?

He got up, went to the railing without a word—"Have we offended the fellow in some way?" Phil asked John— and gazed outward toward the wall of darkening green, his hands trailing abstractedly back and forth over the ebony-stained teak rail, warm and smooth against his palms. The steaming, still rain forest, so much closer here on the Javaro than it had been on the Amazon, slid monotonously by. Below him, the brown river whispered against the metal side of the ship. Gideon didn't see the jungle, didn't hear the water. His mind was absorbed in poking like a prodding finger at this not yet wholly formed idea of his, probing for flaws, testing for soundness, searching for a place to put the piece that didn't fit. . . .

Only yards from his face, a brilliant red macaw suddenly fluttered up from a branch with an indignant squawk and flapped away into the dimness of the interior. It startled him enough that his mind jumped from the unproductive rut it had dug itself into, and the final piece fell into place.

He thumped his fist gently against his palm—an unconscious gesture of self-satisfaction—and turned to face the others. "We got it backwards," he said softly, urgently. "Sonofagun. *Everybody* got it backwards."

"What are we talking about now?" Phil wondered.

"Got what backwards?" asked John.

"The way it happened. The order of events. First we assumed Maggie was thrown overboard *after* Arden. Then we assumed—"

"Still talking about me, I see," Maggie said, coming from the dining room with her refilled bottle. She put her hand to her heart and wiggled her fingers. "Flutter, flutter." Her left eyebrow was characteristically arched, her mouth ironically set, her voice typically mocking, but there was something unmistakably wary in her expression, in her taut shoulders.

Damn, Gideon thought. *Why did I burst out with it like that? Why couldn't I shut up until she was gone?* Surely she'd heard enough to guess where he was going, and it was too late to start waffling now. Maggie was too smart for that, too quick on the uptake. There was but one way to go. He took in a breath and went there.

"Maggie," he said, "you killed Arden. You threw him overboard."

In the charged silence that fell on them John and Phil goggled at him in mute amazement.

Maggie, however, was up to the challenge. "Oh, really?" she said sardonically, her eyebrow arching even higher, her voice falling even lower. "Was that before or after he threw me overboard?"

"Arden never threw you overboard."

"If this is your idea of a joke, I have to say—"

"No joke."

She faltered. Her composure began to disintegrate. A tic jerked beside her right eye. "Gideon, I don't know what you've been smoking, but you're on dangerous ground here. Arden *did* throw me over, or at least *some*body did, but you keep changing your mind about who, and after that he—"

"Uh-uh, Maggie, that whole thing about him, what happened there on the deck—it was all a lie."

Her face had stiffened. Her words spattered out like bullets. "I don't know just who the hell you think you are, mister, but if you think for one minute—"

"We were just up on the roof, Maggie. You left some blood up there. We collected it. What do you want to bet that a lab test doesn't show that it's yours?"

"Hers?" he heard John murmur in astonishment.

Her face eased. Her hunched shoulders relaxed a little. "Oh, I see where you're coming from. My ankle . . . you think . . ." She shook her head and laughed. "I should be angry as all get-out, but it's funny, really. Well, luckily for me, I can *prove* what I said. Give me a minute, let me get something from my room." She walked to the stairs, then stopped and turned as she reached them. "You guys," she said with a crooked grin. "If you don't take the cake." She shook her head as if in wonder and trotted up the steps. "Don't go anywhere," she called.

"Are you serious?"

"Are you crazy?"

John and Phil had both exclaimed at the same time, and Gideon wasn't sure who had said what. Still standing at the rail, his elbows leaning on it behind him, he said, "Serious, yes. Crazy, I'm not sure. I don't know what kind of proof she thinks she has, but I'm damn near certain I'm right. She threw Scofield off, not the other way around."

John shook his head. "How the hell do you come up with that?"

"It's the cut on her ankle," Gideon said. "She said she

got it when she hit her foot on the railing upstairs, in front of Scofield's cabin."

They nodded. "So?" Phil said.

"So take a look at the railing. It's the same down here as it is up there. Smooth, rounded, polished wood." He slid his hand along the surface to illustrate his point. "You want to tell me how you can cut your ankle on that? You could bruise it, break it, sure, but cut it? Uh-uh."

"Well, wait up a minute, Doc," John said. "I've seen plenty of cases where something blunt like that—a bat, a hammer—can cause a cut, and a damn big cut at that. So have you."

"No those aren't *cuts*, those are *lacerations*, and they're not the same."

A laceration was typically a wound from a blunt object, he explained, and was really a rupture, usually from the skin's being stretched over the underlying bone and split open by the impact of the object—an example would be the way a boxer can get a "cut" on his brow from an opponent's soft, padded, twelve-ounce glove. As a result, a blunt-object wound was usually pretty obviously torn, rather than cut, with ragged, irregular, abraded edges. And of course, the area around it would be bruised from the crushing of blood vessels under the skin. A cut, on the other hand (more properly, an incised wound), resulted directly from a sharp edge being drawn along the skin. The edges of the wound were themselves sharp, not messy, and, more important, there was no damage to the surrounding tissue, no bruising.

"And that's what the cut on Maggie's ankle looks like," Phil said, nodding. "Yeah."

"Yes. It looked like a mess before, with all the blood. But now you could see it was clean. And it's been almost twenty hours. If there was going to be any bruising, it would have shown up by now."

"So what you're saying," John said, swallowing the last of his tangerine, "is that she cut herself—lacerated herself—on . . . what, the stanchion?"

"More likely the cut end of the guy wire. Did you see what those wires are like? They're made of—I don't know what you call them—a whole lot of thin, stiff wires twisted around each other and then around a core."

"Wire rope," John said. "Real strong stuff."

"Yes. And the ends are sharp as hell when they're cut off on the bias. Like a hundred little scalpels. That's why they're usually covered with tape or with some kind of sleeve, if there's going to be any traffic around them. But not up there."

"So *Maggie* dumped Scofield in the river, that's what you're telling us?" Phil said, obviously confused. "And cut herself while she was getting him over the side?"

"That's what I'm telling you. You caught your foot on the wire yourself, and you weren't trying to wrestle anybody overboard."

"But then who threw Maggie in the river? What'd she do, toss herself overboard?"

"I believe so, yes."

He came back to the table, sat down, and resumed pulling the white, citrusy wadding out of the cucumberlike fruit. It was like eating a pomegranate. You ignored the bean-like seeds and just ate the sweet packing around them.

Phil shook his head, scowling. "Aw, no. Aside from its being ridiculous, it's impossible, Gideon. It doesn't add up. Listen, there were only two splashes, right? It's like Mel said; the second one came *after* Maggie was already in the water, so how—"

"No, I don't think it did."

"Sure, it did. Think back, right to the beginning. What was the first thing you heard?"

"That little yelp. *Ai!*"

"From Maggie, right?"

Gideon nodded.

"Okay, a little yelp," Phil went on. "And then a splash—that's Maggie hitting the water—and then she yells for help: 'Help, save me, I'm drowning.' And *then* there's the second splash—no? What am I not getting?" he said in response to the slow shaking of Gideon's head.

"What if it didn't happen that way? What if it happened this way? What if—"

"Three *what ifs* in a row," John grumbled. "Oh, that's a great start." He was still attached to his own theory. But he was paying keen attention.

"What if," Gideon continued, "Maggie, knowing that Scofield is likely to still be up there in a stupor after everybody else leaves, goes up with the idea of doing just what she did—pushing him off the back of the ship. But while getting him over the edge, she catches her ankle on the end of the wire—"

"And yelps, which is what wakes you up," Phil put in.

"Correct. And a half second later I hear Scofield hit the water, although I don't know it's Scofield at the time. That's splash number one. So I shoot out of bed and yell that somebody's overboard at the top of my lungs."

"Which *she* hears," said John slowly. Gideon could see that he was getting it, that he was coming over to Gideon's side.

"Right. At which point, thinking fast, still standing on the roof, she yells 'Help, help, I'm drowning, I can't swim!' and *then* jumps into the water herself. Splash number two. End of splashes."

"I'm getting it, I'm getting it," Phil said. "That's pretty smart!"

"So when I come out on deck," Gideon went on, "she's in the water thrashing around, and in I go to get her."

"Wait, maybe I'm not getting it," Phil said. "What was that business with her screaming 'Get him, he's getting away!'?"

"That," John supplied, out ahead of Gideon now, "was supposed to explain that second splash. The first one—Scofield hitting the water—was *supposed* to be her hitting the water. The second one—which was really *her* hitting the water—was supposed to be Cisco."

"Wow, that's fast thinking," Phil said. "But how could

she take a chance on accusing Cisco? At that point every-body thought Cisco was still aboard."

"Not everybody," Gideon said. "Do you remember Tim's telling us that Cisco said that he'd be leaving the ship and maybe wouldn't be back?"

"That's right!" Phil exclaimed. "And Maggie was there when he said it—she told us so. So . . ."

"So all she had to do was double-check Cisco's room first and see if he was there or not. If not, she had a clear field. If yes—well, I don't know, maybe come up with an-other plan. But he *wasn't* there."

"Yeah . . ." began Phil, but then vigorously shook his head. "Nope, nope. She couldn't know she was going to cut her foot, she couldn't know she was going to have to jump in the water herself. So why would she check his room first?"

The question hadn't occurred to Gideon, but after a mo-ment he came up with a reasonable, or at least a credible, answer. "Because she probably planned for the blame to fall on Cisco for Scofield's disappearance—and presumed death—in any case. I mean, who else? And if Cisco wasn't there any more, if he'd fled the ship, that would cinch it. Or so she thought. And then, even if he did come back, he'd still be the logical suspect, being as loopy as he was."

Phil was nodding now. "Yeah, okay, I see."

"And then," Gideon went on, "when Tim came up with the old history between them—who Cisco really was—she must have thought it was Christmas: a ready-made motive. At any rate, no one was going to think Maggie had any-thing to do with it." He paused. "And we didn't."

They all sat there cogitating the scenario he'd put forth. Even to Gideon, it was sounding a little rococo by now, and more than a little fanciful.

"So that scuffling she says she heard," Phil said. "She just made that up? And the guy in the nightshirt, the mumbling to himself? That too? Just made it up on the spot to make it seem more believable? She's that quick on her feet?"

"I believe so," Gideon said.

"And nothing really happened on the deck outside her cabin? It all happened up on the roof?"

"That's what I think. And I'm in the rearmost cabin, remember, practically right under where Scofield was sitting, which is probably why I'm the one who heard it."

Phil scratched at his pepper-and-salt beard, which was growing in even less neatly than usual. "But why get rid of that chair? I doubt if blood from her ankle would have gotten on the chair."

"Because pulling him out of the chair and wrestling him overboard would have been harder than just sliding the chair over the edge with him in it," Gideon said. "That'd be my guess."

John, who hadn't participated for the last minute or so, was looking at his watch. "She's been gone over ten minutes. That's a long time to get to her room and back."

"You don't think she jumped ship?" Phil asked. "No, what am I saying? She can't swim."

"She *says* she can't swim," Gideon said. "But never mind jumping ship. She might have . . . what if she . . ."

They exchanged a look, and before Gideon could get the whole sentence out, they were running for the stairs. At her cabin they pounded on the door. There was no answer. Without waiting any longer, John flung it wide open.

"Aw, jeez," Phil said, turning away.

TWENTY-THREE

"SHE committed suicide?" Julie whispered, horrified.

"Apparently, she couldn't face what she knew was coming," Gideon said, "and it would have been easy enough to do herself in. She had a whole pharmacy full of weird plant compounds in her cabin."

"We'd need an autopsy to make it definite," John said. "The body went to Bogota and they told us they'd do one there, but who knows? And even if they do, whether we'll ever hear about it . . ." He finished with a shrug.

"I suspect we won't," Gideon said. "My guess is the Colombian police aren't going to waste their time doing a full-scale investigation. Why should they get involved in a case involving all US nationals? Besides, Maggie's dead, Scofield's dead, Cisco's dead. There's no one to prosecute. It's all pretty much taken care of itself. I think they'll just write it up, stamp it 'Case closed,' and file it away."

"You said she was alone for only ten minutes?" Marti Lau said. "That was one fast-acting poison."

"It was quick," Gideon agreed, "but you have to remember she'd boiled or dried most of the plants down to very concentrated extracts and, besides, she had stuff in there that—" He barely stopped himself from saying, "that science doesn't begin to understand," and finished instead with "that we've never heard of. Whatever it was, it promptly sent her into anaphylactic shock. She was probably dead in *five* minutes. When we got there, her skin was blue, her tongue was practically . . . well, you don't want to hear the gruesome details."

"Yes, we do!" Marti said.

"No, we don't," Julie said firmly. "John, I think your pizza's ready."

"Good, I'm starving."

They had arrived at Seattle's Sea-Tac Airport within two hours of each other, Julie and Marti fresh off a five-and-a-half-hour trip from Los Cabos, Gideon, John, and Phil not so fresh off a flight that was even more grueling than the one down: Leticia to Bogota to Mexico City to Houston to Seattle—thirty hours, including the stopovers. Phil had left Sea-Tac almost immediately to catch an Airporter bus home to Anacortes, but the others had gone to Pacific Marketplace, the terminal's dramatic, new, upscale food court—fronted by a forty-foot-tall, 350-foot-long, curving window that looked out onto the runways—where each could indulge his or her own desires for a late-evening dinner. Marti had gotten a sushi plate from Maki of Japan, and Gideon and Julie had both gotten chowder and fish and chips from Ivar's Seafood Bar. John, after giving serious thought to a couple of Wendy's hamburgers, had ordered a pepperoni-and-mushroom pizza from an Italian bistro, despite their warning that it would take fifteen minutes. (For John, a week was a long time to go without a pizza.)

"I don't really understand why she would kill herself," Julie was saying when John returned with his pizza. "Dr. Scofield's body was never found, was it? There's no real proof that he's dead, so how could she be convicted of murder?"

"That doesn't matter under Colombian law any more than it does under ours," John said around his first ecstatic, closed-eyed bite. "There would have been more than enough circumstantial evidence to convict her two times over. Especially the blood from upstairs. She knew it'd turn out to be hers. And then there are the lies she told, and the motive."

"What motive?" asked Marti. "Didn't they get along? I thought he was helping her out, getting her a job down in Peru."

"He was," Gideon said, "but she wanted to stay in Iowa City."

"Why, in God's name?" Marti muttered.

"Iowa City's nice," Gideon said, laughing. "But the thing is, with Arden Scofield in the running, her chances of getting the one remaining ethnobotany position were zip. But with Arden out of the picture, everything changes. It's already June, way too late for the department to try to recruit somebody from the outside, so the job would almost certainly fall to her. And with the Great Man no longer overshadowing everything she did, her future there—so she must have thought—was going to be a lot brighter. Her whole life would be different."

"So she came on the trip planning to kill him," Julie murmured.

"I doubt it," Gideon said. "If she had killing him in mind, I don't think she'd have been so free in telling us about the Iowa situation—practically handing us a motive. No, I think the opportunity simply presented itself, and she took it."

"Carpe diem," observed Marti, expertly using chopsticks to insert a bit of vegetarian sushi—rice, tofu, and shaved ginger rolled in seaweed—between her lips. "Well, you two certainly had an exciting time of it."

"What about you?" Gideon asked. "How was Cabo?"

"Great. We slept in the morning, we did a lot of swimming and snorkeling, we ate like horses, we got a few massages. Or at least I did."

"But mostly," Julie said, "we just relaxed, and read

junky novels, and sat on the beach, and baked the North-west chill out of our bones. *That* felt good. It must sound pretty boring compared to your trip, though," she added wistfully. "What an adventure the two of you had!"

"Yeah, it was," said John, pushing back from his now-empty pizza tray and clasping his hands on his belly, a man well contented, happy to be back in a world where pizza could be had for the asking. "To tell you the truth, though, next time something like this comes around . . . no offense to you, Doc . . . but I think I'll opt for the crushed turnip wrap."